THE BUTTERFLY TWINS

A CHARLES BLOOM MURDER MYSTERY

MARK SUBLETTE

JUST ME PUBLISHING

Copyright © 2016 by Mark Sublette
Author's Note by Mark Sublette Copyright © 2016

All Rights Reserved. This book may not be reproduced, in whole or in part, in any form, without written permission. For inquiries, contact: Just Me Publishing, LLC., Tucson, AZ, 1-800-422-9382

Published by Just Me Publishing, LLC.

Library of Congress Control Number: 2016933544
The Butterfly Twins / Mark Sublette
ISBN 978-0-9861902-3-0
1. Fiction I. Title

Quantity Purchases
Companies, professional groups, clubs, and other organizations may qualify for special terms when ordering quantities of this title. For more information, contact us through www.marksublette.com.

Jacket and book design: Jaime Gould
Author photo: Dan Budnik

Printed in the USA by Bookmasters
Ashland, OH · www.bookmasters.com

AUTHOR'S NOTE

The books in the Bloom murder mystery series are all works of fiction. AgraCon World Enterprises (ACWE) is a complete figment of my imagination. Any resemblance to a real corporation is strictly coincidental.

All the characters in The Butterfly Twins are also fictional: the CEO of ACWE, police officers, historians, artists, the art dealers and their galleries exist only in my mind. The Native American characters and references to any of their religious practices or beliefs are fictional as well; any relationship to real life—by name, clan or description—is purely coincidental.

Santa Fe's Historic Districts Review Board is an actual entity committed to preserving the character of Santa Fe, but all personnel, interactions, judgments and other activities of the board as presented in this book are fictional.

The Toadlena Trading Post, a central component of all the Bloom books, is a real working trading post that exists as described on Navajoland. This historic shop specializes in Toadlena/Two Grey Hills weavings and is well worth the effort to visit. I would like to thank its proprietor, author Mark Winter, and his wife Linda for their invaluable insights and Mark's editing prowess.

While some artistic license has been employed in the depiction of conquistador Juan de Oñate's destruction of Acoma Pueblo in 1599, the event is based on the historical record. Oñate's early homestead on Canyon Road, on the other hand, is a construct of my imagination.

No book is complete without a great cover and I'm most appreciative to Jaime Gould for her graphic design skills. I'm also grateful for Patricia West-Barker's careful manuscript editing and thoughtful suggestions.

All the photographs of Santa Fe and Navajoland were taken by me to serve as points of reference correlating to each chapter. Other images are courtesy Medicine Man Gallery Tucson/Santa Fe. I hope they will help the reader experience the same sense of place and moment in time that I experienced when I took them.

PROLOGUE

WHAT'S PAST IS PROLOGUE

The faint whiff of ozone was omnipresent in the cold January air, a promise of life-giving moisture to Acoma Pueblo. In an arid land, any precipitation is usually a harbinger of good fortune. Today, though, the sign was not one of prosperity or nourishment but of death. The sacred watering holes of the sky-high city were about to be filled—not with water but with blood.

A dense winter storm blanketed the usually dusty trail from the snowy peak known as Kaweshtima to Acoma, the picturesque pueblo carved into an impenetrable bluff, obscuring the presence of one hundred-thirty mounted soldiers advancing toward the People of the White Rock.

Don Juan de Oñate y Salazar, the colonial governor of Santa Fe de Nuevo México, a province of New Spain, was pushing his army across the desert floor on a forced march to destiny. Unlike his predecessor Francisco Vásquez de Coronado, who had come to this territory fifty years earlier, Oñate was a realist. Coronado had come in search of the Seven Cities of Gold rumored to lie hidden in the desert north of Mexico—an expedition that ended in failure for both the soldier and his investors.

Oñate came to this same desolate land not to search for precious metals and jewels but to conquer. Acoma's real bounty, Oñate knew, lay not in fool's gold but in slaves and food. Human flesh, full storehouses and revenge for a past defeat were the treasures he sought. As he rode, he thought about the heavy metal trunk jingling along his steed's flank. Empty now, it would soon be stuffed with the spoils of war—proof of his well-deserved victory.

Acoma, jutting out of the pale mesa top, loomed ahead.

The steady rain, occasionally mixed with snow, dripped off Oñate's salt-and-pepper beard, a refreshing reminder to stay alert for the last two-mile trek. There would be no ambush of his soldiers today.

The leathery Spaniard was a veteran of many battles and was not afraid of what was to come. The rhythmic shivers just visible under his wet protective gear hinted at his underlying temperament: heat fueled by anger.

The blank smile of determination fixed on his reddened face spoke volumes. A heavily dented crescent-moon helmet topped his oversized head—a head that ached in the cold, his discomfort yet another warning of perils that lay ahead.

Unlike the early conquistadors, Oñate had dispensed with most of the sixty pounds of traditional Spanish armor. Married to Isabel de Tolosa Cortes Moctezuma, the great-granddaughter of the Aztec Emperor Moctezuma Xocoyotzin, he had instead adopted his wife's people's protective gear—a cotton and leather quilted shirt called *ichcahaipilli*, worn by Aztec warriors. The arduous 100-plus-mile journey from Santa Fe de Nuevo México to Acoma was less taxing in the lighter outfit that still provided ample protection from primitive spears, darts, and clubs.

Armed with the advanced technology of the fifteenth century—horses, cannons, swords, and muskets—Oñate knew that his campaign's success was all but guaranteed. His superior military power was no match for a people stuck in the Stone Age. A few days of continuous cannon fire would reduce five hundred years of human existence to rubble—and pound the proud People of the White Rock into submission.

A professional military man, Oñate should have been focused on the battle plan, but the conquistador was bent on revenge.

The thud of the horses' hooves on the wet ground provided a hypnotic background beat for the soldiers moving toward the village in the sky. Engagement was now just a mile away, and the reassuring song of battle readied the warrior's nerves for what was to come.

With the target in view and no opposing forces to stop him, Oñate's mind drifted back to an event three months earlier. It was October, and there was no hint of humidity in the air; instead, the pungent odor of golden chamisa set off the sparse yellow cottonwood leaves dancing in the dry, crisp air.

That fall he had come in peace—at least that was what Oñate told himself—to replenish the food stores of the hungry constituents huddled in their miserable adobe huts back in Santa Fe de Nuevo México.

"It was no raid; it was a good-faith trip for my struggling colony," he thought. And the puebloans were, after all, required to pay a "food tax" to the Spanish crown.

Mexico City was a thousand miles away and Spain across an ocean—yet here he was burdened with the responsibility of not only governing a settlement of misfits but also with trying to keep them alive.

The summer had been brutal. A poor bean and squash crop was followed by the complete failure of the even more important corn harvest. Oñate was a soldier, not a farmer, yet he had been charged with ruling a colony of peons who didn't have the skills to keep themselves fed.

It was not their fault the crops had shriveled and died, the settlers said. They had been praying daily to the patron saint of gardeners since spring; still, when no water fell from the sky, their gardens failed in the summer heat. The usually vibrant Santa Fe River was reduced to a mere muddy trickle. There was not enough water to nurture the thirsty plants, much less sustain the colony's scrawny animals.

So, beseeched to do what he did best by the settlers, Oñate had gone in search of food to buy or appropriate as needed. Acoma was laden with Mother Nature's gifts—or so he had been told by neighboring

Indians along the Río Grande—inspiring the soldier to ride toward the sky-high city.

But the conquistador's first trip to Acoma was a disaster.

"I was rebuffed as if I were some leper," he recalled. "The Acoma Indians ordered me—a colonial governor!—to stop and come no further. My silver *macuquinas* were of no interest to them. Food and clothing were the commodities of trade, they said, and their one thousand-five hundred occupants had barely enough of each to get them through the coming winter."

Still, he couldn't help but covet the pueblo's riches: rooftops were laden with dried beans and roasting corn scented the air. Acoma's plaza was filled with strong, healthy women adorned in fine cotton blankets—and they didn't have enough?

Oñate decided to insist on the crown's (his!) due with a show of force, but the pueblo's inhabitants had been prepared for him and attacked from their advantageous position off the mesa's steep canyon walls. Too late, he realized it had been foolish to approach Acoma so ill-protected, with no significant weapons and not enough men.

It was a mistake he would not make twice.

Thirteen men died during that first encounter, including his wife's beloved nephew and a close confidant.

Today's battle would be sweet revenge for both his failure and his loss. Today, he would slaughter many and take what he liked—women slaves for trade and treasures for his *cofre del tesoro* to remind him of this day. This time, he vowed, no man or Pagan god would stop him.

Rivers of blood would flow by day's end.

The battle went as predicted. The cannons wreaked havoc on the ancient mud and stick multistory buildings, leaving their rustic pot chimneys in shards, sacred kivas destroyed. Three days of pounding was all they could take.

Some Indians tried to escape and were picked off, one by one, as they stumbled down from their protected position.

"An isolated fortress can cut both ways," Oñate thought.

The sounds of pain and suffering filtered down to the Spaniards, and when the cacophony reached an audible hum, Oñate knew it was time. He ascended the rock, this time from the south. When he entered the pueblo, he found 800 Acoma dead—and not a single Spanish soldier had been lost.

At daybreak on day four the final retribution was exacted: all men over the age of twenty-five were stripped, then laid face down. In a horrifying mass butchery, each man's right foot was amputated as other members of the pueblo were forced to look on.

Rivers of red flowed into a shallow sandstone depression. Once used to grind corn, it was now a pool of human misery. A week later the receding mass left a red discoloration on the stone—a permanent reminder of Juan de Oñate's visit.

With his *cofre* filled and his slaves in tow, the governor was pleased for the first time in months. The loss of his wife's nephew had been vindicated—and he now had enough food and slaves to get his constituents through the winter of fifteen ninety-nine.

❋ ❋ ❋ ❋

Four hundred-fifteen years had passed since the streets of Acoma ran red, but the full impact of Oñate's wrath was only now coming to fruition. The Santa Fe art dealer Charles Bloom would soon bear witness to the heavy weight of the first New Mexico governor's destructive legacy.

CHAPTER 1

DAYS OF OLD

It was not unusual for Brazden Shackelford to daydream—a man with no real job has the luxury of such pursuits.

Today he enjoyed the warm spring sun, his dark brown skin betraying a life spent outdoors. It was a good day, one on which his breathing was less labored.

The Santa Fe Farmers Market could be excruciatingly slow in early May. The tourists who filled the aisles would still be scarce until the Texas heat became too much and the out-of-town visitors and second-homers migrated back to the higher elevations of New Mexico. There was even an occasional free parking spot to be found near the market pavilion, a rarity in the railyard district.

Brazden only showed up at the market when the weather was favorable, so his booth had been delegated to the last row of vendors. His meager spring garden offerings included snap peas, some now-wilted lettuce, potatoes (from last year's crop), and a few scraggly ears of dried native corn displayed in colorful arrangements he had constructed over the winter.

Examining a thumb-sized ear of corn with multicolored kernels, Brazden closed his eyes and reflected on how the seed had come into his possession.

In his mind's eye, the early spring day morphed into fall, steam rising in sheets off the warm ground. Brazden was no longer a 60-plus-year-old man with an unkempt beard, gray ponytail and arthritic joints slumped in a dilapidated green lawn chair at the New Mexico Rail Runner station in Santa Fe's Guadalupe district, but an energetic kid with a blonde buzz cut on a great adventure. He was once again hiking the remote Navajo reservation with his beloved grandfather Sidney, a well-known and respected pothunter.

He was young again and had his entire life in front of him.

Brazden ached for those days, a time before the Native American Graves Protection and Repatriation Act was signed into law and enforced. Before NAGPRA, a hard-working man with an intimate knowledge of prehistoric Indian culture could hunt for artifacts and make a good living without having to worry if the Feds were going to raid his home and handcuff him in front of his friends.

Brazden was a pothunter by profession—a person who digs up prehistoric pots and artifacts and sells them to dealers at a wholesale price.

Looting prehistoric archaeological sites was the trade he learned at his grandfather's side. Once he had made a decent living finding and selling pots; for a few years it was downright lucrative. But with the crackdown on the sale of prehistoric art, the last ten years had been especially lean.

Reflecting on his life was not easy for Brazden, but the warm Santa Fe sun relaxed his mind, and he traveled back in time to a day when he was twelve and first learning his trade. It was a pivotal moment in his life.

Grandpa Sidney had discovered the stash of a lifetime, and he was there to witness the find—three large, fully intact, corrugated storage vessels filled with treasures that had been hidden on a remote ledge adjacent to the Wupatki National Monument near

Sunset Crater. Just outside Flagstaff, Arizona, the find was a pothunter's wet dream.

The two had hiked to the area of interest under cover of darkness and arrived at first daylight. Even fifty years ago, hunting for illegal pots on federal land could get one into big trouble, so caution was advised. The flash of first light hitting the concealed pots on the high ledge had been the tell—and his grandfather recognized it instantaneously. It was a sight not lost on a man who had spent his life walking the back slot canyons of the Navajo reservation.

The glint of micaceous pottery meant money for those who could recognize hidden gold. So Sidney sent his only grandson scurrying up the steep cliff wall to confirm what he already knew. Like a desert gecko, Brazden climbed, using the faint remnants of an ancient Anasazi handhold, now mere depressions in the sandstone, to make his way to the top—the first human in a thousand years to do so.

Three hundred feet above the high desert floor sat three unbroken mica-rich pots buried in fine volcanic sand, each angled at 20 degrees, each filled with gifts from its long-deceased owners.

The smallest pot was a massive twenty inches in diameter and had a well-fitted lid that protected its contents, which included a large macaw skeleton, a cache of feathers, child-sized wooden effigies and large quantities of corn covered in a fine mist of corn pollen.

The middle-sized vessel had no lid but was filled with dozens of handspun cotton strings laden with turquoise beads and two pairs of earrings that may have come from the faraway mines near Santa Fe—all trade items of great importance.

The third and largest vessel was thirty inches in diameter, a masterful accomplishment for any artisan. The lid was topped with a three-inch carved turquoise butterfly fetish and had been sealed to the lip of the pot with brown piñon pitch.

Using the smallest blade of his most prized possession, an Old Henry pocketknife, Brazden wedged the steel under the edge of the lid and loosened the now-crumbling sap, freeing the unharmed ceramic cover from its one-thousand-year bondage. The release of air that followed was marked by a pungent odor that invaded the small closed space, making the boy gag. The smell of death was recognizable even to a teenager.

Brazden peered over the massive pot's rim and immediately realized he was looking at something that must have been sacred—a human skeleton.

The hardened flesh had been freeze-dried to ancient bones, but this was no ordinary skeleton. Pinched into a crouched position was a small torso clothed in a magnificent two-panel manta, each half made of the finest handspun cotton, the luster intact a thousand years after its execution. Except for a small stain at one corner where the body fluids had collected, the weaving could have been a recent construction. The outside was adorned with red ochre pictographs of dozens of stylized butterflies similar to the one on the lid. But these were no ordinary butterflies; here, two insects were attached by a single body—a metamorphosis in process.

What had truly frightened Brazden was not the sickly smell of human death, or the fact the pot contained a skeleton, a sight he had seen before while hunting pots with his grandfather. His fear emanated from the sight of the skeleton's skull. It was not a single human head but two!

The mummified remains were those of Siamese twin girls. Strands of long brown hair flowed in rivulets halfway down their spine, two sets of pearly white teeth smiled back at Brazden. Their skeletal arms were crossed in front of a bifurcating chest—the whole effect reminiscent of a cross protecting the magnificent dress.

Brazden's pulse quickened as he remembered the image of the pots and skeleton that had been burned into his mind's eye. Almost absentmindedly, he rubbed the turquoise butterfly amulet he wore around his neck—a constant reminder of his great find and the beloved grandfather who had taught him how to make a living off the land.

The pots were worth a lot of money but were too large for a boy or an elderly man to move. The climb up and down the treacherous path with an awkward load was a two-person job and would require ropes. The pots were safe in their hidey-hole. They could be extracted another time when money was tight and a plan was at the ready.

Brazden gave his grandfather a detailed description of his findings, then made three round trips to carry out the goods he considered valuable from the pots. The full skeleton was too cumbersome and not deemed valuable enough to remove, but Brazden wanted a trophy and his grandfather wanted the dress.

To extract the white manta intact, the boy had to separate the skeleton's arms at the shoulder joint. Once separated, the bones were tossed aside on the cliff floor. The dress was removed from the body and bundled with a shoestring. The lid (minus its fetish) was replaced on the large olla.

The heads connected by two cervical spines merging into one at the chest were removed at the first thoracic level—a young boy's trophy. The girls' faces were at a compelling—and terrifying—45 degrees to each other. The skulls were stuffed into Brazden's large backpack, unbeknownst to his grandfather, who avoided human remains whenever possible.

The looted manta, jewelry, and wooden offerings were a valuable haul. An empty pork and beans can that had held the young pothunter's lunch was filled to its jagged top with corn kernels coated in pollen. The seeds had no intrinsic value, but they were so intriguing to young Brazden that he couldn't help taking them. As he stuffed them into the can, he saw himself planting the seeds, like Jack and the Beanstock, just to see what would happen.

A half-century had passed and the kernels he had stolen did indeed produce plants: the wreaths in his farmers market were the offspring of those one-thousand-year-old artifacts. The small ears were minuscule food offerings for the average consumer; woven into wreaths, they provided colorful decorative accents for fancy Santa Fe front doors.

Brazden discovered that dryland farming suited the seeds well and they thrived during the short summer Santa Fe monsoon rains. He had kept the meager corn production for his own use until this year, when he was forced to sell the gifts of the Butterfly Twins to tourists.

His trance was broken by the sound of that rarity—a paying customer.

"How much for all three corn wreaths? That corn looks unique—Is it?" The questions came from a well-dressed white man in a new pair of Ferragamo loafers.

"That's Indian corn, my man," Brazden replied. "Supposed to be the same stock the Anasazi used, or so I'm told." He wasn't about to give any trade secrets away.

"I must admit it does look different. Where did you get the seed?" The middle-aged man lifted the wreath to the sun for a closer inspection.

"An old farmer down near Mesilla Valley who used to grow it gave me some seed years ago. It's pretty to the eye but not much of a producer, unless you got no irrigation. Then it's perfect."

"Dryland farming, huh?"

"Yep, it's good desert stock, the best I've ever seen. I need five dollars a wreath, but if you take all three, I'll knock it down to four bucks apiece."

"I'll take the whole lot; they should make a fine posole. If you give me your card, I'll call you later and buy some more. They'd make great gifts."

"Yes, they do indeed—but I'm afraid I don't have no business cards and this is pretty much all the corn I got available till the first of August. But tell you what—Give me your number and when I get more I'll let you know."

The buyer seemed put off but wrote his Santa Fe phone number on a stained Starbucks coffee sleeve.

Brazden was good with people—one had to be when eking out a living off the land. He realized this overdressed man asking detailed questions wasn't your ordinary farmers market patron. And there was something odd out about the way he looked at the corn, like a doctor. He wouldn't call the man anytime soon, not unless he was desperate for money. The last few wreaths he had squirreled away were not for sale.

Brazden hated selling his special stock and didn't want some city slicker with too much seed to start competing with him. The corn decorations were paying the bills better than digging pots these days and they didn't require as much physical labor.

✳ ✳ ✳ ✳

Little could Brazden know how dead-on his instincts were. The well-dressed man returned unnoticed to the market when the vendors were loading out, tracking the reluctant farmer to his worn-out Ford truck. The two would meet again—and the next time it might not be so cordial.

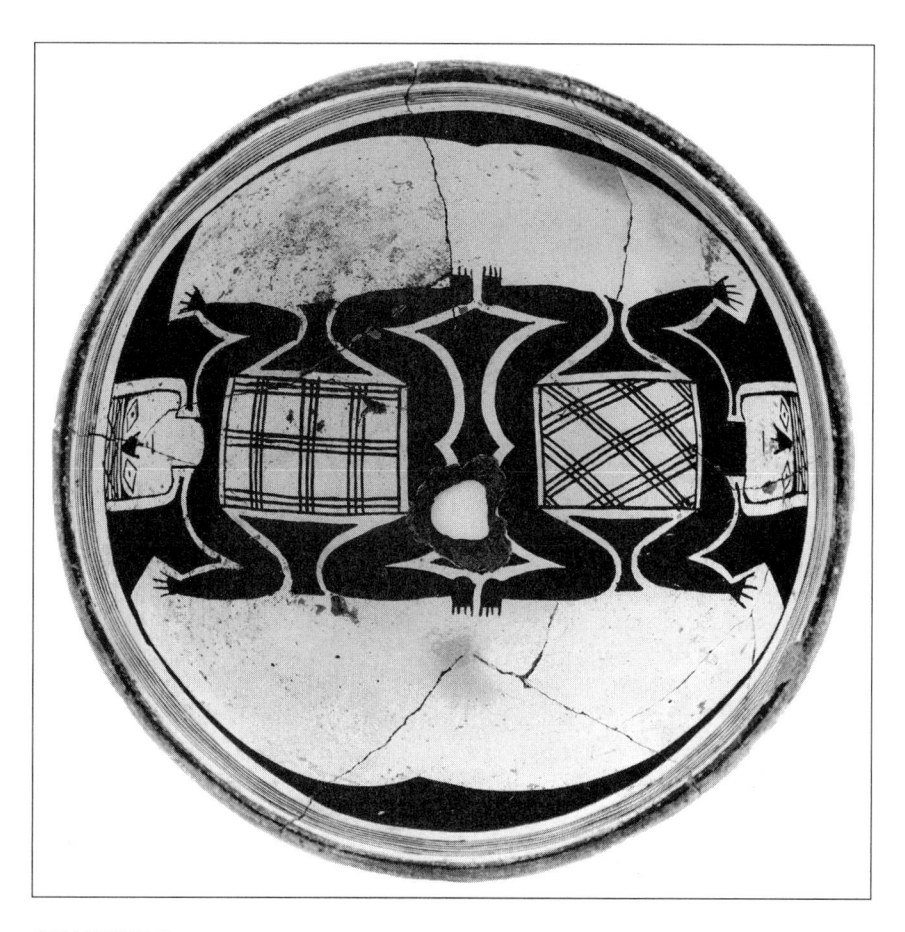

CHAPTER 2

A HARD LIFE

Sixty-five dollars and change for six hours of work at the farmers market—it was gas and beer money and nothing more, Brazden thought to himself—but it was still better than a sharp stick in the eye, something his grandfather would say when he came up empty-handed on a dig.

Once upon a time Brazden had made a $5,000 profit on a good Mimbres picture bowl that took less than an hour to dig. But the old days of digging by hand for ancient artifacts had been replaced by backhoes raping the sites under the cover of darkness. Breakage was just one of the hazards of the job, although the ability to make a fast exit was also paramount to avoid the law—often tribal cops who were bad news for pothunters. Brazden's skilled repairs were almost impossible to detect, so it didn't matter if a few pots got damaged in the collection process; they would still bring good money.

For Brazden, the prehistoric pottery market was a sweet business up to the mid-nineteen-nineties, affording him the occasional new truck, some extra cash and plenty of inventory. Then the Feds decided the party should end.

A dicey or nonexistent provenance was no longer acceptable; the bigwig Indian art dealers in Santa Fe wouldn't touch any prehistoric pottery unless there was a clear, notarized chain of provenance. The few dealers willing to skirt the laws were only interested in the kinds of high-ticket items that would end up with overseas buyers.

No federal or Indian land could be touched. Pottery had to be excavated from private property to be legal. In New Mexico, which had passed additional grave robbing laws, nothing could be taken from burial sites even if they were on private land.

The market for ceramics with a spotty history had dried up, putting an end to Brazden's heyday. Now he could only sell pieces dug with the permission of a rancher, and even then he had to produce a certificate to back up that claim. The extra steps took time and cost money, making the profit margins too narrow for a wholesaler like him.

Pieces that had been looted required special treatment that was too risky for the poor payoff in today's Indian art market. Forging documents was only worthwhile for large pieces or Mimbres picture bowls, which were scarce.

The bottom-feeder dealers who didn't care about niceties like papers would occasionally buy if the price were right, but for most it was no longer business as usual. Brazden now struggled to survive, his saving grace a small plot of land and a seasonal garden to fill in the gaps in his income.

But he never stopped thinking about those three big pots on national monument land outside Flagstaff. Brazden was convinced they were still there, untouched on the hidden ledge. He would have heard about it if something that extraordinary had hit the market—even if it had been an underground transaction. Pothunters would have bragged about a find that important and thrown their money around.

When he last checked on the pots more than twenty years ago, he was able to find their exact location with no problem because Sidney Shackelford had constructed a small marker out of caliche. The stone outlined a stylized butterfly motif, the head pointing in the direction of the cliff. Because of the way the light moved across the land, the ledge that housed the pots was only visible at sun-up.

The jars had been left in peace for a quarter century and now, Brazden thought, was the time to retrieve his personal cache. Two men with good climbing gear and a hoist of sorts would be able to extract the huge pots intact. There was only one small problem: the pots were located within a national monument that was now heavily visited. It would be hard to convince others to take the risk of moving them unless they were as desperate as he was.

If they were caught in the act of stealing pots on a national monument, the punishment would be severe, and no doubt include prison time. Brazden's health was poor; he would not do well in a cold, damp cell. He would rather die then get caught.

But the potential rewards were great. With quality forged documents, the three pots could bring $250,000 from the right buyer. Brazden could buy a first-class set of forged papers for $10,000 or—if he gave up a piece of the action—no upfront money at all. Even if he sold a part of the find, he would have enough cash in reserve for his so-called golden years, which were just around the corner—or so he hoped.

He knew the best outlet for the pots would be overseas, with France having the friendliest laws, and a large pool of buyers, when it came to selling questionable Indian art.

A hard life of alcohol, tobacco, and no medical check-ups ensured that Brazden's retirement would be a short one. He was a cash-and-carry kind of guy, with no social nets to catch his inevitable free-fall from life. The time to figure out how to retrieve the pots was now, while he was still able to scale the cliff.

If he could get some photos of the pots, he thought, he could negotiate a presale—and he knew just where to go to unload merchandise of this high-dollar value.

Tomorrow he would shave, put on a clean shirt and visit one of the big-time dealers he had done business with in Santa Fe in the past. The dealer was a man of questionable scruples. A big fish in the art world, this individual was willing to cut corners as long as the risks were calculated and the payoff significant. A dealer known to skim money off the top of deals and never think twice, he would be the perfect match for Brazden's plundered artifacts.

Dealing with a man of questionable integrity was the price you paid for swimming with the sharks, Brazden thought. He might take a chunk of flesh, but if you got what you needed everyone wins. He knew the man with the high, tight haircut and penetrating blue eyes would work with him; he had done so before and they both had made great money.

Brazden would just need to watch his back. This sale would be the aging pothunter's last big score—and there was no room for error.

CHAPTER 3

A FRESH START

Bright green tree buds, signs of life on a barren brown landscape, spattered the Navajo reservation with color.

Spring, a time of rejuvenation, was Rachael Yellowhorse's favorite season. Lambs were giving birth and Spiderwoman's guiding force was helping her start a new rug.

The winter had been long. Now it was time to come to terms with promises she had made to her husband, Charles Bloom, back in February. By May, she promised, they would move to Santa Fe. Rachael understood that Bloom needed to be challenged and that his business needed impetus. She could weave rugs no matter where they lived as long as her precious sheep were safe and nearby. And having two young children who were not yet enrolled in school made this the ideal time to make the move.

Reflecting on the beauty that surrounded her gave Rachael pause. From the tip of Shiprock peeking over the open prairie that greeted her with the morning sun, to Tsénaajin and Tsénaajin Yazhi, the two buttes she passed going to town for groceries, her daily life was embedded in the matrix of the land.

It would be hard to walk away from a landscape so deeply embedded in her soul. To leave might place her *hózhó*, or inner balance, in jeopardy. For a woman who had not lived outside the four sacred mountains for more than a dozen years, a new home was unthinkable—yet she knew she must leave Toadlena. The decision had not been made lightly. Rachael believed a husband's happiness should come first, and the move would solidify the family unit.

She knew she had made the right choice. New living quarters would make family life less contentious and, with the two of them engaged in full-time work at the gallery, it was sure to pay off in spades. Money was a necessity of life—even for a woman who didn't place it high on her list of essential needs.

Her one concern was that not being around native Diné speakers would affect her children's ability to learn the Navajo language. Even though she spoke Navajo to them during the day, the potential loss troubled her.

It was clear Bloom was excited about the move.

He loved the reservation and looked forward to his daily runs. He had learned a great deal about Navajo weavings from Sal Lito, the Toadlena trader, and from his intimate relationship with Rachael. His wife was one of Dinétah's best weavers.

He now understood the effort that went into making a single small rug and could share that information with buyers. He knew how hard it was to raise, care for, and shear sheep—not to mention the skill required to spin their wool by hand. These insights would help Bloom sell textiles, and he planned to add Navajo weavings and jewelry to his new gallery concept.

A few months earlier, Charles Bloom had a forced indoctrination into the world of Stone Men, individuals who dedicated their lives to the art of turquoise, and their tutelage had given him the confidence to carry Indian jewelry at Bloom's.

Bloom's biggest issue at the moment was where to find adequate accommodations for his family of four and Rachael's growing flock of sheep.

His second pressing concern was to find a larger gallery space, something that would be necessary if he were going to have a year-round presence and expand his offerings.

Brad Shriver, who ran the gallery next door, had been generous in allowing him to rent the smaller casita on the property. But now that Bloom's concept had changed, he would need more room, which meant finding a new space—unless Shriver wanted to give up his gallery, something Bloom highly doubted.

Bloom loved his hideaway on Canyon Road. The gallery had charm, history and, most importantly, was set far enough off the busy road that he didn't have to contend with tourists looking for ice cream or a bathroom. The people who came to Bloom's wanted an art experience. For them, he was happy to provide both inspiration and the occasional restroom.

Next week he would leave Toadlena and begin his quest for a new gallery space and a place for his family to live. He hated the thought of leaving Canyon Road, but it was time for a fresh start and it didn't look like he would have much of a choice. Good retail space on Canyon Road was scarce—even in a recovering economy.

CHAPTER 4

A BIG SURPRISE

Like Charles Bloom, Brad Shriver was a confirmed bachelor. Unlike Bloom, who had found his soulmate in Rachael Yellowhorse, Shriver was still satisfied with casual relationships that allowed him to focus his energy on his true love, which was art.

When it came to his business, he preferred to sell paintings without worrying about another person's input—other than that of his friend Bloom, of course. His life had always been about the gallery—at least until Madeline Sandoval wandered into his viewfinder. Sandoval was a vivacious fifty-year-old widow who, as fate would have it, also happened to be Shriver's and Bloom's landlady.

The Sandovals were a prominent Santa Fe family. Northern New Mexico's Sandoval County, which encompasses Bernalillo, Rio Rancho and counts twelve Indian reservations within its borders, was named after her ancestors. The family could trace its roots back to the conquistadors.

Madeline was land rich, with properties that included a tidy bit of Canyon Road and Camino del Monte Sol. Her rental and business ventures provided her with an ample income that allowed her to spend time on her favorite pastimes: art history and travel.

Shriver had forgotten to take his April rent check to the Santa Fe post office. So, even though he had never met his landlady in person, he figured he had better hand deliver it or face a possible late payment charge, a thought that irked him to no end. He didn't mind spending money on rent but saw no reason to throw good money away on late charges.

Shriver called Madeline to let her know he would drop the check off, but she offered to pick it up instead. This pleased Shriver immensely because he was short-handed and it was one less hassle to deal with.

When Madeline arrived at the gallery, he was deep in selling mode with a rare late-season snow skier who had decided to forfeit one day on the mushy slopes to visit art galleries. The potential customer was showing serious interest in a large, expensive painting by Sheldon Parsons, an early Santa Fe artist, which Shriver had just purchased from a local estate.

The piece, painted in 1943, was of a snow scene featuring a stretch of Canyon Road near the entrance to Shriver's gallery.

"This was one of Parson's last paintings," Shriver said to the client. "It's a provocative title, don't you think? TREASURES OF CANYON ROAD."

Shriver would use any ploy to help sell a painting and the unique title was perfect sales fodder. That it was a snow scene, something the skier probably loved, didn't hurt either.

He talked at length about the importance of Canyon Road in America's history.

"It's one of the ten most historic roads in America," he exclaimed, and that was a fact, not a sales pitch.

He pointed out all the landmarks in the painting, discussing how the chimneys were still in place on the old adobe building that was now

Ernesto Mayans Gallery, noting that the road was a rough dirt lane lined with telegraph poles in 1943.

Canyon Road, he said, was an artist's haven and Sheldon Parsons had lived at the top of it. The studio of Fremont Ellis, another well-known artist, was only a few houses down from Shriver's gallery.

Bringing up Ellis' studio may have been a tactical mistake, though, as the client then asked to see some of the second painter's work, throwing him off the scent of the Parsons piece.

"Ellis... Hmmm... I don't currently have any of his pieces in stock. He's good, but I must say this Parsons is great!"

A well-dressed middle-aged woman had quietly entered the gallery during Shriver's sales pitch, and was intrigued by his perspective and persistence.

Madeline had been around sales long enough to realize the tall, handsome gallerist was leading the client down the path to purchase.

Shriver first detected a sweet perfume in the air, and then he noticed Madeline.

He did a double take, smiled and decided to include the unexpected guest in the conversation. Maybe he had more than one potential buyer—and on a cold, snowy day in April! Two heads were better than one when it came to closing a sale.

It worked. Madeline Sandoval chimed in. "You know, Mr. Shriver..."

He was surprised she knew who he was. He didn't recognize her but wanted to know more about this lovely visitor.

"You are correct. This painting is very important and better than most Ellis pieces from the same time frame. Parsons wanted to depict the road accurately. Look at the details. Each building has been represented.

"The irony is that Parsons was a realist who lost his job at Santa Fe's art museum for his support of modern art."

Shriver's mouth fell open. This was something he hadn't known, and she certainly sounded like she knew her facts.

Madeline continued her commentary.

"Though I must wonder why he put *my* little gallery in such a prominent position in the painting. It's like he was saying. 'Look here...'

"Who knows? Maybe this very space we are standing in is the treasure he refers to in the title."

Madeline smiled, then blushed. She had upstaged the maestro and hadn't given him any time to respond.

Shriver couldn't help but smile at her perceptive and utterly excellent sales pitch. She was a gem, he thought, a special person, and her blush spoke volumes about her.

He was impressed and intrigued by the elegant and well-spoken woman he now realized was his landlady. He had assumed she was a cranky old lady counting her money as it rolled in off the backs of working stiffs like him and Bloom. The reality, now standing before him, was quite the opposite.

Shriver was so enthralled with Madeline he forgot to close the sale— a rare slip for a seasoned salesperson.

"Interesting observation," he responded. "Mrs. Sandoval, I presume?"

"Call me Madeline," she laughed. "My mother was Mrs. Sandoval."

"I would never confuse you with your mother. Madeline it is."

Shriver was now completely ignoring his potential buyer.

"I've also wondered why Sheldon Parsons felt it necessary to make the little casita that is Bloom's gallery a focal point of this painting— although, in my opinion, that's why this piece works so well: it's both a composition and a statement.

"The fact that the painter made the effort to document an insignificant adobe building supports my theory that he's capturing a slice in time on one of the most important roads in America.

"Not unlike AMERICAN GOTHIC, don't you think?"

"Well, that might be pushing it. A Sheldon Parsons-Grant Wood correlation is a bit of a stretch. I don't see the common thread, Mr. Shriver."

Madeline winked at him, knowing full well this intellectual banter was tinged with a hint of sexual innuendo.

Shriver blushed. "Call me Brad."

He smiled, then regained his composure, backing off the mental gymnastics with his landlady. It was time to get back to the matter at hand—closing the client.

He tried to reopen the dialogue with the buyer, but the moment had been lost and he knew he had blown the opportunity. The man took a printed sheet with gallery information and crumpled the glossy paper into his oversized parka.

A blown April sale! A bonehead move for a professional like him. Shriver even followed the skier out to his Land Cruiser, pressing an additional business card and cell phone number on him just in case he decided to purchase the painting before he left town or wanted to return after hours. Then the Texan was gone forever and Shriver had no one to blame but himself.

"I appreciate the help, Madeline. You were brilliant. I just lost eight months rent in one fell swoop. Totally my fault. Performance anxiety, I guess." Shriver grinned as he spoke.

"I shouldn't have been so vociferous," Madeline replied. "I'm afraid it knocked you off track."

"No, if anything your insight added to the conversation. I was taken by your line of reasoning and forgot about the task at hand."

Shriver was no longer worrying about the lost sale. Now he was focused on the attractive women he was so drawn to.

"You're a wonderful salesman by the way. Your passion comes through. And he didn't seem like a man with money to me. That parka must have been ten years old and he kept all his ski tags. The empty can rings the loudest in my book."

Both laughed.

"By the way, Brad, you never said how much you were asking for your wonderful painting."

Shriver's sales instinct kicked back in.

"I have $55,000 on it but was going to let him have it for $50,000. It comes with handwritten letters Parsons penned to a close friend, the man to whom he gave the painting right before he died. I got the piece from that family. It's never been on the market.

"The letters make for an interesting read. It appears Parsons was quite sick at the time, and they are more than a bit cryptic. There's lots of detailed information about the painting's composition and color. And the artist reflects on his choice of title, saying he 'hoped they found the treasure of Canyon Road.'

"If I had been a better salesperson I would have brought this up, don't you think? Buried treasure in Santa Fe makes for a good story, I'm told."

"Yes," Madeline agreed. "Buried treasure is in vogue in Santa Fe these days."

"Maybe, Madeline, you and I can strike a deal on my painting. I could sell it to you in lieu of rent money.

"What do you say?"

"I like the idea of a fair trade with you, Brad Shriver. I'm sure we can work something out though it might take some time and effort on both our parts."

Madeline's wicked grin was the equal of Shriver's own delighted smile.

❋ ❋ ❋ ❋

From that day on Shriver and Sandoval were inseparable. Their relationship matured quickly. Given their ages, neither felt there was time to waste and it was clear they were intellectually and physically compatible.

Madeline, it turned out, did indeed like art. She had amassed a significant collection of her own, built on the bones of her family inheritance.

A trade was worked out, not for rent but for a down payment on the entire Bloom/Shriver gallery complex on Canyon Road. Neither Madeline nor anyone in her family had ever sold a single piece of property before—but somehow it now seemed right. There were no longer any direct heirs to the Sandoval legacy.

By the end of April, the relationship had gotten serious and the two had set a wedding date. It was to be May 7th—the same day Bloom had almost died three years earlier.

The wedding would take place at Madeline's estate on Camino del Monte Sol, a few blocks from Canyon Road. A large early adobe home with multiple buildings, low-slung doorways and aspen as large as oaks graced the property. An expansive vegetable garden filled the back yard, along with a long lap pool.

Madeline spent most of her free time in the garden.

More shocking than the spur-of-the-moment nuptials was the fact that Madeline convinced Shriver to close his gallery and travel the world with her exploring art museums.

She would leave her garden if he would give up his gallery.

To entice him to accept her proposal, Sandoval Inc. agreed to purchase Shriver Fine Art's entire inventory and use the work to decorate her restaurants. And the great deal she had given him to purchase the Canyon Road complex would allow him to either sell the buildings or rent them out. Either way, he would do well and could retire. It was Madeline's wedding gift to her soon-to-be husband.

A closed gallery and no inventory were a new and freeing concept to a man who had never stopped buying in thirty years. For the first time in his life, he had no responsibilities and plenty of cash in the bank.

But what should he do about Bloom?

The wedding invitations were soon to be delivered. The marriage would not be the only surprise for Bloom. Little did he know he had a new landlord who was making big life changes—and one of those changes was about to rock Bloom's world to the core.

CHAPTER 5

MUST FACE EAST

The mountain of boxes stacked in the Ford truck confirmed to Rachael that she was really leaving Toadlena. The final load contained the things had filled her tiny home with meaning—a lifetime of memories.

Even empty, the hogan sang to her to stay.

The old wooden door gave a high-pitched squeak of protest as she pulled the handle shut and locked the persnickety front latch. Rachael's usual security consisted of a bent inner screen door fastened with a hook to a small metal eyelet. She had always felt safe and had no use for locks until today.

"Another abandoned hogan on the rez," she thought to herself as she hid the key under a nearby pile of broken bricks.

Once settled into Santa Fe with her husband and kids, there was no telling when she would return home other than for a holiday visit, so the house was secured to keep nosey neighbors at arm's length.

She wondered if she would ever feel as safe in Santa Fe as she felt here. It was a big city compared to Toadlena.

This move was for Bloom—no, for both of them, she reminded herself. The goal was to keep the family unit happy and grow the art business. The fact that the move made sense didn't make it hurt any less.

A final walk around the house completed, Rachael hopped in her truck and revved the engine. The hot air spewing from the vents felt good on her dusty feet. She was ready to leave, but the land's magnetic force field was so strong she just couldn't put the Ford in gear and drive off.

Rachael's tears bounced off the plastic seat cover as she tried to get her feelings in check. Something was missing, she thought. Part of her needed to be grounded to Mother Earth in a very tangible way.

Getting out of the truck one final time without waking her warm, sleeping kids, she found what she needed—a spiritual and emotional cure of sorts. A burlap sack stashed under the front porch step would work as a container. She gathered up few precious mementos—a slick moss-green rock she had played with for hours while tending sheep as a girl; a fine set of bleached deer antlers her late brother Willard had found on the Chuska Mountains when he was fifteen; and a now-useless broken painted gourd her grandfather had once used as a metronome for healing ceremonies—and tenderly placed them in the makeshift medicine bag. Removing the deer antlers from their mountain home might bother a few traditional Diné, but in her heart Rachael felt it was just the medicine she needed to stay grounded to Toadlena.

Now she could leave and begin the next chapter of her life in Santa Fe. These reminders of her past would help smooth her transition to an as yet unknown future.

✺ ✺ ✺ ✺

Compared to her old home on the rez, the new house looked pretty grand. It was located south of Santa Fe, just off exit 271 on Interstate 25, near the village of La Cienega.

Bloom had searched for weeks for the right rental property, one that could accommodate Rachael's ever-growing flock of sheep and his growing family. Finding a match wasn't easy.

Rachael had insisted their new home face the east. Bloom understood leaving Toadlena was a huge move for her, requiring many adjustments in the way she lived. He also knew that no matter where they lived, she would raise their two children in proper Navajo fashion—which meant having an entrance oriented to the east so they could greet the morning sun. This commitment to following the traditions of her people was serious business in Rachael's mind and Bloom respected her wishes.

Bloom had already moved into the house and Rachael's sheep were happily secured in their new pasture of buffalo grass and snakeweed.

The adobe structure was one-hundred-fifty-years young, with a roof that bowed in the middle. The low-slung, eastern-facing entrance was pleasing to Rachael, even if Bloom's six-foot-plus frame might have to endure numerous clunks to the forehead.

The last time Rachael had lived in Santa Fe, she was in her twenties, attending the Institute of American Indian Arts on a sculpture scholarship and rooming with two other Native students. The three young women had shared a small brick home in the South Capital district. The building was charming and its proximity to the plaza was perfect. One of her roommates, a Jicarilla Apache girl, still lived in Santa Fe, so Rachael knew she would have at least one ready-made friend in her new home.

Still, a lot had transpired in the sixteen years since Rachael left school. She had raised her late brother's son Preston to adulthood, found love with a wonderful husband, and given birth to two rambunctious young children.

Rachael knew Bloom had always wanted to live on the outskirts of Santa Fe and her sheep gave him the perfect reason for doing so.

Seeing his face as she entered the house for the first time told the story—no one could have had a wider grin. Bloom was thrilled to have a large tract of land and ample space for a growing family. The children would have separate bedrooms and abundant outside space to roam. There were four giant cottonwoods gracing a silt-laden farm pond and rich soil for a summer garden. A nearby horse stable was available for occasional rides.

There was plenty of good, fenced pastureland for Rachael's sheep. The Blooms' new landlord, Rocky Martinez, used to own sheep himself and was fine with free grazing as long as Bloom paid the rent on time and promised to keep all the gates shut.

While it was not Toadlena with its majestic two gray hills and rugged horizon, the La Cienega homestead had unmistakable charm that Rachael could not resist. She felt at ease—not home yet, but content with her family, her nearby sheep and a home with an entrance that faced in the right direction.

There were worse places to live, she told herself as she surveyed her new domain. This was Santa Fe, after all. How bad could it be?

CHAPTER 6

BREAKFAST AT CAFE PASQUAL'S

The Yellowhorse-Bloom mail had been rerouted from Toadlena to their new address, so Madeline and Brad's wedding invitation arrived a week late.

Bloom had been so busy getting the new home ready for Rachael he had barely visited the gallery. Dr. J, his manager and only employee, had the place under control.

Next week was the beginning of May and free time soon would be a distant memory. Bloom was no novice dancing to the Canyon Road rhythm. The art road's beat was consistent—slow in the winter, steady in the spring and fall, and rapid during the summer.

When he finally made his way to downtown Santa Fe, Bloom's first stop was at Brad Shriver's gallery to catch up on the local gossip and get a feel for how this year's sales were going.

But Bloom's next-door neighbor and best friend was nowhere to be found. A large yellow card in the gallery window said to try Shriver's cell phone, and Bloom considered calling him. Shriver's was never closed, he told himself, but he had known the man for more than twenty years and knew Shriver would have called him if there had been a problem. The gossip would have to wait.

When Bloom returned home, a five-inch bundle of forwarded mail filled the beat-up mailbox. He picked through the stack, sorting out bills and art magazines. One envelope stood out from the rest, a gold-embossed wedding invitation addressed to Sir Charles and Lady Rachael—Shriver's idiosyncratic sense of humor.

Opening the envelope released dozens of multicolored paper bells that fluttered down to Bloom's feet, many disappearing through the wide cracks in the floorboards, never to be seen again.

"What the hell?"

Bloom smiled as he shook the confetti off his bare foot. Stunned, he had to read the invitation several times before he could comprehend its meaning.

"Madeline Silvia Sandoval and Brad Eugene Shriver request your presence at the blessed event of their marriage on May 7, 2014."

"Shriver is getting married—and to Madeline Sandoval, my landlady?" Bloom said out loud as he plopped into an overstuffed bomber chair, still trying to comprehend what it all meant. He had talked to Shriver for a half-hour a few months earlier and his friend had said nothing about dating someone, much less marrying her.

Bloom figured the invitation must be a joke—Shriver's way of messing with him and welcoming him back to the fold. The date of the wedding confirmed the prank in Bloom's mind.

May 7th was an important milestone for him. On that day, three years earlier, Bloom had come perilously close to bleeding to death at the hands of a homicidal New York City art dealer. Bloom had threatened to expose the alpha art dealer for whom he truly was, a psychopathic killer of artists, and it had nearly cost him his life. The ordeal had made national headlines for weeks and damaged Charles Bloom both physically and emotionally.

One year later, the deadly date was redeemed by the birth of Rachael Yellowhorse's and Charles Bloom's first child, also on May 7th. They named the boy Willy in honor of Rachael's deceased brother, Willard

Yellowhorse, a famous contemporary painter who had died twenty years earlier.

Since that time, May 7th had become a date for healing old wounds and giving life to a family, a special day to be remembered and celebrated each year.

Shriver knew all too well how the arrival of the first week in May pulled on Bloom's heartstrings—the so-called May 7th nuptials had to be his way of ribbing his best friend for finally moving back to Santa Fe full time. Canyon Road was where Shriver had always felt Bloom's heart belonged, not the remote Navajo Nation.

Bloom picked up the phone and speed dialed his number three entry—Shriver's cell.

"So what's this I hear about you getting married on May 7th. And to the landlady?"

Bloom waited for his friend's deep, uninhibited laugh, but none was forthcoming. Shriver was playing it very cool, Bloom thought. Bravo for him.

"Yep, following in your footsteps," Shriver finally responded. "Except this is better. No kids. Madeline bought my entire art inventory, and guess what—I'm *your* new landlord!

"Pretty trippy, wouldn't you say Mr. Bloom? Or should I say tenant Bloom?"

Bloom could feel Shriver smiling at the other end of the phone.

"It's trippy all right! Let me guess now: You're done with the gallery business and you're going on a world cruise?" Bloom baited his best friend.

"You're more intuitive than I gave you credit for, Charlie Bloom—except it's not a world cruise, just Italy and France for now, a three-month sojourn. First time in thirty years I won't be in Santa Fe for Indian Market—and frankly, I can't wait!"

"You're good, my friend," Bloom parried. "If I didn't know better, I could believe you were actually leaving town instead of blowing smoke up my ass."

Shriver couldn't help but laugh. Bloom rarely got it so wrong.

"Admit it. You're screwing with me," Bloom said, thinking Shriver was laughing because he had pulled one over on his old friend.

"Charles James Bloom, I have known you a very long time and let me make this as clear as possible. I'm marrying Madeline Silvia Sandoval on May 7th and want you to be my best man. No joke, my friend. I'm really getting hitched!"

Bloom was speechless—and silent—as he reran the conversation through his mind.

"Bloom?"

"Damn, I don't know what to say! It seems congratulations are in order, and it looks like we have a lot to catch up on.

"What in the f***ing world did you mean when you said you're *my* new landlord?"

"Yup, that's true. And we need to discuss your rent. How about we meet for breakfast tomorrow at Cafe Pasqual's—my treat?"

"Now I know I'm in trouble! You never treat—especially not at Pasqual's."

"See you at 9 a.m. Bring your checkbook as well as your good appetite..." and Shriver was gone.

✱ ✱ ✱ ✱

Bloom hung up not knowing what to think. His best friend was now his landlord? And it looked like his rent was about to go up. But least he would get a world-class breakfast out of the deal. Shriver could be guaranteed a large tab.

CHAPTER 7

WOW!

Still in shock, Bloom shared the stunning news about his new landlord situation with Rachael.

"Maybe he's going to boot me out? Maybe he needs more room, and now money isn't any object? Do you think that's possible?" Bloom confessed his growing worst-case scenario fears to Rachael as they lay in bed getting ready to turn off the lights.

"Listen, Charles. Didn't you tell me recently that you need more space and higher ceilings? This change could allow you to move out with no hard feelings.

"You've known Brad Shriver for a very long time—and he doesn't strike me as a person who would treat a friend that way. Have you ever thought that maybe it's good news that he wants to discuss with you?"

"Well, I'm not counting on a decrease in the rent," Bloom responded. "He's giving me a screaming deal already and he's a great businessman."

Bloom had to admit he didn't know what he would do if the tables were turned and he was standing in his best friend's shoes.

"Don't sweat it, Charles! He's your best friend; he's probably just screwing with you."

"I'm sure you're right, Rachael. I know I shouldn't worry but we just signed a one-year lease with Martinez, and it's May and I can't afford to scramble for a new gallery space this late in the game—plus moving would mean coming up with a two-month deposit.

"Things could get dicey—it's not like I have only myself to think about anymore."

Rachael stroked Bloom's graying temples, letting him know by her gentle touch that everything would work out for the best.

"Honey," she sighed, "Don't worry. You still have one of the best weavers around and I'm not going anywhere. In fact I'm kicking it on this new rug and it might—just *might*—be ready for Indian Market."

Bloom smiled at his wife's confidence and tenaciousness; she had only recently started her current weaving.

"A rug for market—wouldn't that be nice." Bloom admitted he had never considered the possibility.

Rachael turned off the light and snuggled up to Bloom, moving her hands from his temples to his shoulders.

Tomorrow would be better, he thought. The night already was.

✺ ✺ ✺ ✺

The usual herd of early morning tourists was huddled around Pasqual's front door waiting for a table. Shriver, as expected, had managed to secure a prime spot on the rise by the geranium-filled front windows. He looked anxious, though, something Bloom thought was not a good sign.

"What's up buddy?" Shriver boomed. "Can you believe I'm going to get married—me, the last of the lifelong Santa Fe bachelors?"

The two men gave each other a bear hug and sat down to catch up. Bloom felt more at ease when he saw how his friend's face lit up with the news of the upcoming wedding.

Shriver filled Bloom in on the details of how he and Madeline met and confirmed that he was indeed closing his shop, most likely for good.

The aroma of fresh tortillas filled the room and Bloom's stomach churned with the anticipation not only of the food but also some closure on his questions about the ownership of the property and his lease.

He proceeded right to the business at hand.

"So where does this leave us, Brad? What are you going to do with your old space, not to mention my little casita—something I've about outgrown again?" Bloom waved off the waitress who had come to refill their water glasses.

"Well, since you asked, I'm thinking of maybe turning the gallery into a coffee shop or hair salon, maybe taking a piece of the action. I'm sure you will land on your feet; you always have, buddy."

Shriver's toothy grin told Bloom not to worry, and to get the waitress back so she could take their orders. Bloom felt a rush of hunger and happiness.

"I recommend the hair salon. It would make a bundle, and no one else has seven parking spots on Canyon Road. You could definitely take a piece of their action over rent."

The two returned to some less stressful small talk as they snacked on a gift from the chef.

"Hot plates," the waitress warned as she approached their table. Both men took the arrival of their food as a cue to get back to business.

"OK, Here's the deal Mr. Charles Bloom. Madeline and I want you to buy the entire property. It's mine to do with as I like now, and I want you and Rachael to be set—not to mention that with you two as the new owners I could walk away without having to worry about a bad tenant. You know these damn art dealers—they're either always late on payments or hightailing it out of town."

Bloom gulped down the first bite of his delicious *huevos rancheros*, the egg yolk and green chile sauce running together and dribbling down his chin.

"Brad, that's a really nice offer, but I doubt first of all that I can get a loan and second, even if I could borrow the money, I couldn't afford the price. It's got to be about $1.5 million."

"$1.8 million is closer to it, but who's counting? So here's the deal: I'll sell the property to you for $1.4 million and carry the property payment using the current interest rate of, say, 4.5 percent. And you don't have to give me anything down—zip. You can't beat that, my friend!

"I'm happy to make the monthly payment plus the 4.5 percent juice on the principal."

"What if I can't make the payments and I default?" Bloom countered. "It's been known to happen to art galleries in Santa Fe, even the good ones like Bloom's."

"I'm not worried about you defaulting," Shriver replied, but if you decide to sell the property in less than five years, we will split the profit if there is any. And if for some reason you do blow up and can't pay me, I'll take back the property and you can give me half interest in your small Willard Yellowhorse painting. That's worth $150,000 to me I would think, and the deal would give you plenty of incentive to not screw up because I would want to sell my half of the painting —and Rachael would make Rocky Mountain oysters out of your manhood.

"What do you think?"

"Wow!" Bloom gulped. "It's a very generous offer. What do you think the payments would be?"

"Five thousand dollars a month plus utilities should cover it, not including property tax. Sell a couple of good paintings each month or a have a great Indian Market week and you'll be in the clear.

"This will give you an extra showroom to sell those Navajo weavings and jewelry you have become so enchanted with of late. At worst, you could move into the casita if things get tight and save the money you are spending renting a home.

"I'm set now and can retire—and I want you to have something you can fall back on, too. A great property on Canyon Road is always going to be valuable."

Bloom knew that Shriver was selling him on the deal, but, in this case, he also knew his friend was right.

"Can't argue with you there! I'll talk to Rachael. When do you need an answer? And I assume you'll take a credit card for my rent payments..." Bloom grinned at the thought, knowing all good business people hated to loose that 2 percent.

"I'll give you a week. If you don't want to buy the property, I can just be your landlord—and then I will take your credit cards for an additional 5-percent fee, of course. But my advice is to take the deal. You won't get an offer like this again."

A satisfied smile came over Bloom's face, in part because he had just downed a plate of the best *huevos rancheros* in town, but also because owning a building on Canyon Road was something he had always dreamed of—and that dream now had a strong possibility of becoming a reality.

His ship had come in and he had his landlady to thank!

He hoped Rachael would be as receptive to the deal as he was. On impulse, he got another order of *huevos* to go. It never hurt to prime the food pump.

CHAPTER 8

SOMETHING'S UP

Bloom arrived home cradling a hot tin of *huevos rancheros*, and Rachael knew something was up. Take home from Pasqual's? There were never any leftovers.

Her husband was spontaneously generous with his love, but he usually didn't come bearing gifts. She felt like Bloom was a roadrunner presenting her, his mate, with a snake. He was after something and knew Pasqual's was a powerful aphrodisiac.

Rachael was willing to play along as long as she got to eat the meal.

The red and green chile-covered delight was presented on a picturesque old picnic table at the base of a one-hundred-fifty-year-old cottonwood tree. Small parachutes of white fuzz—one of the things that gave the trees their name—filled the air with each passing breeze.

"OK, Charles Bloom—What gives? I know you love me and all, but takeout from Pasqual's?" What does Mr. Shriver have planned for us—and did he pay for this?"

Bloom smiled then repeated the entire conversation as he dipped the end of a warm blue-corn tortilla in the corner of Rachael's red sauce.

Rachael listened quietly while she ate, then asked: "So you're the money guy. Can we pull this off or will we be giving half of my late brother's gift to your best friend?"

Rachael avoided using her brother Willard Yellowhorse's name, respecting the dead in the Navajo way.

"I think it's a great deal," Bloom enthused. But I'm trying not to let my emotions sway me. I've always wanted to own that gallery space, but the few times I broached it with Mrs. Sandoval, she laughed it off, saying something to the effect of 'over my dead body.'

"So now that it's being served to us on a plate, it seems stupid not to grab the opportunity." Bloom smiled at his ongoing food metaphor.

"So what you're saying is that this is a good deal?" Rachael asked, her mouth half filled with a corn tortilla.

"Hon, I wouldn't be able to finance even a crappy building for zero down and honestly, I'm tired of being a renter. Even if this season sucks because of depressed oil prices in Texas, I still believe it's a good deal."

Rachael pondered both his heartfelt confession of his desire to be an owner rather than a renter and his evaluation of the offer.

"It would be nice to have something for the kids, but this deal could tie us to Santa Fe forever instead of for the two years we agreed on. And you know how hard this is for me."

Rachael teared up. Bloom came closer, gave her a long hug, then snuck another taste of her red chile sauce.

"Listen. I love Toadlena, too. It's magical, and we will always have your hogan to fall back on. You told me yourself that the school system here in Santa Fe is better than the one in Newcomb, and the kids will be starting school in just a few years. If business is a bust, I think we can sell the property and make some money. Quite frankly, I think we would be foolish not to take the chance."

Bloom's mind was made up and the high-powered salesman in him was looking to close the deal.

"If we do it right, Rachael, we can set up a place on the property for you and the kids to work during the day and bring a couple of sheep to the gallery to promote our Navajo weavings. It will be a great attraction and we can be together every day."

He knew he had her at "Rachael."

"OK, I'm in—but you have to promise you'll keep me in the loop if things aren't going as planned."

Bloom nodded his head in agreement and tried to make one last dip into Rachael's food. This time, she swatted his hand. "We can buy the property, but the rest of this sauce is mine!"

Both laughed and Bloom gave up his chile quest. But Rachael didn't touch the rest of her food.

❋ ❋ ❋ ❋

The two spent the next hour-and-a-half discussing their plans for improving the gallery and making it their own. What the couple couldn't have foreseen were the other forces at work, the current of anger that would soon be flowing down Canyon Road. Someone would not appreciate being shut out of the historic buildings—and he would stop at nothing to turn the tide of events in his favor.

CHAPTER 9

A TO Z

Bloom called Shriver back that same evening and accepted the deal. He did not want Shriver—or worse, his ex-landlady—to change their minds and backtrack. A good salesman knows when to close; wait too long and deals have a tendency to go south.

The next week was a whirlwind of gallery-sale related service people —a building inspector, appraiser and handyman to name a few. In Santa Fe, the routine was to make appointments, wait and reschedule when no one showed up.

Since they weren't using a Realtor, both men figured it was best to do this transaction by the book so if any issues arose they would be on the table.

The property was in surprisingly good shape considering its age, which was as yet undetermined. Parts of the building probably dated from the eighteenth century, but the house had been added onto so many times it wasn't clear what date to use.

It was your typical Santa Fe homestead on Canyon Road. A portion of the casita's back wall was shared with a neighbor, a newer gallery owner on the road, Felix Zachow. The surveyor had assured Bloom this was not uncommon and he should not worry about it. The shared wall didn't seem an issue, so Bloom didn't fret: After all, this was Santa Fe and all the historic homes had some weird easement or another.

Bloom decided not to bother Zachow about the common wall—at least not while he was in the process of closing, and especially because he never planned to sell the property.

Felix Zachow was a serious art dealer, a big fish in the Santa Fe gallery pond. He made both the local papers and the national art rags on occasion. The articles were often not very flattering, but they made it clear the man had money and made major art transactions. Bloom understood that a sour deal wasn't always the dealer's fault, though in most cases there was probable cause for unkind media exposure.

Zachow had three galleries: New York, Zurich and Santa Fe. A relative newcomer to the City Different, he had arrived on the Santa Fe scene eight years ago. He was only in town for the summer season and, since most the galleries in Santa Fe—including Bloom's—didn't play in his elevated sandbox, they weren't a threat to him.

Still, in the art world, Zachow was feared as well as respected, and the word on the street was to watch your back when doing business with him. Since Bloom had never had any transactions with him, he kept an open mind about his neighbor and decided it was best not to make an issue out of the shared wall, which was primarily on his property.

Moving against the latest trends, Zachow had recently moved from the up-and-coming Santa Fe Railyard arts district to Canyon Road, where many of the well-established galleries had their roots.

A to Z, Zachow's gallery, was obviously well capitalized. He had purchased the two expensive buildings that surrounded Bloom's, right on the main thoroughfare, and almost immediately began significant construction projects. This was surprising to Bloom, as the buildings were magnificent structures to begin with.

Appropriately, A to Z's inventory covered the gamut of contemporary paintings, sculpture, and tribal art. A nineteen-fifties abstract painting juxtaposed with a nineteenth century Zuni kachina was the typical décor scheme. Zachow mixed and matched artistic styles, with the only common denominator being quality. Everything he showed was the best of type, including his collection of pre-Columbian art, one of his favorites. His display skills were immaculate and his prices eye-popping.

Zachow's clients rarely ventured back to Bloom's shop. Bloom figured his inventory wasn't expensive enough to merit the short walk. These collectors wanted deceased and rare, and were the dealer's invited guests, so to speak.

The crucial information Bloom needed to consummate the deal with Brad and Madeline was the appraised value of the two buildings. The information would be important if an exit strategy were needed.

The numbers that came in were realistic, quoted by a person who understood the uniqueness of Canyon Road property—not a lowball, computer-generated Zillow-like price. The gallery/casita appraised at $1,750,000 and, as promised, Shriver did the deal at $1.4 million.

An agreement was written, all terms and conditions signed-off, and Bloom gave $5,000 to Shriver as his initial mortgage payment—the first one of many. Bloom would be eighty when he paid off the property unless he lugged on it, a daunting proposition.

Dry elm samaras piled against a sandstone fence crunched under foot as Bloom walked the property boundaries for the first time. He had always hated elm-tree debris; the tiny winged seeds caused nothing but extra work. But now he looked at the pods with new eyes. Now that they were his, the elms were no longer springtime pests but valuable shade-giving trees. Scraggly as they might look at the moment, the trees were his responsibility and their seeds reminders of his newfound wealth.

Bloom's life had been more intertwined with the historic property than he ever could have imagined.

Over the years, he made many thoughtful renovations to the property even though he didn't have title to it. Fruit trees on drip irrigation were fresh with color; brick gardens with mature plantings were created out of love for the land he didn't own.

Had he somehow known that one day the planets would align in his favor? If he hadn't invited Shriver to share the property two years ago, he would never have been in a position to purchase the buildings now. At the time, it was a big decision to give up the main gallery to Shriver, but he had trusted his gut. Committing to buy property he could barely afford was no less a leap of faith. A higher power must be involved, Bloom reasoned; being married to Rachael allowed him to consider such possibilities.

Now that the transfer was complete, Bloom's first order of business was to expand the smaller casita that had been serving as his gallery since he gave the main space to Shriver. The casita would become the new Indian art gallery where Rachael could work and care for their children. They would enclose and expand the ancient portal, creating a playroom and adding needed storage space. The children would be safe, only a step away from their mother.

The small casita would be transformed into a sizeable rug room laced with jewelry. Preston Yellowhorse and Billy Poh would show their jewelry and Bloom would add a couple of other smiths and weavers to the mix. Dr. J would help Rachael Monday through Friday with this more traditional portion of the business, which meant Bloom could continue to man the contemporary art gallery, something he had done for years. They decided to call the casita space "Bloom's Traditional" so as not to confuse old clients.

Reluctantly, Rachael agreed to apply the kids' education fund to build out the casita's portal to create a playroom. Bloom assured her that the increased sales would allow them to recoup the money in no time. Tourists would respond positively to seeing Rachael at work on her rug with the kids in the background—and that would lift sales for the rest of his inventory.

Sal Lito, the great businessman who ran the Toadlena Trading Post, had agreed to supply the bulk of the new Toadlena/Two Grey Hills weavings for the rug room, and Bloom figured he could fill the gaps with weavers from other parts of the rez. With Internet advertising for old rugs in place, he would soon have a respectable inventory of Diné weaving covering the last hundred years.

Bloom's Traditional and Bloom's were now open and ready for business, officially listed on the CanyonRoadArts.com website. All he needed now was for summer to arrive, the plummeting West Texas crude to stabilize, and nothing to go wrong with the build-out of the casita.

But getting a permit to modify the historic building would turn out to be more challenging than he could ever have imagined.

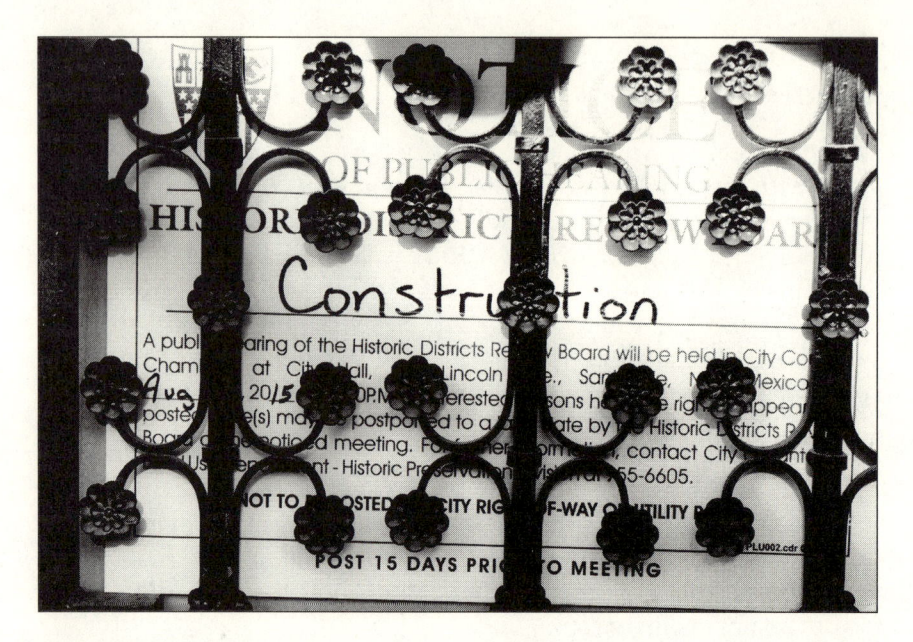

CHAPTER 10

YOU NEED A HISTORIAN

Enclosing a porch in most cities in America can be accomplished with a couple of day laborers and a six-pack of beer. But in Santa Fe's historic districts, and especially on Canyon Road, making a change of any kind is much more problematic. Bloom and Rachael no longer lived on the rez, where there was no question that a nineteen forty-eight trailer dumped behind your home made a fine guesthouse.

In Santa Fe, any alterations to historic buildings have to adhere to strict rules and regulations.

Founded in sixteen hundred-nine or sixteen hundred-ten, Santa Fe is the oldest capital city—and the third oldest settlement in the United States overall—its unique culture and style influenced by the Native tribes and Spanish colonists who called it home and the Americans who followed the railroad West.

When New Mexico became a state in 1912, Santa Fe looked nothing like it does today. But farsighted city fathers, moved by the need to enhance the region's budding tourism trade as well as preserve its unique multicultural style, began an adobe-centric architectural revival that took a giant leap forward when it was codified into law forty-five years later.

As any home or business owner in the affected districts can tell you, the Historic Zoning Ordinance of 1957 requires any new construction in the downtown and Canyon Road areas to conform to one of two specific architectural styles: Spanish Pueblo Revival and Territorial Revival.

Today, "Santa Fe Style," with its earth-toned adobe and fauxdobe facades, graces everything from strip malls to barbershops, Southside apartments to multi-million dollar mountain homes.

Bloom was a supporter of keeping Santa Fe's historical architecture intact—and preserving the buildings on Canyon Road was a big part of that process. He had heard the Historic Districts Review Board—often referred to as the hysterical committee by locals—could be hard to deal with. If they took a dislike to you or your plans for any reason, there was certain to be trouble.

So Bloom was prepared for a long approval process and the need to spend extra money out-of-pocket to move things along.

An on-site evaluation of the property was the first step to getting the ball rolling. Bloom's evaluator was to be a woman named Wendy Whippelton. He envisioned her as an erudite, elderly white woman armed with a measuring tape and a camera, looking for reasons to shut his project down. Even her name—Wendy Whippelton!—sounded like trouble.

On the day of her visit, scheduled for 9:30 a.m., Bloom arose early and made some sun tea using his family recipe. He planned to be on top of his game today. He figured it wouldn't hurt to soften up the old gal with a cool drink since she held his future in her scrawny hands.

At 9:45 a.m. Bloom began checking the calendar on his phone, assuming he had gotten the day wrong, when a Toyota Prius tore into his driveway, tossing gravel knee-high. A young woman with frazzled red hair jumped out of the car, talking on her cell phone, barely pausing to breathe between sentences.

"Sorry, so sorry," she gasped when she caught sight of him. "I got stuck at the DeVargas Starbucks, the line was out the door, and then, on top of that, they're doing construction on the Paseo—can you believe that? Major construction in May, on one of the busiest roads in Santa Fe? You'd think they could wait until winter when no one's around..."

Bloom liked her immediately—a city worker bashing the road crews' timing—this was a woman he could work with.

"No problem! I'm Charles Bloom. I own this place."

Bloom smiled widely as he introduced himself. This was the first time he had given voice to his new status in public.

"Nice digs. You're so lucky," Wendy gasped. "So let's see what you've got here. Sorry to rush but I have four more properties to evaluate this morning and one of them I can't even find on Google Maps— How is that even possible?"

She didn't wait for an answer as she ran toward the casita.

Bloom showed Wendy around as she peppered him with questions about the building's age, the existence of architectural plans and documentation, and whether he was aware of any archaeological concerns regarding the property.

The last question—the one about archaeological findings—was the one Bloom had been hoping she wouldn't broach.

"So, Wendy, say I hypothetically found something of archaeological interest on the grounds here. Could that stop my small project from going forward?"

"Listen," she laughed. "You can't put a spade in the ground around here without turning up something—a piece of Spanish porcelain or Indian pottery. As long as it's not human remains, it shouldn't be a problem.

"So, 'hypothetically,' what've you got?" She flashed him a toothy grin.

Bloom told her what he had found a few years ago when he had a problem with a raccoon family that had taken up residency underneath the portal. He tried everything to rid the place of pests, including digging a large hole for a live trap. The contraption was of no use, but the excavation turned up a medium-sized old wooden box containing two early Spanish coins and the head of a large pre-Columbian figure. He couldn't believe the items were original to the property, but he hadn't investigated the find beyond a few simple Internet searches.

Living in Santa Fe, Bloom had seen plenty of pre-Columbian ceramics that had little value, and the Internet was filled with inexpensive colonial coins for sale. The trunk was the most interesting item but was in poor condition. He could find nothing comparable online.

Bloom had hung onto the artifacts even though they didn't belong to him. He thought that if he ever stopped renting the property, he'd return them to Mrs. Sandoval, their rightful owner.

Right now, telling Wendy about the find, he felt like a thief—but he had forgotten about the objects until last night when he realized he would probably need to disclose their existence at today's meeting.

Bloom went into the casita and retrieved the goods and handed them over to city's evaluator, hoping she wouldn't judge him too harshly.

"It's probably nothing, but here's what I found. The hole was right about here, three feet from my last pear tree."

As it turned out, Whippleton was not only a city employee; she also had an archaeology degree from the University of New Mexico. Sometimes, Bloom thought, it seemed like everyone in Santa Fe was an archaeologist.

"Interesting," she said as she looked at his finds. These are from the colonial period. The Spanish coins date from somewhere between fifteen and sixteen hundred. The pre-Columbian head is earlier than the coins, but that's not really my area of expertise.

"It's a very odd and very interesting find," she continued. "I'm not sure how the head could have gotten into the box with the coins. I'll take some photos to do some research—gratis of course—and you can hold on to the objects.

"The artifacts shouldn't stop your construction as you're not doing any excavation other than for landscaping purposes, and you're not going to be altering the integrity of the building. But because you don't have any architectural plans or drawings, or a good, documented history of the property, we will require a historical review before we give you permission to move ahead."

"What's that entail?" Bloom, who could see the money starting to flow out, was now regretting disclosing the existence of the trunk and its contents.

"In Santa Fe," Wendy responded, "we often need to hire a historian to give us background information regarding structures like yours, buildings that have no clear date of construction. I'll investigate the archaeological finds as a fun project, so that won't cost you anything.

"I can recommend four historians that meet the city's requirements. The best credentialed is Jonathan Wolf. He's been around forever, he's good at getting projects like this fast-tracked, and he's very thorough, which the board likes.

"I'll make my recommendation to approve your project today. Then, once you have the architectural drawings and the historian's report, you'll just need to go in front of the Historic Districts Review Board for approval. Because your building is off the road, you shouldn't have a problem getting a permit."

Wendy thought for a moment, then continued: "The A to Z gallery next door was approved for construction and those buildings faced Canyon Road, so I don't see why your proposal wouldn't fly through. But I'm afraid it's going to cost you some money."

Bloom and Whippelton parted on an up-note and, for the first time, Bloom felt confident he would survive the review process. Tomorrow he would call Jonathan Wolf. He hoped the historian wouldn't be too expensive.

It was also time, he decided, to come clean about his archaeological finds. In the morning, he would pay a long overdue visit to Madeline Sandoval.

CHAPTER 11

PREHISTORIC TAKE OUT

Walks with a Limp was pushing hard to return to the clan shelter before the rain began. Dark purple storm clouds were percolating behind the sacred volcano rim only a few miles away. She remembered such a storm as a child when two people had lost their lives. Mother Earth's power was not to be taken lightly. Her people called this season a time of plenty, a time when the sun was high in the sky, a time when heavy male rains came in force and corn plants thrived.

Walks with a Limp was in her last trimester of pregnancy. She looked like a giant brown squash—to the point that members of her clan had started calling her "Big Gourd" as a joke. She took the ribbing, and the pregnancy, in stride. In twelve hundred C.E., life was hard for all and especially hard for women. Her role in the world was determined by tradition: She was to gather food and prepare it, tend to the fire, raise children and help care for the elders.

Her mate, Tall as Corn, was a leader in the community. He had lived for many seasons and was strong and wise. At thirty, he was one of the elder statesmen of the village.

When he chose the exiled club-footed girl as his life partner, the people were surprised but did not question his judgment. Tall as Corn recognized that she was wise beyond her seventeen years and felt her deformity was a sign of power.

Walks with a Limp was strong and decisive. She had been on her own since age twelve, when her parents died in a cave collapse during the long winter of pain. She would have perished, too, if it were not for the strong will to survive that allowed her to dig herself out of the snow and rock tomb. Of her family of five, only she lived, the youngest and a cripple.

The clan was divided on her fate. How was it possible, they asked each other, that she could have breathed under all that dirt. Was she infected with evil from the Third World after her near burial? Was she blessed with powerful magic or cursed? They would let the gods decide.

So, in the depth of winter, Walks with a Limp was cast out of her village and told to stay away until three seasons had passed—a sentence not all agreed with. If she survived, it was reasoned, it would be proof she was free of evil, and she would be allowed back into society. The elders did not consider this a harsh punishment, but a necessary test to protect the whole village from bad spirits.

Walks with a Limp not only survived the severe sanction cast on her by her people. Free of the rule of a man or the community, she thrived.

High above the pueblo-style settlement built into low canyon walls, she found her bastion of safety. Her new home was a ledge on a cliff wall ten miles away, a ledge she discovered as she walked east to greet the morning sun while praying to the god of safety. The morning light had revealed the otherwise hidden sliver to her, almost three-hundred feet straight up from the desert floor.

It took most of her reserves and a day of laborious work to peck out a few key handholds of sufficient depth to reach her goal. The ledge offered protection from the elements and wild animals. A constant drip of water from a crevice seep was clean and, most importantly, reliable.

A crack in the wall that ran straight down from the high cliff to the hard desert floor provided an occasional small game morsel she could capture without actually hunting—prehistoric take out of sorts. A colony of bats that shared the ledge was another source of nourishment in the hot season.

Her new home didn't require her to search for substance or shelter—five-star accommodations for the time—and it saved her life.

✱ ✱ ✱ ✱

Walks with a Limp had time to work on her hunting skills, not a usual female skill set but an important one if you're alone. Three seasons stretched into twelve and she grew strong and fearless. She had been menstruating for twenty-five moon cycles when she realized that if she wanted more from life than the solitude of her ledge, she'd have to rejoin her people on the flatlands. A woman now, she yearned for children and the touch of a mate.

Packing her meager belongings, she left her high, safe home on a chilly morning to return to the village.

She was afraid she might be ostracized again—or worse, deemed an evil spirit and killed—because she had been gone so long. Her plan was to arrive at sunrise chanting a curing song her father used to sing. He had been a well-liked man of vision, and she believed that singing his song might help win over the unbelieving and provide her with some important spiritual cover.

Tall as Corn was the first to spot the young woman, who appeared to be floating in the daybreak mist. Her striking features took him off guard: a strong chin accentuated by white teeth, long straight black hair that flowed past bare breasts to a taut stomach. He recognized her by her odd gait and was immediately smitten with her beauty and poise.

He had recently been left alone and childless, his mate killed in a fall. Although he felt a deep hole in his being, no new match was of interest until that early morning chill brought him a memory from the past.

The central courtyard filled with people as the girl's presence became known. But most of the villagers did not react to her approach with the interest and charity of Tall as Corn. A rumble of discontent and fear filled the moist air, and there was a call to stone the demon into oblivion. She could no longer be of this world, they said. She must be an evil spirit coming back to take revenge on them for banishing her.

The frightened woman who called for her death threw the first stone, hitting Walks with a Limp in the side with an audible thud. Others, not sure what to do, watched the girl coming toward them. Walks with a Limp winced but never faltered. Instead, her voice grew stronger. She was determined to be taken back into the tribe or perish in the process.

Before another stone could be flung, her soon-to-be mate blocked Walks with a Limp's path and turned to face the mob.

"I know of this woman," he said in a strong voice. "She is Walks with a Limp. She has returned to our camp and will become my mate. Do not fear her. She has survived the wilderness and is fitter than most. She can teach us much and is a blessing for our people—a great gift from the gods."

There was a hush in the crowd.

"Is this true, Walks with a Limp?" a voice in the back asked.

"Yes, Tall as Corn speaks the truth. I have come back to be at his side. I will bear his children and teach all of you the ways of survival on the land. If you allow me to come home, I'll share my wisdom with you. My knowledge runs deep and our gods have blessed my return."

Before anyone could respond, Tall as Corn let out a loud shout of joy and proclaimed: "Today the gods have spoken by the return of Walks with a Limp."

The two clasped hands and Tall as Corn walked his new mate to his rock enclave at the head of the large canyon where they would start their new lives as one.

CHAPTER 12

TWO HEADS ARE BETTER THAN ONE

Waves of pain crashed over Walk with a Limp's huge abdomen, her amniotic fluid returning to Mother Earth through the packed dirt floor of her home.

"It's OK. Don't worry. I am very skilled and will help you pass your child." The old woman attending Walks with a Limp tried to reassure her, but this would be no ordinary delivery—something Tall as Corn recognized when he summoned the sometime midwife to assist with his mate's impending delivery. She arrived just as the baby struggled to be born.

Graying hair, bad teeth, and foul breath made standing close to the old woman unpleasant; at forty-five, the woman was one of the oldest members of the tribe. Her help would cost Tall as Corn a week's worth of food. It was a high price to pay, but worth it for the safety of his firstborn and the woman he cherished.

For prehistoric women, the birth process normally didn't receive much attention or consideration. Like grinding corn, producing babies was just something expected of them. Isolate yourself, squat and deliver the newborn, then bring home the afterbirth for a rare protein meal and be ready to work the next day—that was the drill. But Walks with a Limp's pregnancy was not normal. The size of her belly made it clear there would be something very different about this delivery.

Two years had passed since she returned to the community and, after the initial trepidation had faded, Walks with a Limp had been well received. Most felt she had special powers and she did nothing to dissuade them of this idea. It gave her more prestige than women could generally garner, so she embraced this misconception, never again wanting to chance being banished and alone. The gods would summon her at some point and she would make sure she had the ability to accept whatever destiny they had in store. Her higher status was part of the equation.

The people did not question her huge abdomen—only the outcome of the birth was unknown. The midwife had been called in for help. It would take all of her years of experience to avoid disaster.

The baby finally arrived in serious distress. A breach delivery is a major problem no matter what millennium you lived in. The midwife had attended three such births, and only one resulted in a living child. The other two brought death for both mothers and babies. For the first time, the odds of surviving were not in Walks with a Limp's favor.

The old woman pulled at the two little blue legs with each contraction, slowly extracting the baby one tug at a time, applying just enough pressure to avoid injuring the newborn. It looked as if she might succeed until the head became stuck in the birth canal. Try as she might, the midwife could not move the pliable skull beyond Walks with a Limp's pelvis.

Finally, with as great determination to survive as she had exhibited twice before, Walks with a Limp repositioned herself from a squatting position to a prone one.

She readied herself, wedging her feet against the rock wall of the doorjamb for maximum leverage. With outstretched arms holding onto the hearth, she used all her legs' strength and bore down hard to deliver the newborn. To fail would mean certain death for them both.

Her legs, which had climbed a nearly vertical cliff for three years, did not disappoint her. A gush of bright red blood and a sucking pop signaled a large tear in the vaginal perineum and the baby was free. But Walks with a Limp's relief was immediately followed by a scream.

The old woman's face spoke volumes. A fearful expression replaced her earlier look of concern. Her shriek penetrated the morning heat like a coyote's call at a kill, and concerned villagers began gathering outside Tall as Corn's home.

"What is it? Tell me!" Walks with a Limp implored, fearing the worst though her pain was now slowly subsiding.

"I don't know. This is beyond my knowing," the midwife replied. "Here. You can see for yourself."

She handed the pinkish baby, still gasping for air and attached to the placenta by an uncut umbilical cord, to Walks with a Limp. What then became clear was that this was not a single child, but a child with two heads and two necks attached near the base of the shoulders, each mouth breathing in fits and starts.

Without hesitation, Walks with a Limp commanded the old woman to get back to work.

"My daughters are a sign of god's will, so cut the umbilical cord, you old fool, and help me deliver Tall as Corn's dinner. This is a great day for our people. Let all in the village be summoned so they can come to see the gift of the gods. Tonight we celebrate our good fortune as a people."

The old woman snapped back into action, her fears alleviated by her magical patient's confidence. She finished the delivery and pasted a patch of juniper bark onto Walks with a Limp's jagged laceration with a generous amount of mud, which helped slow the bleeding to a minor trickle.

Walks with a Limp relaxed and sat up. Still biting her lower lip to control the pain, she forced a smile on her face for the benefit of those now looking into the room. She knew she must be strong for her newborn daughters. They would be known as the Butterfly Twins, she decided, and would represent a metamorphosis from the human womb to a new type of being. Fertility would be their mission in life.

She couldn't have been prouder.

CHAPTER 13

SACRED BEGINNINGS

The night was filled with celebration. A chunky placenta stew was shared by all, the first gift of the Butterfly Twins.

The girls were only a few hours old, yet their distinctive personalities already showed through in their sleep patterns.

Tall as Corn's status was enhanced with the girls' birth. It was an important event in the people's history, something to be remembered along with the great volcano eruption four generations earlier, the resulting crater sitting just a few miles from the village. The volcanic ash had changed their world by increasing the land's fertility—something Walks with a Limp assured the people her daughters would also do.

At sunrise the next day, Tall as Corn greeted the morning sun with prayers at the great picture wall north of the communal kiva. The sound of chipping rock filled the air for two days as the sacred birth was recorded for his people's history. When the pictograph was complete, the black and red sandstone rock face was decorated with dozens of butterflies emerging from cocoons. Each butterfly had two heads and one body, a symbol of his daughters that would now represent fertility.

Another few days passed and it was clear the two heads indeed represented separate individuals. They ate and slept differently and each hand appeared to be independently controlled.

The word of their birth had spread as fast as a summer fire, and the newborns were a hit. Watching each head grasp a nipple and feed soon became a rare entertainment in a world of want. Within a week, a member of a nearby community heard of the event and came to see the spectacle; soon all in the Four Corners region would visit the blessed girls.

Walks with a Limp enjoyed the attention and made sure all knew her daughters should be treated with the utmost respect. Their powers would grow as they matured, she said, and she would look unkindly on those who spoke ill of their unique physique. She did not want her daughters endangered by any talk of evil. Unlike her disfigurement, her daughters' perceived disability would be treated as a rare and positive gift.

Never before had a conjoined twin birth been recorded in a tribe's history. The phenomenon was not unheard of in the animal kingdom, but for a human it meant there was a direct link from the animal world to the human—powerful medicine of the most visceral kind.

❈ ❈ ❈ ❈

Many moons passed and the Butterfly Twins reached adolescence. They were slow to develop gross motor skills but, beyond their physical awkwardness, they were as adept at life as their dynamic parents.

Song was second nature to them, coming from deep within as it had for their long-departed grandfather and Walks with a Limp, and they spent much time perfecting their chants. When they sang in narrow slot canyons, they produced an eerie sound that could resonate long distances, a sound the people had never heard until their birth.

The girls talked as if with one voice and could finish each other's sentences, which the people interpreted as being able to read each other's minds—something that proved they were not of this world.

Unlike other women, the Butterfly Twins were free to lead a more creative life. Food was provided in their honor by the villagers, so they were never in need. They were celebrities among their own people and those living in surrounding communities.

A parrot from a southern tribe had been brought to the central kiva as a gift. The Butterfly girls shared the bird with everyone in the tightly knit community, allowing each family to take a turn feeding and protecting the bright beast. If a feather fell while the bird was being cared for, it was given to that family as a blessing.

The Butterfly Twins referred to each other as Ish and Osh. Ish had the higher head and could see frontally and side-to-side. Osh spent much of her time looking backward. Their combined vision gave the girls a unique 360-degree perspective that allowed them to act as lookouts, a duty normally reserved for a man.

The people interpreted this ability to look forward and back to mean they could see things others could not, and they were respected as visionaries. Because the girls didn't have to work for food or clothing, their powers of observation became keener and more insightful, solidifying their reputation as powerful medicine.

During the first part of their life, there was significant and positive change in the northern Arizona environment. There had been an increase in both food and the population directly after the Butterfly Twins' birth—something the people attributed to the girls' fertility gifts. But, as the years passed, a significant drought hit the land.

Through the Butterfly girls' visions, Walks with a Limp encouraged her people to save as much corn and beans as possible and to avoid having sex except during menstruation to decrease the number of hungry new mouths to feed. She also told them to focus on improving their dryfarming skills. One particular corn variety they developed did very well in the drought. Over the next two years, it was the only plant to produce enough seed to see the people through the harsh winter months. The people looked at this new corn as a blessing, a testament to the Butterfly Twins' powers.

By year three of the drought, it became apparent that the people were in a severe predicament. The elders came to the Butterfly Twins and asked them to help safeguard their future. The girls were mature women by then; they were fifteen and ready to have babies themselves.

It was decided that the strongest man in the community would become their mate and that they would be allowed to have a child during this time of need. If the child were strong, the people too would be strong and could stay put. If the child struggled or died, they would take it as a sign that they needed to leave their ancestral land and look for another place that could nourish them.

The most skilled craftsman wove a special dress from the finest cotton to coincide with the occasion of the birth. The dress represented a gift from the tribe, a tribute to the Butterfly Twins' powers. It was decorated with red lines of ochre and butterflies to help the new mothers be strong enough to meet their people's needs.

Walks with a Limp, who at thirty-two was reaching late middle age, was worried about her daughters. She knew of the pain and risk of delivery—something she had experienced just once—and it was unclear if being a conjoined twin would increase the dangers of childbirth. But she believed it was up to the gods to decide the outcome of both the birth and the prophecy for the community.

Thanks to Walks with a Limp's counsel, her people had enough corn saved for the winter, and soon the newborn would deliver the needed sign for the future.

CHAPTER 14

DAY OF RECKONING

A low rumble of concern flowed through the corridors of single-family rooms as the Butterfly Twins went into labor. The midwife with the bad breath had long ago died and Walks with a Limp had taken over her position. Today would be her most difficult delivery, though—on this day her own grandchild would come into the world.

The baby turned in the womb and seemed to be doing well, slowly making its way down the pelvic canal right on schedule. But the Butterfly girls' discomfort produced odd, writhing movements. Twisting and jerking, each girl's leg and arm movement was independent of the other's. Villagers hovering around the birthing room's window reported on the patients' condition to the crowd waiting behind them. The odd movements they observed, similar to those of a snake in a muddy pool, were not a good sign. And the more anxious the people became, the louder the rumble grew.

"Human to animal spirit—the village is doomed!" proclaimed an agitated woman—the same now-elderly woman who attempted to stone Walks with a Limp when she returned from her banishment.

Walks with a Limp could not help but hear the fearful gossip, especially from the woman she most despised. She stood up from the squatting position she had taken next to her daughters, stretched her bad leg, then pushed her strong arms against the old women's torso. The mop of gray hair snapped backward and the woman was ejected from the open window, landing outside with an audible thud.

"Today is a great day, so stop this foolish talk," Walks with a Limp demanded. "Go about your business and get ready for a big meal, for all will partake of the afterbirth with roasted agave leaves on the side. I will summon you when we are done here."

Tall as Corn was sharpening a piece of flint just out of earshot, lost in his own thoughts. Today's outcome had huge ramifications for the tribe, far beyond his grandchild's birth, and this was not lost on the de facto leader of the village. If anything went wrong in the next moon cycle, it would mean a great and perilous move for the community.

The Butterfly Twins worked as a team, looking at each other without speaking, nodding, then pushing in tandem. Walks with a Limp put pressure on the perineum to slow the exit of the head so her daughters' vaginal vault would not be damaged as hers was during their delivery. She hoped they would have many children and did not want them to have the kind of painful strictures she still carried.

"Slowly, my girls," she said softly. "You must have control. Concentrate on the rhythm of the clouds above and you will soon be mothers."

With a final concerted effort the baby, a boy, broke free of the birth canal, announcing his arrival with a strong, bellowing cry.

"A great sign for our people!" Walks with a Limp declared loudly enough for all outside to hear—especially the naysayers.

The baby was affectionately named Caterpillar Boy, as he had numerous wrinkles of fat and had come from the womb of a butterfly.

The meaty placenta that followed was placed in a corrugated brown ceramic serving bowl to be roasted in agave leaves for the night's festivities. The worn-out twins lay down for a well-earned rest.

It was not until a few hours after the delivery that Walks with a Limp became gravely concerned. The baby was doing well, but her daughters were still hemorrhaging, even with lots of abdominal massage and applications of the juniper-bark salve. If the bleeding did not cease soon, she knew, her daughters would die.

Tall as Corn was summoned and the entire camp grew quiet as all waited for the gods to decide the Butterfly Twins' fate.

The gods made their decision and the outcome was life-changing for all concerned.

The last words Ish and Osh said after bidding goodbye to their cherished mother, father and Caterpillar Boy, were to each other and their community. They smiled, gripped each other's hands, and announced that while they had always loved their people, it was now time to leave their earthly embrace.

"Please watch over Caterpillar Boy," they pleaded, "as he will be a great leader some day. Leave this land and find a new beginning. Go east. Follow the rising sun and you will come to a high mesa with abundant ponds of water seeping from its rocky breast. Let all you meet along the way know they too must find new shelter or die. Remember us in your prayers as we will remember you from above."

Their eyes simultaneously fluttered shut and they passed into the great world beyond. The people's crying became loud, knowing their future was written and they must now leave their home.

There was no community feast that night. The placenta was buried at the north end of the girls' home—the first of the community's many gifts to the gods.

CHAPTER 15

THE MIGRATION

It had only been a day since the Butterfly Twins' demise, but the people respected their wishes and prepared to move quickly.

Walks with a Limp had slashed her arms in mourning but was also aware she was now responsible for Caterpillar Boy. It was fortunate that one other woman in the tribe had given birth that year and could suckle the baby. Caterpillar Boy took to the breast with great enthusiasm. Like his mothers and grandmother before him, he was a survivor.

Her daughters' burial would be at the sacred canyon hideout only Walks with a Limp knew. It was not only a place where their body would be safe, but also a marker for any members of the tribe who might come back to resettle this beloved land.

The red earth that laced the now-dormant volcano's cone had been Walks with a Limp's guiding force, a beacon she had looked to for guidance when she lived in isolation high above her village. The color of the earth pervaded her dreams and tinted her waking consciousness. In a way, the cinder cone was her mother's breast, and it would be difficult to leave it behind—but leave she must if the people were to survive.

It comforted Walks with a Limp to know her daughters' body would be in the red earth for all time, a testimony to her people's existence in this place.

To make the Butterfly Twins' journey easier, she had provided jewelry, gifts for the gods, and corn for prosperity and nourishment. Someday, she hoped, another sign would appear, and the people could return to the land of her birth.

Tall as Corn begged her not to leave so much corn, but Walks with a Limp was steadfast. "I'm leaving enough corn so the people will have nourishment and a seed crop at the ready if they return," she said. It was dangerous to leave so large a cache when it was not clear if and when more food would be forthcoming. But Tall as Corn had learned to respect his wife's intuition; he knew she could see things others could not.

The process of getting three gigantic pots laden with bounty to the ledge was no easy feat. It took two days of hard work and much ingenuity on Tall as Corn's part.

A grandfather juniper at the edge of the mesa acted as a lever for hauling, and yucca twine was used to fasten a harness around the great vessels. Twice the couple almost lost the load when the tree limb buckled under the weight.

Since they were abandoning the camp, the large pottery ollas were no longer of use and had been freely given to the distraught parents. The people did not ask about—or even want to know—what would become of the Butterfly Twins. The girls were sacred, and this was not the sort of discussion members of their tribe undertook.

Each person in the village gave a necklace or other gift to the dead girls, thanking them for the wisdom that came with their passing. The number of beaded necklaces was the largest ever collected for a burial, a testament to the Butterfly Twins' standing in the community.

Walks with a Limp bathed the girls and drained all the blood from their body. They were then eviscerated and their bodily contents buried at the north end of the pueblo under a juniper tree leaning toward the east. The community gathered and prayers were chanted as the people mourned their loss.

The small, now shriveled, body was outfitted in a pristine white cotton dress that matched their now-bloodless porcelain skin. The manta's surface was covered in diagonal red ochre stripes and butterfly designs that brought color to the somber affair. After rigor mortis had passed, the body was placed in a fetal position and covered with Tall as Corn's rabbit-skin coat. The coat acted as a pack, allowing the girls' body to be carried up the cliff by their father.

Once the girls were safely on the ledge, Tall as Corn carefully placed the small body in the largest pot, gently folding their delicate hands over the once-beating heart. A community treasure in the past, the olla was now the girls' tomb.

After the three pots were in position high above the desert floor, Tall as Corn said goodbye to his beloved daughters. In a final gesture of love, he placed a live butterfly cocoon inside the tomb. It would hatch and become part of the girls' journey, helping to guide them to the afterworld.

He sealed the pot's special top, adorned with a turquoise butterfly fetish he had carved—a stylized butterfly comprised of conjoined human figures, each looking in a different direction as they emerged from their earthly bounds. Tacky piñon pitch was applied to the lid to seal the vessel for eternity. It was a mausoleum fit for a god.

Leaving his woman alone to say her farewells, Tall as Corn felt her immense pain and was glad he had sealed the pot. He hoped that would make her leaving somewhat easier.

Walks with a Limp sat quietly with her arm on the large jar, her fingertips caressing the turquoise fetish on the lid. The vista was comforting; it had been her place of reflection when she was young and alone and life looked bleak. She had come a long way from her teenage struggle for survival and had acquired the wisdom of an elder.

"I will miss you my loves—the smell of your fine black hair full of yucca soap after a hard summer rain, the way you gazed into my eyes, your love piercing my heart with every blink. Your song will be missed the most. Now wind and rain will carry your voices. When I hear the summer downpours, I will know you are close by and our people will remember the gift of knowledge you have left us.

"The world is the worse for your passing, but I look forward to one day seeing your smiling faces and telling you all about Caterpillar Boy and our journey to the sacred new lands you have promised.

"We leave you gifts for your journey and corn for those who may come after we leave. Your people sacrificed these precious kernels so your spirit and those who follow will be nourished for as long as our children walk Mother Earth."

Tears flowed over Walks with a Limp's brown skin, making small circles in the fine red dust.

Gathering herself together, Walks with a Limp finished preparing her daughters' final resting place. She took dirt from the surrounding floor and steadied the pots so no great wind or water seepage could dislodge them from their high sanctuary.

She sat for a long time gazing at the red cinder cone and thinking of her daughters' faces. As her final act, she placed her hand in the dirt, leaving a print, a memory of sorts. Then she made her last, long climb down the precarious cliff face.

She would never see her beloved ledge again.

CHAPTER 16

BACK DOOR FOR YOU

Felix Zachow's nose was raw, and hurt as he wiped it for the umpteenth time with his favorite pink monogrammed handkerchief —a square that was always neatly folded in the front pocket of his jacket.

Santa Fe's single-digit humidity wreaked havoc on his sensitive mucous membranes, and the extra dust from the construction that surrounded him made everything worse. Still, he reminded himself, the pesky dirt will be well worth the drippy nose.

Like his father Wilhelm and his uncle Boris, both respected European art dealers, Felix appreciated order and neatness. The gallery makeover now underway would provide him the aesthetic perfection he desired.

Felix grew up in a family of art dealers whose fortunes dramatically increased after World War II. Wilhelm specialized in contemporary art and Boris in antiquities of all sorts. When it came to art, the Zachow name was synonymous with the best of type.

There had been talk for years of shady practices, the looting of historical sites, and fencing of stolen Jewish heirlooms, but no charges had ever stuck to the men or their galleries and, over the years, the family had made tens of millions of dollars.

After the war, the Zachow brothers moved from Vienna to Switzerland and opened separate galleries that shared a common entrance. They exported that concept to New York City in 1966, and then to a small Santa Fe satellite location for Felix in 2006.

Shortly after opening their Santa Fe gallery, both Wilhelm and Boris died when their private plane experienced mechanical failure and crashed over the Sangre de Cristo Mountains after leaving Santa Fe airport. The only heir to the family business and fortunes, Felix inherited all three galleries. He had worked with his father and uncle all his adult life, and the galleries thrived under his watch.

One of the first changes Felix made when he took over the business was to change the name of the Santa Fe shop from Zachow's to A to Z Galleries. He also combined the two brothers' specialty areas into a single shop concept, adding considerably to his holdings of antique Native American art. Santa Fe was once known for having the best inventory of early Indian art, but the number of high-end dealers had dwindled and Zachow wanted there to be no doubt about who was now the top dog.

Wilhelm Zachow had collected Native American art along with the modern art he sold, and he left Felix a few stellar pieces from his prized personal collection. While Felix appreciated the Native art form, he was much more interested in money, and in what extreme wealth could bring to the table.

His father's collection was in a Swiss bank vault. He had been dead for eight years now—long enough that Felix could start selling off assets without attracting attention or arousing suspicion. He planned to sell the best items first and invest the proceeds in an oceanfront property in Maui.

Although his feet were planted in Santa Fe, Felix's internal clock was still running on Zurich time. But, regardless of the circadian disjoint, he was determined to be on hand as the last of the gallery construction was completed—even if his nose didn't much like the idea.

It was May and August's summer show—a major exhibit—was just around the bend. Zachow's strategy was simple: presale the best works early and quietly before the exhibit opened on August 1st, then sell some of the leftovers to the tourist crowd before the show closed in September.

❋ ❋ ❋ ❋

An unplanned—and highly prized—addition to the summer show appeared when Brazden Shackelford strolled through A to Z's front door without an appointment.

"Hi—Can I help you?" The well-manicured receptionist greeted the pothunter tersely, assuming by the man's appearance that he was of no consequence.

"I'm looking for Felix. Is he around?"

"Mr. Zachow is in his office. May I say who would like to see him?" Her tone was still icy.

"Brazden Shackelford. Tell him I have something he will definitely want."

"One moment, please."

"Mr. Zachow says to have a seat. He will be here shortly." She turned her back to Shackleford and resumed paging through the magazine open on her desk.

Thirty minutes went by and Brazden was considering leaving. He didn't have a mobile phone with which to entertain himself, and the low-slung Milo Baughman scoop chair he was scrunched into made breathing difficult.

"Sorry about the wait old man," Felix said as he finally appeared in front of Brazden. "I've got a lot of pressing issues to deal with. I'm sure you can understand the gallery world time-suck." He then smiled broadly, resembling, just for the moment, his cartoon-cat namesake.

Brazden nodded and made an appropriate facial expression in response to the dealer, even though he didn't have a clue what owning a gallery entailed.

"Let's retreat to the inner sanctum and you can fill me in. You've got something tasty for me, I hope." Felix ushered the pothunter into his plush private office.

At close to one-thousand-square-feet, with fifteen-foot ceilings, Zachow's office was as large and elegant as most of the galleries in Santa Fe. A massive mahogany George Nakashima table dominated the room. There was a large, colorful nineteen-fifties abstract painting behind the desk and numerous artifacts of varying ages and origins on tables and cases carefully placed throughout the room. The setting made clear that this was where the big deals went down —not the sterile showroom floor decorated with the mannequin-like sales staff.

Standing there observing each other, the two men could not have been more different. The athletic, well-healed art dealer's custom Italian suede suit, silk tie, pink socks and Tom Ford loafers were the polar opposite of Brazden's pot belly encircling low-riding jeans, untucked corduroy shirt and well-worn Tony Lama cowboy boots.

Art sometimes makes strange bedfellows.

"Can I offer you a drink? Beer, coffee, sparkling water perhaps?" Zachow made the first conversational move.

"It's early, but if you're buying beer, I'm drinking," Shackleford sighed.

"Hope German beer will suffice; I can't stand your local Mexican brands."

"Dandy by me. I don't care what flavor it is as long as it's cold and wet," Brazden said, a genuine smile lighting his face.

"So, tell me, my old friend—What do you have that will interest a man like me?" Felix watched Brazden's face for cues.

"I'm sure you remember that white cotton Anasazi blanket, the one with red stripes and butterflies, that my grandpa Sidney sold your dad, forty-plus years ago," Brazden started...

"Of course. That weaving was one of my father's favorites. In fact I inherited the piece eight years ago and planned to sell the textile this summer. Why do you ask?"

"That's good news," Brazden said, "because I can make that fine little manta even more valuable. I have something you will want to add to that deal."

Shackleford then told Felix the story of the Siamese twins, a story his grandfather had never disclosed to Wilhelm Zachow.

Felix's father did, of course, know the textile had been collected on federal land, but the crafty dealer had false documents drawn up to take care of this pesky detail. And the passage of nearly a half-century had helped make the manta appear even more legitimate.

Sidney had never discussed the pots with Wilhelm. He first sold off the jewelry and offerings to the gods taken from the pots, and then, ten years later, when he was in need of extra money, he parted with the exquisite cotton manta knowing Wilhelm would pay top dollar.

"My God—That's a fascinating story! Is it true?"

"Yes, sir! As my maker be my witness, it is all true!"

Felix took another long, hard look at the man seated across the table, swigging his expensive imported beer. He could detect no sign of treachery in the pothunter's face.

"I have to ask you this, Brazden. I'm sure you will understand. Are you working with the FBI in any capacity? Are you wearing a wire?"

Brazden's face turned red as he choked on the dark brew. He understood the high-profile dealer's concern with getting into more detail about the prize he was offering.

"Nope. You can frisk me if you want, Felix," he finally responded. "I'm not a fan of the Feds. You know they busted me once. I was lucky to get off with my pottery and a warning."

Felix's eyes locked on Brazden's face. "I will do that if you don't mind. It's just business. I'm sure you understand…"

Felix had Shackleford stand up and gave him a very professional once-over.

"OK," he retorted. "I'm satisfied. Now how can we help each other with this most interesting development?"

Brazden explained he had the twins' skulls and that the pots were where he had left them fifty years before. There were no other relics on the ledge but the twins' skeleton and the cache of corn—assuming the kernels hadn't been eaten by animals in the intervening years.

"I would like to purchase the heads and the skeleton," Felix said smoothly. "It's such an unbelievable story. And you're right, they will add to the price of my now very expensive manta—if sold to the correct person, of course.

"The pots will be difficult to extract. I think the easiest way is probably to break them into large pieces and then backpack them out. It's obviously not an ideal solution but, if done skillfully, it shouldn't affect their value too badly. You'll have to retrieve the pots on your own. I can't have any part in the operation other than buying them from you once they are out."

The dealer took a deep breath before he continued: "How much are you asking for the heads and skeleton and the pots? Maybe you should retrieve the skeleton first, just to see how it goes, and then go back for the pots."

Brazden hadn't been prepared to tell Felix how much he wanted for the cache, so he winged it.

"I want $20,000 to retrieve and turn over the skeleton. I can give you the heads now. Then, once I get the pots and they sell, I want 15 percent of the profits from the deal."

Felix pretended to ponder the offer. He knew he could get an extra $250,000 for the skeleton alone, which would add to the manta's value and desirability for certain people. And he could easily cream money off the top when pricing the large pot artificially low. Skimming was second nature to him, as it is for many art dealers.

"OK, Brazden. I can work with those numbers on the condition the pots are equally priced at, say, $50,000 each retail. That will give you an extra $22,500 and I'll settle up with you as soon as they are in my possession. You don't have to wait for them to sell to get your money."

Felix figured he might get double that price for the pots, but once they were his Brazden wouldn't be the wiser. The pothunter would never see the sales receipts and the clients the dealer worked with would never appear in Brazden's circle—or so he assumed.

"That's a good deal for you, Felix. We both know the pots are a bargain at that price, but I'm good with it because I can use the money now. Any chance I could get a $5,000 advance when I bring you the heads?"

"Sure, I can do that. We can call it a loan for now, then settle up when you give me the rest of the skeleton and the pots."

"What do you want me to do with the corn and pollen, assuming it's still in its pot?"

"That stuff is no use to me. You can feed it to the birds for all I care."

"But don't forget those arms you tossed to the ground. Let's hope they're still there. I want to restore the old girls to their original condition.

"Deal then, Mr. Shackelford?"

Felix stuck out a hand encrusted with antique gold and diamond rings to close a deal that favored him—as they always did.

"Sure thing, Mr. Zachow."

The two shook hands and Felix showed the pothunter out through the office's back door, Brazden still clutching his half-full Dunkel's beer bottle.

"Brazden," Felix added with his catlike smile, "be a good fellow and use this door the next time you come—and please call ahead. The front door is for paying guests. I'm sure you understand..."

Brazden understood all right. He was only as good as the valuables he could produce. He would never be a front door kind of guy. He chugged the rest of the beer and considered smashing the bottle into Mr. Fancy Pants' wall, then thought better of it.

"This has got to be worth at least a dollar recycled," he mused.

CHAPTER 17

PRAYER TO THE GODS

The high-octane beer set the pothunter on a drinking jag that lasted the rest of day—something that wasn't all that unusual for Brazden.

Being shown the back door when he was bringing Felix a six-figure deal didn't sit well with him, even though he was used to this kind of treatment. Pickers were considered second-class citizens by many top-notch art galleries.

But the Zachows and Shackelfords had a history going back a generation. The manta his grandfather had sold Felix's dad now had to be worth a small fortune. Brazden figured the blanket might make $500,000-plus with the skeleton and a buyer who would want that sort of trophy.

A First Phase Navajo blanket had recently brought $1.8 million at auction and it only dated back to the eighteen-forties. The prehistoric manta was over eight hundred years old and had been owned by Siamese twins! Sidney had sold the textile for $5,000—a large sum in its day—but the added value from the skeleton he was selling to Zachow made Brazden feel like he was being cheated.

Shackleton's mood turned even blacker after he polished off the last of his store of 24-ounce Pabst Blue Ribbon. He was getting screwed! Forty-two thousand dollars was an enormous amount of money—and he hadn't seen that kind of cash in ten years—but it was a small snippet of the overall take. The rich always got more than their fair share, he grumbled.

The beer buzz made Brazden reconsider his options. He decided he would retrieve the artifacts as agreed and then renegotiate the deal. He would no longer be a passive bottomfeeder; instead, he would transform himself into a lamprey riding on the shark dealer's underbelly. It was a dangerous place to ride, but that's where the easy food was to be found—if you didn't get eaten in turn.

The money from this deal was his last big score and it could last him for several years. Brazden had not expected to negotiate the deal so fast and he had shaken on it! He hated to go back on a handshake; he despised those that did. Even in the world of pothunters and thieves, a man had a reputation to uphold. More then once he had regretted his poor choices in life, but he tried to keep lapses in character to a minimum.

Some of the things he had done would always trouble him, like plying teenage Pueblo Indians with liquor so they would sell him their grandmas' goodies. Brazden wasn't proud of his choices, but hey—it was survival of the fittest and if he were going to live, this type of conduct might be required.

Convinced he was in the right, and forced into a corner, Brazden would give Felix the skulls as agreed. He was ready to let go of that childhood trophy, convinced the evil juju in his life came from those twins. Let Felix bask in their spirit, he thought.

When he retrieved the complete skeleton, Brazden would renegotiate with Felix for a larger percent on the sale of the pots. No location would be divulged until the money was in his hands. Then he could turn over the rest of the skeleton and fetch the pots. He might even try to bring the ceramics down in one piece, which would add to their value and reassure his partner that he was getting his money's worth.

Tomorrow would be a better day, he thought. He would hand over the heads and plan a trip to Flagstaff—assuming his own head didn't hurt too much.

❋ ❋ ❋ ❋

Memories flooded Brazden as he removed the girls' skulls from the metal hook in his closet where they had been hanging for twenty years behind an army of winter coats. When the Feds had raided his home, they had missed the skulls and, after that encounter, he had made sure his trophy was well concealed.

He even developed a winter ritual: Anytime he retrieved a coat, he took time to peer into the Butterfly Twins' sunken eyes and wonder what they might be saying.

"Get us out of this god-damned dark coffin and take us back to our pot," was the request he most often heard echoed in his mind.

Successful pothunters can't take Indian lore about curses and demons too seriously, and, for the most part, Brazden didn't. The twins were different, though. Retaining most of their facial skin and hair gave them personality. Silverfish and mice had nibbled at their skin in a few places, but, for the most part, they still felt human.

What were their lives like and how did they perish? His guess was natural causes. He had once seen a Siamese-twin baby in a show called BODIES. The exhibit explained that these rare individuals often died young. But maybe the Butterfly Twins' death was more sinister. The Anasazi were not known for human sacrifice, but the macaw skeleton and turquoise fetish suggested distant trade had occurred and that their manta might also have been a gift.

What he suspected was that the twins' life had been hard, something Brazden could relate to. Being an outsider is never easy, no matter what century you're living in. So he couldn't help but feel empathy for the girls, even though he wasn't exactly sure why.

Removing the skulls from the dark, dank closet, Brazden felt a twinge of remorse—a new feeling for him when it came to artifacts. The skulls should have been relocated years ago, he thought. These were human beings, not trophies.

He rolled the twins' braids in tube socks, taking care not to damage their original Native cotton ties. The skulls and spine were covered in butcher's wrap and then placed in a brown paper Whole Foods bag that had strong handles.

Whole Foods had been a recent go-to location for Brazden; the store's free food samples and superior paper bags were a boon in his lean times.

The pothunter tossed two of his last corn wreaths into the bag as well—a kind of thank-you for doing business, a match to Felix's gift of the German beer. There was nothing wrong with forging a good relationship even if your scruples were impaired, he thought cynically.

Brazden had not shown Felix his precious turquoise butterfly fetish, and he would keep it a secret—at least for now. Touching the cool turquoise figure that hung around his neck at all times was a form of prayer for the man who had rarely attended any formal church. The stone ornament provided him with a form of meditation during times of stress. With a hand on the fetish, for the first time in his life the pothunter asked to be forgiven for treating the girls' heads with such disrespect—even though he had no problem with the grocery bag delivery system he had devised.

Shackleford was to meet Felix at 6 p.m. at the dealer's secondary gallery, which was closed to the public for construction—the building that shared a wall with Bloom's casita.

Felix had told Brazden to enter the lot off Canyon Road and park there. He would be waiting for him.

CHAPTER 18

TREASURES OF CANYON ROAD

Bloom was crafting the right words to explain the existence of the antiquities he had somehow forgotten to turn over to Madeline Sandoval.

He called ahead and was evasive about why he wanted to visit her. Madeline figured Bloom had a special wedding present for her and Shriver. After all, the blessed event was only a week away and he was the best man. Bloom didn't do anything to dissuade her thinking.

No matter how he tried to rationalize his lapse, it sounded weak. The best he could come up with was, "It's been a few years. I must have forgotten?"

Bloom knew it was bullshit and she would too. It would be best to be straightforward about the whole thing. He had a terrible face for lying—not a good trait for a salesman when so many dealers made it an art form.

A hand-forged knocker was the only form of a front door bell on Madeline's house. When he hit it, the thick mesquite door resounded with a THUD.

Bloom wasn't sure anyone heard him, so he knocked a second, then a third time, as hard as he could. Finally, he heard a metallic sound in addition to the dull metal-on-wood tone.

"I'm coming, I'm coming!" The voice behind the door sounded as if it were in a long tunnel.

Madeline Sandoval—immaculately dressed and looking much younger than her 50 years—struggled to open the heavy door. A broad, welcoming smile spread across her face as she recognized her soon-to-be husband's best friend and the ex-tenant she had known only tangentially for over twenty years.

"I love that door," she gasped, "it's so gorgeous, but in ten years I don't think I will have the strength to open it, much less hear the knocker. Few people can make it ring the way you did."

Bloom blushed. "Sorry. I wasn't sure you heard me."

"Not a problem. You Type-As are good door ringers, I guess."

Bloom responded with a weak smile.

"Please come in, Charles. It's so nice to see you. Are you taking care of my little place?"

Madeline couldn't help but feel the property would always be hers. She never questioned Shriver's motives in selling the buildings to Charles Bloom at less than market value—and so quickly after acquiring them. But Madeline loved Shriver and, even though they hadn't been together long, she trusted his instincts. Unbeknownst to Bloom, she had not only agreed to the deal but had also endorsed Brad's generosity.

Even though she hadn't known him well, Bloom had been a loyal tenant who respected her property. Her father had always warned her not to get too chummy with either the tenants or the help, and she had followed his instructions—at least until she met Shriver. The man had touched her soul in a way few had, so Daddy's rule was amended just to pertain to the help.

Bloom stepped in the large entrance hall and immediately set the tone for his visit.

"I wanted to thank you personally for letting Brad sell your place to me. I know it must have come as a surprise to you, and I want you to know Rachael and I are grateful for the opportunity you've given us."

"You're welcome," Madeline smiled. "The property had been yours for so long it was high time to make it official.

"Please, Charles, have a seat. Can I offer you something to drink?"

"Thanks, I'm fine."

They headed to the living room to chat. This was Bloom's first time in his ex-landlady's home, and he was stunned by the great art that graced the Venetian plaster walls. He had no idea her collection was so extensive, and he wondered why he had never sold her anything.

"Impressive collection, Madeline. Shriver must have done a double take when he saw this room."

"You're right he did. Good thing I waited until he put a ring on my finger before I brought him home."

Both were familiar with that perverse art dealer mentality and laughed.

"Madeline, you have them all—the Taos Founders, Los Cinco Pintores, the Taos modernists—and in spades."

Early paintings by Northern New Mexico artists can easily bring six figures or more. Bloom didn't normally handle these works as the artists were not Native American, not to mention very expensive.

"Yes, Papa was a fan and so am I. He had a personal relationship with most of these artists—many were tenants like you—and he often traded rent and food at our restaurants for paintings.

"You see this lovely piece over my fireplace?" she continued.

Bloom nodded.

"That is the painting that brought your best friend and me together. Isn't it lovely?"

Bloom could see the admiration Madeline had for the image, which he believed boded well for a successful marriage.

"I recognize the location, it's Canyon Road—and that's my gallery. Very cool. What do you know about the piece?"

"Its title is TREASURES OF CANYON ROAD. It was Sheldon Parson's last painting, a gift to a close friend. There's some correspondence between them about it, but I haven't had the time to examine it closely. This wedding thing is eating my life."

"You're the best man I heard?"

"Yep, that's me. But I promise there will be no bachelor party. You needn't have any concerns."

"At my age, Charles, I don't worry about much but where to find a public restroom on the plaza."

They both laughed at that, knowing the challenges of finding public bathrooms anywhere in Santa Fe. Then Bloom became serious.

"Madeline, I'm trying to add a room for the kids to the casita, and yesterday I met with the city representative reviewing my case…"

"That must have been fun," Madeline quipped. "I've been through a few of those inspections in my day—definitely a love-hate relationship."

Her comment made Bloom even happier Wendy Whippelton was his inspector.

He continued: "The lady doing the interview on the property asked whether I knew of any historic artifacts that had been uncovered there, and the fact was I did. Remember that raccoon problem I had a few years ago? I tried to trap them myself until I came to the conclusion they were much smarter than I."

Bloom gulped as he came to the part he wasn't proud of—and there was no way he could stretch the truth to ease his pain.

"When I was digging a hole to capture the varmints, I found these near the casita portal."

Bloom pulled the artifacts from his oversized man bag and handed the small trunk, pre-American head and silver coins to Madeline.

"I should have given them to you at the time I found them. I didn't do that, and I'm sorry. Wendy Whippelton, my liaison with the Historic Districts Review Board, looked at them and took some photos. She's not sure how the head got buried in Santa Fe—it's probably an outlier—but the coins and small chest are definitely from the early Spanish colonial period."

Bloom watched Madeline's face closely, expecting a grimace or look of disgust, but neither was forthcoming. She examined the artifacts carefully and handed them back to Bloom.

"Well," she said, "That's interesting. I know that Papa found some similar coins and other miscellaneous artifacts when he did a renovation in the nineteen-fifties."

She walked over to a large oak cabinet and pulled out a velvet bag.

"These are also early Spanish material, conquistador period, like the ones you found. That compound you now own is very old—no one knows for sure exactly how far back it goes. Some think it was once owned by relatives of Diego De Vargas."

"THE De Vargas? The guy who was thrown out of Santa Fe in sixteen hundred-eighty during the Pueblo Revolt and came back in sixteen hundred-ninety-two with a better game plan for working with the Pueblo Indians?"

"Yes, that very one. My guess is there may be even more artifacts buried beneath that property. Old Hispanic men used to bury their valuables when there were no banks available. Even my own Papa had that kind of rainy-day mentality.

"Hey," she said, excitement rising in her voice. "Maybe Sheldon Parsons knew about the cache and that's why he called his painting TREASURES OF CANYON ROAD."

Bloom was trying to let all this new information soak in. He wasn't sure what to think.

"That's amazing," he finally replied. "Well, I figured you would want these back as they were yours when I found them—and I should have given them to you at the time. I wish I could say the find slipped my mind but that would be a half-truth at best. Honestly, I held on to them because I found them interesting—and I apologize."

"Don't sweat it, Charles," Madeline smiled. "It's your property now, and you can keep them. In fact, I would like you to have the pieces my Papa found as well. It's all part of the building's history."

"I'd say it's time to dig another raccoon trap. Who knows? Maybe you'll find Sheldon Parson's treasure."

They both laughed—and Bloom wondered how he had failed to appreciate the beautiful Madeline Sandoval.

CHAPTER 19

HI, NEIGHBOR

Charles couldn't wait to show Rachael Madeline's generous gift—two additional Spanish silver coins, a crucifix, and a small brass bell. The heavy ingot silver coins all seemed to be from the same period. He would try to determine their value, but they would stay with the building and not be put up for sale. Like Madeline, he would pass the cache on to the next owner, who he hoped would be one of his children.

Bloom emailed photos of the recently acquired artifacts to Wendy Whippelton, along with a quick summary of the history Madeline had shared with him. Maybe it would help her identify the provenance of the finds.

The idea that the De Vargas family had owned his place at one time was an exciting proposition—although it might turn out to be a double-edged sword. If the property turned out to be historically significant, the board might not allow him to make any changes, although Wendy said that was unlikely to happen because too many alterations had already been made and the casita didn't face directly onto Canyon Road.

Rachael didn't like him to be late for supper, but he wanted to run by the gallery before heading home. Pulling in, he saw his neighbor, Felix Zachow, leaning against their common wall. He was sipping something in a martini glass and obviously waiting for someone.

Bloom stuck his hand out, waved, and said, "Hi, neighbor!"

Felix didn't know what Charles Bloom looked like and didn't seem to care. He gave him a half-hearted smile.

Bloom pulled his Ford pickup two parking places away from Felix's Mercedes-Benz S550 sedan. It was clear which gallery made more money. Felix was less than thrilled that Bloom was now headed his direction. He took a large slug of his vodka martini and prepared himself for the kind of friendly neighbor talk he abhorred.

"Hi. We've never met. I'm Charles Bloom, your next-door neighbor."

"Ahh, yes. I do recognize the name if not the face. You used to represent Willard Yellowhorse, didn't you? Got into a bit of a sticky wicket with his former New York gallery, correct? THE CUTTING EDGE, I believe?"

Bloom hated to discuss his near-death experience at the hands of a psychopathic art dealer three years ago. Wishing it weren't still a topic of interest, he weakly replied, "The one and only, I'm afraid."

"I did a few transactions with THE CUTTING EDGE," Zachow said, "but that man always wanted the last cent on every deal. Turns out he was a really bad guy. Happens in our business, doesn't it?"

Bloom was finished with this part of the conversation and moved on.

"Felix, the reason I walked over is that I wanted to give you a heads-up that our neighborhood may have one more construction project in the works. I'm doing some minor renovations to the casita. It doesn't look as if a little banging will matter much as you're doing the same, but if you have paintings hanging on our shared wall, let me know and I'll be sure to warn you if we are doing any construction in that area."

As soon as Bloom said "shared wall," he regretted it. He didn't want to get into that discussion if Felix didn't already know about their overlapping ownership.

"Is Mrs. Sandoval doing the work?" Felix asked, his attention now fully focused on Bloom.

"No, I am. It's my property now. I bought the compound from her recently."

"Well, that bitch! I've been interested in the property as an extra the buffer for my annex. She didn't even have the courtesy to let me know it was on the market."

Felix was clearly perturbed, and Bloom was wishing he had gone straight home. His stomach was growling, and this conversation sucked.

"Sorry about that. The building never came on the market. It was offered only to me. A rather sudden sale, I'm afraid. The good news is that I'm a great neighbor—you can ask anyone."

This did not seem to placate Felix a bit.

"So, Mr. Bloom, how about making a handy profit? I'm interested in your place. You could flip it and do really well."

"Sorry, but I'm not interested in selling at the moment. If I change my mind, I'll let you know."

Just as Felix was about to say something else, a beat-up blue Ford pickup crawled into the parking lot and a man carrying a Whole Foods bag got out of the cab.

"You'll have to excuse me, Mr. Bloom. I'm afraid I have an appointment now, but I would like to discuss the neighborhood with you in more detail. I'll come over and say 'Hi' in the next week or so."

Felix smiled, then turned his attention to the man with the scruffy gray beard.

Bloom had witnessed his fair share of back parking lot transactions —and had done a few himself. Even if it was nothing illegal, it always felt that way. A picker or private seller bringing in something they don't want others to know they are offering for sale, meeting in a parking lot or the back of the store, away from prying eyes.

Bloom had seen the man in the blue pickup before. He didn't know his name, but was pretty sure he dealt in antique Indian art. Something was going down, and Bloom couldn't help but wonder what kind of man Felix Zachow was.

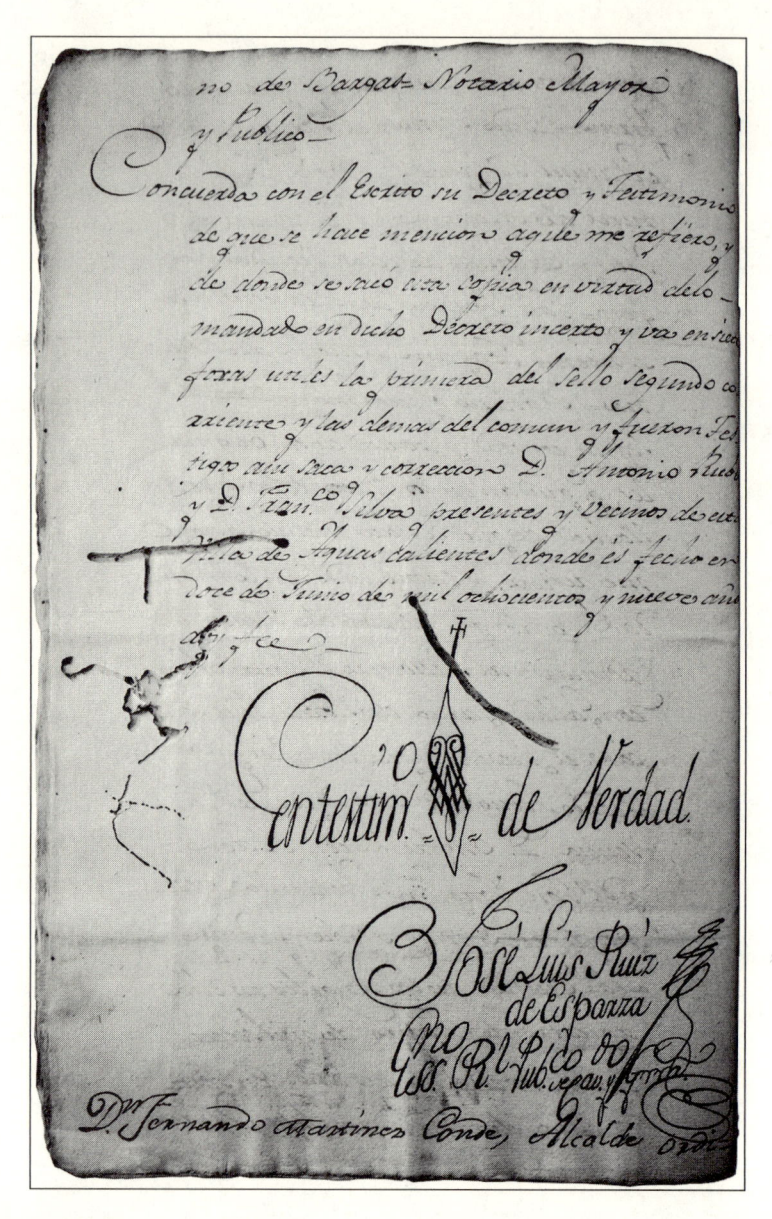

CHAPTER 20

TROPHY

Felix was peeved that Bloom had witnessed the paper-bag deal. Charles was no novice gallerist and would have recognized all the signs. Whether he would investigate or not was another matter.

A to Z was in a different league than Bloom's, so it was doubtful he would come snooping around. If he did decide to delve into it, that was another matter. Felix didn't like nosey neighbors poking around in his business—especially the illegal business.

That Sandoval had gone behind his back to sell the property infuriated him. Felix had made it clear to the woman that he was interested in purchasing the buildings. He had spent $4 million on the adjacent gallery spaces that were currently under renovation. A savvy businesswoman, she would be well aware of any sales in the neighborhood, and would know he had plenty of capital.

Bloom couldn't have paid more for the property than he would, could he? Felix had figured it was simply a matter of time until Sandoval came forward with a proposal. If that didn't happen, he would make an offer she couldn't refuse.

But now he had to deal with Bloom, who presented him with a different set of problems. He had a long-standing and what appeared to be a successful gallery and would not be easy to buy out, even at a handsome profit. Galleries become personal and Bloom didn't impress him as someone who would value money over pride. Felix would do some research on Charles Bloom and then make a run at buying the gallery once he understood what made him tick.

Getting back to the deal at hand, he now turned to Brazden, who had followed him into his office through the private back door.

"Well, let's see what you've got in the brown bag. Can you imagine if you'd been pulled over and the Santa Fe cops saw your taste in groceries?" Felix cracked a smile, breaking through his terrible mood.

The two men took a seat in Felix's office and Brazden placed the bag on the large oval table.

"First, I brought you a little gift—a couple of wreaths for your bathroom doors or what not. I grew these here ears of corn from the Anasazi kernels in that one big jar. Pretty cool, don't you think? One-thousand-year-old corn stock—wrap your mind around that one."

Brazden was smiling at the thought of his dryland farming accomplishment, one of the few successes he had managed in his 60-plus years on earth.

"Yes, that's quite interesting, very attractive. I'll make good use of them, thank you. They'll be a nice addition to my gallery decor.

"Now for the big finale: Let's get a look at what I've agreed to purchase from you sight unseen."

"Here you go. I call them the Butterfly Twins, which of course they were."

Brazden pulled the skulls and cervical neck out of the bag by their jerky-skin encased scalp and unfurled the girls' long braided hair.

"My god, that is incredible. There's no doubt they were conjoined twins—undoubtedly one of the oldest recorded oddities of early man. One would think that during prehistoric times deformities like this would simply have been eliminated at birth as unnatural, god's will and all. But that was obviously not the case with this tribe. They showed more capacity to accept differences than I would have ever expected."

"Yes, sir! In fact, from what I can tell from all the turquoise and gifts and that butterfly-covered manta, the twins were considered something special. It took hard labor and real engineering to get those pots up on that ridge all in one piece—and that much corn was quite a cache in times when food resources weren't easy to come by."

"So to be clear, Brazden: As far as you know, the rest of the twins' skeleton is still in the big vessel?"

"Correct. I would doubt anyone could find that place, not to mention that it's on the grounds of a national monument with strict rules about where you can hike and so forth. That ledge is totally invisible from the ground except at dawn. My guess is the pots are sitting there pretty as you please."

"When will you retrieve the skeleton?"

"Soon. The weather's been decent but not too good, and I want to get there before the tourists start arriving en masse. I figured I'd get the skeleton first, then go back to break up the jars and bring them out one at a time—unless I can figure out how to get them down in one piece, which seems unlikely.

"The Anasazi got them up there in one piece, so it seems like we should be able to get them down in the same condition. Do you know of any drones big enough to carry one of those pots?"

"I don't know the answer to the drone question, Brazden, but I'll look into it. Let's start with the skeleton, because that will help me sell the manta for a good price. Then we can focus on the pottery."

Felix picked up the heads and brought them close to his face, delicately sniffing the hardened skin.

"You know, you can still catch a faint hint of flesh," he whispered. "It's leather now, but it has the distinctive aroma of homo sapiens. Did you know that human leather is quite durable? During World War II, skin taken from Jews in the internment camps was used to make lampshades and sundry other goods. Did you realize that?"

"No, and I wish I didn't know it now. It's pretty creepy if you ask me." Brazden wrinkled his nose in disgust.

"Now, really, Brazden. Is this skull I hold in my hands that far removed from the Nazis' operation? You didn't kill the poor girls, but you've kept human skulls as a trophy for almost fifty years. I believe you said you kept them in a coat closet—it doesn't seem too far off in my book."

"I guess when you say it like that, it doesn't. But these heads were so unique I just felt like they needed to be saved. It would be a shame to simply put them back where no one else would see them. The heads change the way we look at early man, you know, and in a way that making leather wallets out of innocent Jews does not."

"The Nazis said their experiments were to benefit science too; the leather was more of an afterthought, not wanting to waste valuable resources during war times. Personally, I don't see much difference between them and you. But it's a nice trophy old man. I'll take possession of the Butterfly Twins and get you the money I owe you for fulfilling this part of our agreement. You'll receive the rest after you bring me the remains of the skeleton.

"Agreed?"

Brazden nodded his head affirmatively, knowing good and well he was planning to change the terms of the agreement. But for now he would play it straight.

Felix took the skulls and placed them next to his own head, laughing at how it must look. He was tempted, momentarily, to take a selfie.

"I'll get your cash. Now say goodbye to the twins and I'll see you next week. Call my cell when you get back to town. The number is on the back," Felix said, handing him one of his gold-embossed personal business cards.

"Call and we'll set a time and place to meet. Next time, let's find an out-of-the-way location. I'll have the money and you'll have the rest of my girls' skeleton."

Felix gave him a pre-bundled block of cash, which Brazden counted before he stood up. Felix then showed him the way out, locking the back door behind the pothunter.

A freshly lit Camel cigarette sent gray smoke spiraling upwards in the calm, warm air as Brazden climbed back into the cab of his truck. He rolled down the passenger window and turned on the radio, a country western song filling the courtyard.

The rough man seemed lost in thought as he blew small smoke rings through the Indian corn wreath hanging from the rear-view mirror. Perfect circles floated through the round hole created by the tiny ears of corn until the vacuum from the open window sucked them outside.

Bloom could smell the toxic tobacco smoke from his position behind his casita's coyote fence. There was no grocery bag in evidence when the man came out of the gallery. It was a deal for sure and definitely meant to be private. Felix's annoyed expression told Bloom the whole story; he did indeed recognize what was going down.

The man in the truck seemed content, so it must have been a decent transaction for him. Bloom figured it wouldn't hurt to know who the picker was—after all, his wife and kids would soon be spending most of their days in the casita, often on their own. He used his iPhone to take numerous shots of the truck and its occupant, then zoomed in on the man's features. He was amazed at the quality of the shots he could take with the camera on his phone. He could clearly see the man's face, torso, hands, and the contents of the truck's dashboard. He even got a shot of a smoke ring drifting through its circus routine—a rather arty image, Bloom thought.

Billy Poh, a Santa Fe police officer and silversmith, was supposed to drop off some jewelry for Bloom's Traditional tomorrow. He would show the pictures to Poh and see if the cop recognized the man and thought he might be someone to be concerned about.

CHAPTER 21

THE FIVE-SECOND RULE

The list of historians Wendy Whippelton provided included a curriculum vitae and photo of each candidate. The four older, bookish men wearing glasses looked a lot alike, but one résumé stood out—that of Jonathan Wolf.

Wolf had worked for numerous well-heeled institutions before opening his own practice thirty years ago. Bloom liked the idea that the man had spent decades in the archives going through deeds. The tipping point for Bloom—if the historian's rates weren't too high—was that this candidate also had an archaeology degree and could provide certificates for provenance.

Bloom was interested in additional information about the pre-Columbian head, Spanish coins and other artifacts unearthed on his property. Wolf might be able to figure out how the cache ended up under the front portal of his casita.

He called Wolf and left a detailed message on his answering machine to discuss fees and the possibility of hiring him. Ever since a wealthy client had told him that he would never listen to any message longer than five seconds, Bloom tried to avoid lengthy communications. From that time on, all his messages started with his name and phone number in case the recipients also followed the five-second rule of successful business practice.

❋ ❋ ❋ ❋

There were two messages on Jonathan Wolf's answering machine when he arrived home from a day of research at the New Mexico Records Center and Archives. He didn't own a cell phone—too invasive, he reasoned. "They can track you on those things; Snowden proved that."

A suspicious nature was a useful trait for one who steals documents from important institutions.

Message one was from Bloom. Jonathan wrote down the number, then listened to the voice mail in its entirety. Message two was from Felix Zachow, his best client, who kept him on retainer to respond to special needs.

"Jonathan, we have to talk!" There was an angry urgency in Zachow's voice.

"Bloom's gallery got sold and guess to whom? First hint: it wasn't ME! Try that second-rate art dealer, Charles Bloom. Sandoval—that bitch!—screwed me!

"I'm sure Bloom is going to be looking for a historian since he told me he plans on doing construction on the casita, the building that's adjacent to mine. We need to talk! Call me when you receive my message."

Wolf picked up the landline and dialed Zachow.

"Mr. Zachow, it sounds like we have an issue here. Please fill me in on the details."

Jonathan was not one to waste time with small talk. There was nothing to be gained, he believed, from chatting about the unimportant details of someone's life. He was acutely aware of his biological clock ticking, a fact that permeated his consciousness and influenced his decisions.

Felix explained what he had learned and how he had offered to buy Bloom's on the spot—but Bloom didn't seem interested, at least not yet.

Jonathan had a good relationship with the Historic Districts Review Board, which meant his reports could sway consensus. The A to Z gallery evaluations for the current restoration project were personally handled by Wolf, and the changes had gone through without a hitch—something that was not usual given that both galleries had direct access to Canyon Road.

With his off-the-street location, Bloom's construction wouldn't be an issue either, and Jonathan told Felix as much. What Jonathan didn't share was that Bloom also had left a message on his answering machine. Sometimes, he thought, it was better to get as much information as you could and keep both parties in the dark, at least for now.

"Jonathan, I'm sure Bloom will call you. He seems smart and will pick the most qualified person to support his case—which is you. When he does contact you, you'll need to lower your hourly rates to be competitive. I've seen his car, or should I say truck, and I doubt he's swimming in extra cash. I'll make up the difference in your fees—just make sure you get on this case. I need some eyes and ears on my payroll. Take the man out for dinner for all I care, and I'll cover the expenses—just find out what you can."

"I'll let you know what happens, Felix. If Wendy Whippelton is his liaison, I'm sure she has already signed off on the preliminary inspection. Don't worry. If Mr. Bloom calls, I'll do whatever is needed. I always do. Talk soon."

Jonathan hung up before Felix could respond. He was on the case and time was of the essence.

The historian considered his options, then dialed Bloom's number. He hoped the dealer wasn't as long-winded as his voice message.

"Bloom's. This is Charles. How can I help you?"

"Hello, Mr. Bloom. This is Jonathan Wolf returning your call. Is this a good time to talk?"

"Thanks so much. I have a renovation project on Canyon Road, a minor redo, pretty straightforward, I believe. I'd like to discuss your doing the historical review. Any chance you could drop by the gallery? I could show you the property and the few records I have, and talk about how much this will cost."

As usual, Felix was right. Fees were an issue. So Wolf cut his rates by 25 percent to be competitive. Bloom had no problem with the proposed price structure. Jonathan hated to be on the same pay scale as his subpar, milquetoast competitors—even if Felix's subsidies meant it wouldn't cost him a thing out of pocket.

Bloom and Wolf arranged to meet the following morning, and Jonathan called Felix to let him know how things were developing.

Tomorrow would be a turning point in Bloom's construction plans—and not for the better.

CHAPTER 22

WORLD DOMINATION

AgraCon World Enterprises (ACWE) was one of the largest suppliers of seeds, fertilizer, pesticides, and farm equipment in the world. The corporation specialized in genetically modified organisms (GMOs), spending more than $130 million a year on research and development. It had single-handedly invented the seed gene-splicing industry.

Only a few large agribusinesses control the world's production of seeds, and AgraCon was the biggest player in that market. Their aggressive protection of their seed patents was legendary, and feared by those who might otherwise challenge them. The company routinely searched the globe looking for new products or technologies to increase its bottom line and feed the ever-growing needs of farmers worldwide.

American farms used AgraCon products if they wanted drought- and pestilent-resistant crops—a necessity if they were to compete in modern-day food wars. Under ACWE rules, farmers were no longer allowed to grow a crop and keep a portion of the harvest for seed, as they did in the not-so-distant past. The new hybrid seeds were classified as patent-protected intellectual property—and the courts took the side of the corporation if anyone dared challenge it.

On the rare occasion that a new plant was discovered with no transgenic contamination, the varietal find was worth millions to the Chinese, who had both banned some and allowed some genetically engineered agricultural products, while investing heavily in research.

The top three criteria for seed quality were pest resistance, drought tolerance, and yield. The ability to affect any one of these variables meant big money for a company's bottom line.

ACWE was able to incorporate its genetically modified products deeply into the big-agra food chain. Any resistance by farmers to the use of the company's seeds was viewed as a serious threat. When the people of Kauai attempted to ban GMOs from their island, a federal judge shut them down. The activists were still fighting the ruling, but money talks and, as CEO of AgraCon, David Rolland was one of the loudest men on the block. He had an almost unlimited budget and didn't like to lose—which made him a fearsome foe.

Rolland loved the title of CEO, along with his high compensation package and the power that came with both. The money was important, but it wasn't what drove Rolland. The real high was the exhilaration that came from beating his competition to the market with the next great product.

He had absolutely no tolerance for the Hawaiians. "If we let the anti-GMO side win," he opined, "then what's next? The Philippines? We make a stand and pay our lobbyists whatever it takes to get ACWE seeds approved—and once we're a fixture in the marketplace, they're sunk."

After Rolland and his army of lobbyists and lawyers had defeated the protestors in Kauai, the hard-charging CEO allowed himself some downtime and took a month off.

David lived for a few weeks each summer in his Santa Fe retreat in the hills above Hyde Park Road. Like most driven businessmen, he had a hard time really turning work off. You could only play so much golf at the Club at Las Campanas. So, to entertain himself, he would peruse the Santa Fe Farmers Market looking for trends he could potentially incorporate into his long-term strategy.

Organics were big money now. David had seen this trend emerging five years ago through walk-and-talks with market customers and farmers, and had made organics part of the conglomerate's big picture.

Rolland was making his weekly pilgrimage to the Santa Fe Farmers Market—though today's reconnaissance was for dinner, not business. He had purchased a variety of fresh vegetables and fruit, many advertised as GMO-free, which he darn well knew they were not. He didn't care if the farmers lied as long as they used AgraCon's products.

During this visit, though, he had stumbled onto an odd fellow tucked away in the back row. The man was selling a few common garden crops, but what was unique was his Native corn. David had never seen anything quite like the small, dried ears of corn bundled into decorative wreaths. The phenotype was baffling, even to a man with a Ph.D. in agro-science. The small blue and red kernels were too minute to be a sub-variety of Indian corn, and the colors weren't right either.

The disheveled man didn't seem like a farmer. He wasn't interested in talking about his crops. Rolland knew from long experience that farmers live to talk about what they grow, so this man did not fit the profile. He also stonewalled David when he asked about the history of the corn. All the vendor would say was that it was Native corn of some nebulous origin.

David had written down the vendor's license plate number, and was in the process of tracking the man's information through corporate headquarters. He also overnighted one of the ears to his lab for DNA analysis. It could be a couple of weeks before they knew much, but he was sure it was a unique species, a rare find in today's world.

Having set aside enough seeds for analysis, David decided to also do a taste test and asked his cook to prepare a mild posole stew with the dried kernels. He found it tasty, with a more nutty than vegetal flavor.

Was it possible this was an ancient strain of pure Indian corn that no one had seen before? Any corn that had unique properties—and especially one that tasted good—was worth millions. The key was to make sure that AgraCon licensed the corn first.

Santa Fe was not a stronghold of agricultural secrets. It was purely by chance that he had stumbled upon the enigmatic find. David Rolland was not the type to take "No" for an answer. He would track down the farmer and get the real story of his unique Indian corn. Until then, he would enjoy his traditional New Mexican stew.

CHAPTER 23

HO, HO, HO

In mid-May, Santa Fe's temperature was rising and tourists started creeping up Canyon Road again after a long hibernation. The full summer visitor spigot wouldn't be turned on until the opening day of the Santa Fe Opera season—usually the last weekend in June or the first weekend in July.

Bloom was looking forward to the summer season. He now had two galleries from which he could sell art: the casita (his old space) was now Bloom's Traditional, with his mainstay, Bloom's, remaining the galleries' contemporary arm. Rachael was next door, selling at Bloom's Traditional and having a built-in lunch partner, as well as the ability to see his kids during the day, was an exhilarating prospect.

Bloom was venturing into a new area of art in earnest—traditional Navajo weavings and Indian jewelry. A jewelry show was on the schedule for Indian Market week, with his wife's nephew, Preston Yellowhorse, and Billy Poh, the Santa Fe police officer/silversmith, providing much of the stock.

It looked to Bloom as if Rachael's rug also might be finished by Indian Market, despite her insistence that "There's no way, Charlie Bloom!" He had watched his wife work long enough to know when she was in the groove, and there was no doubt her creative juices were flowing full force.

Rachael's rejuvenated sense of family was centering her *hózhó*. The new home in La Cienega and the two buildings on Canyon Road were the nests she had craved. Bloom figured her maternal instincts would soon kick into full gear as well, given her asides about how lucky they were to have a guest bedroom that could accommodate another child. Bloom was convinced this extra room was as an important a factor in Rachael's choice of housing as the east-facing door.

Ownership had also renewed Bloom's interest in the Canyon Road property. Owning was different, better. He was familiar with everything about the place after renting it for more than twenty years. Many of the trees he had planted as saplings were now tall providers of shade and great fruit.

Appreciating the complex life of their buildings was intriguing to Bloom, who loved history, and he embraced his part of the provenance trail. No longer would he describe his gallery as "Santa Fe funk," but as a fine historic enigma waiting to be deciphered.

The artifacts and family tree Madeline Sandoval had provided suggested a very early dwelling. With a Jonathan Wolf probing the old files, the puzzle might be solved. He hoped the truth wouldn't stop the construction project, but, if it did, then maybe it was for the best. He would let the chips fall where they should.

The first step was research, and Wolf seemed to be the right historian for the job.

Bloom hadn't recognized the man from his photo, but once his six-foot, two-inch frame stooped down to enter the ancient gallery doorway, a light bulb went off. He had seen him at Whole Foods on a few occasions and often wondered what his backstory might be. Wolf's hair was wild and matched by his oversized Santa Claus beard and belly. Reading glasses on an expensive handmade silver chain dangled over his protruding abdomen. A noticeably rounded spine that suggested childhood scoliosis completed the picture.

Bloom remembered he had once made a lame attempt at humor on a Christmas Eve by greeting Wolf in the checkout line with a hearty, "Ho, Ho, Ho! Merry Christmas!"

The historian's remarkable likeness to Santa Claus was undeniable, but the joke bombed and Bloom wondered if Wolf would recognize him as the Whole Foods asshole. It would be embarrassing, but Santa Fe was a small town, and one got used to these types of awkward encounters.

"Charles Bloom, I presume." Wolf stuck an oversized hand over the front counter. Bloom was relieved. The man either didn't recognize him or was a great actor.

"Yes, that would be me. And you are Mr. Wolf?" He already knew the answer, but had to resist a strong impulse to say, "And you're Santa Claus, I presume."

"Call me Jonathan."

"Sure, Jonathan. I reviewed your fee sheet and it's in line with what I would expect to pay, but I must say you have quite the pedigree. A degree from Harvard and past employment at the Smithsonian?"

"Yes, it's all true, but that was many years ago. I gave up the rigors of academia so I could focus on my own interests, primarily sixteenth and seventeenth century New Mexico history. I'm working on the definitive manuscript in the field, forty years of research. Once I publish, it should be quite eye-opening. I've uncovered lots of misconceptions about the whole Santa Fe-San Juan Pueblo timeline, who settled where first—bragging rights you might say.

"Your casita, in fact, is one the older buildings on Canyon Road, though you wouldn't have guessed it by its outward appearance."

"Really? How do you know?"

"I did some research on the A to Z place next door and the homes in this neighborhood are quite old, older than one might think."

"Like the eighteenth century?"

"Maybe older. I believe there was a small enclave on Canyon Road that was never fully documented that dates back to the time Santa Fe was founded—and yours may be one of those early buildings."

Bloom's face was alive with interest.

"One of the reasons I wanted you to work on this project was because of what I was found on the property," Bloom said as he pulled the chest with the head and other artifacts from under the counter.

Wolf's eyes grew large and his giant hand trembled slightly.

"These were found where?" Jonathan cocked his head like a dog looking for a treat, and Bloom threw him one.

"Follow me and I'll show you."

Bloom led Jonathan to the casita that was now Bloom's Traditional.

"Here's where I found two of the coins and the pre-Columbian head in that small trunk," he said, pointing to the edge of the portal. "Two similar coins, a bell, and crucifix were also found in the same general area in the nineteen-fifties."

"What do you think?" Bloom watched Wolf's expressive face closely to gauge his reaction.

"Don't hold me to it, but the Spanish material would fit with the early occupation I believe occurred on your property. These things are not terribly valuable—they might total $1,000 on a good day—but they are very interesting from an archaeological standpoint.

"The head is an oddity, and I'm not sure what to say about it. I'm happy to do some extra work on this case for no charge as I'm very interested in the history of your holdings from an academic standpoint."

"Great. Let's start right away. The sooner I can get a report from you, Jonathan, the faster I can get my construction permit."

"What exactly are you looking to do?" Jonathan asked.

Bloom explained his plans to put in a new portal floor with radiant heat and push out the roof overhang, adding 400-square-feet and an air-conditioning unit to the casita. He was hoping to have the project completed by the beginning of August, when the summer season would hit in full force. He thought it was possible, but recognized that in Santa Fe it could just be wishful thinking.

"OK, let me get going, Mr. Bloom. If I need to get into the property on short notice, are there any extra keys I can have or should I come bother you?"

Bloom could tell the old man didn't want to be tethered to his schedule any more than he wanted to be tied to the historian.

"I have an extra key underneath this old Mexican pot that you can use. The code for the casita if the alarm is activated is 1610, and then hit the 1 key to turn it off. That should be easy enough for a historian like you to remember."

"Indeed it is!" Wolf retorted. We all know when the Palace of the Governors was founded, sixteen hundred-ten. I like how you think Mr. Bloom."

Charles smiled and they walked into the gallery to sign the paperwork.

CHAPTER 24

NOT AS YOUNG AS I ONCE WAS

Brazden arrived in Flagstaff on a cold afternoon, something he considered a positive omen; there would be fewer people milling around the ruins.

He would spend the night at one of the sleazy motels off old Route 66, wake early, and be in the national park by 5 a.m. He would enter through the back road, where there would be no attendant taking money—and no one noting his comings or goings. Most tourists assumed you had to come in through the park service road, so the unadvertised back entrance was free and unmonitored.

If he arrived early, Brazden could be at the cliff by sunrise and out with the skeleton before the air warmed up and the tourists filtered in.

The looter brought a small camera to document the pots and the location. He knew this was risky as it could also be used as evidence if he were caught, but he figured that Felix might be more receptive to paying him extra if he saw how large the vessels were.

Intermittent sleep and frequent urination made for a poor night's rest. Flagstaff was almost as high as Santa Fe, and the altitude affected his health. Swollen lower legs were a bothersome new symptom. Something was wrong, and Brazden knew it was serious. His breathing was more labored and he was excessively tired.

Brazden attributed his health issues to the upcoming task and a lifetime of smoking. Without health insurance or Social Security, there were few options for a man who grew up on the wrong side of the economic pyramid. The reality of his situation weighed heavily on his mind of late. The butterfly fetish reassured the spiritual side of his nature and, ironically, provided his only medical treatment. He was glad he hadn't sold it—at least not yet.

❋ ❋ ❋ ❋

Finding the right cliff was trickier than he expected. It had been many years since he visited, and his grandfather's rock marker now looked more like a question mark than a butterfly's body.

The sun had been up for nearly thirty minutes when Brazden located the ledge. The sun's rays had passed the optimal viewing angle to see a glint from the pots' micaceous surface, but the crack of the hidden ledge was visible. He hoped the pots were still up there.

Faint human handholds lined the edge of the cliff, but he was no longer a one-hundred-pound young man. At one-hundred-ninety pounds, his weight made scaling the precipice both difficult and dangerous, but there was no looking back. He could only move onward and upward. Brazden knew the Anasazi made patterns with their handholds so he had to be careful to get the right pathway up the steep cliff face or risk having to back down.

Brazden was grateful he had lost twenty pounds in the last four months, even if he didn't know why the weight had just fallen off. The lighter load made climbing to the top of the ledge possible.

Peeking over the sandstone lip for the first time in almost a half-century was exhilarating. A rush of adrenaline coursed through his body and he felt a little younger—until his heart sped up and taxed his breathing. Still, the symptoms felt good in an odd sort of way: he was alive again.

The three pots were in his line of sight, greeting him like old friends. Their positions were unchanged; they were just as he had left them. Glancing side to side, he saw nothing suspicious. The print of a kid-sized sneaker left there fifty years ago was still visible in the fine sand behind two of the pots.

Awareness of his mortality and the touch of time flooded in on Brazden and he started to tear up. The most important moment in his whole life was here, preserved in the red sand from nearby Sunset Crater, along with the remains of a mysterious set of Siamese twins.

The two arms that Brazden had considered worthless and tossed to the side like so much garbage no longer contained any skin. Ravaged by flesh-eating insects over the years, they were now bleached white. A wave of guilt flooded over the old pothunter for not returning the bones to the large vessel where they belonged. His childish behavior would cost him money when he tried to sell the skeleton, and worse, it showed his complete lack disregard for human life. The Butterfly Twins had lives and a place in society.

Brazden inhaled deeply and lifted the top of the largest vessel. The faint scent of human decay was still present, but years of smoking had taken its toll on his nasal receptors and he could barely register the aroma. Inside the pot lay the headless skeleton of the girls' body. Somehow, it didn't feel the same. With the twin skulls taken away, first to hang in a ramshackle home's closet and now in an upscale gallery, the forlorn little torso lost most of its identity. The hardened skin was attached to the bones as he remembered, but it all looked so much sadder this go around.

The pothunter took a moment to reflect. He pushed off his shoes to relieve the pressure on his swollen legs. Dangling his two elephant-sized feet over the ledge seemed to help relieve the deep calf pain. A Camel cigarette relaxed his nerves, and he reviewed his life as he stared at distant Sunset Crater.

Finishing the smoke, he flicked the butt into a corner of the cave.

"Human detritus," he thought, amused at how future explorers on the hidden ridge would account for this red herring. Brazden had taken two community college courses on prehistoric man and recognized the ramifications of polluting the site, but figured the added layer would give some graduate student an interesting point to elaborate on in his dissertation. Despite his occupation, Brazden was a bright person who understood the nuances of the situation he was setting up.

Getting up slowly, he stretched his painful joints, then shuffled around the cliff floor in his bare feet. He placed a foot into one of his old shoe prints—"new clues for those who care, more layers," he grinned.

He surveyed the ledge to see if he might have missed something—young boys often do. But even as a teenager, Brazden had been thorough.

Feeling he had overstayed his welcome, Brazden pulled the J-shaped human remains from their tomb and stuffed them into an oversized bag. It crossed his mind to offer some prayers, but the pothunter in him took over: self-preservation came first.

That's when he saw a previously missed piece of the puzzle at the bottom of the largest jar. The remains of a butterfly had been under the cadaver. It must have been placed there by the original inhabitants, which made sense in terms of the butterfly motifs and the turquoise amulet. It was a goodbye gift and lucky charm from those who cared to ease the twins' entry into the next world.

Brazden picked up the fragile carcass, retrieved an almost empty Skoal can from his front pocket, and placed the last chaw in his mouth. He then replaced the tobacco with the desiccated butterfly for safekeeping and documentation. Last to go in the bag were the twins' arms. He slid them in gingerly, knowing that they could easily fall apart without any ligaments to hold them together.

Brazden replaced the lid on the now-empty storage vessel and shuffled to the jar containing the corn cache. A fine trail of dust followed his tracks—more clues to mystify future scientists. The rest of the corn kernels he had taken as a teenager and that had fed him for fifty years were untouched.

The wealthy art dealer's words played over in his head and pissed him off.

"Give it to the birds for all I care," Felix had said.

"Screw the birds," Brazden said out loud. "This is worth planting at the very least. These kernels were left here for humans. It was a huge sacrifice at the time, not something to be wasted."

Using the tin water cup clipped to his oversized backpack, he scooped all the contents of the pot into four large freezer bags, closed them, and nestled them against the skeleton. A mist of one thousand-year-old corn pollen filled the chamber. The rising morning sun intensified its hazy presence and caused Brazden to cough violently.

Catching his breath, he focused on the three pots and tried to envision how drones could retrieve them. It didn't seem possible.

Brazden snapped back to reality. He wasn't much younger now than grandfather Sidney had been when they first discovered the ledge. No way would he be able to extricate the massive ceramics, not even in pieces. He was lucky to get the corn and skeleton out.

He took photos of the pots with his small camera, using his backpack as a reference for size. After he had documented the entire ledge, he put the camera back in his pants pocket and headed down the cliff.

It would be the last time he would visit this sacred place. Brazden knew his time was short—and he knew what he needed to do.

CHAPTER 25

TRACKS

It was pushing 11 a.m. as Brazden lumbered down the cliff. He had dallied longer than was safe and he recognized his mistake. No decent pothunter would ever be caught carrying out looted objects in the middle of day. He had let nostalgia get the best of him and now he was asking for serious trouble.

Voices bounced off the cliffs below, a bad sign.

"Tourists in search of ruins," Brazden said to himself.

His legs were game, but his crappy lungs could only be pushed so hard. He needed to stop to rest periodically, and the sounds of human conversation grew louder.

With the truck now in sight, Brazden made a final effort to reach safety but the noisy family of four rounded a large sandstone precipice before he got there. He pulled his cowboy hat down low as the family walked by single file, tipping their hats to say "Hi!" the Western way.

Brazden wanted to avoid eye contact and did not return the gesture. The truck was only a quarter-mile away. A teenager about Brazden's age when his grandfather first found the pots turned, looked at the hiker, and said to his father, "That guy's kind of a dick."

The pothunter's hearing was fine even if his lungs were not. He wanted to say something to the kid but kept on task. Deep inside, though, he knew the boy was right.

Reaching the pickup, Brazden hid the bag full of loot under a pile of dirty clothes. You never know when you might get pulled over. He figured he could be back in Santa Fe in six hours. Once home and rested, he would let Felix know he had been successful and arrange an exchange.

The ride back was uneventful. Brazden set the speed control on seventy miles-per-hour and inserted a tape into his truck's out-of-date console. Indian music was followed by a deep, melodic voice, which started the audiobook—A THIEF OF TIME by Tony Hillerman—one of Brazden's favorite authors.

He was soon lost in the story and his imagination. The day had been pretty successful for a man running out of options in life, he thought. Soon the Butterfly Twins would be whole again—and maybe he would start sleeping better at night.

❋ ❋ ❋ ❋

Brazden pulled into his tiny adobe home on the outskirts of Santa Fe with a couple of hours sunlight left. The trip had tired him out more than he had expected. He had hoped to renegotiate the terms of the deal with Felix today, then hand off the skeleton—but to do so exhausted would be a mistake.

"Rest and a good hot meal of Anasazi stew are better than money any day," he thought to himself.

As the pothunter reached for the door, the hairs on his neck stood up. The screen, which was always stuck in the frame, was ajar. Brazden was always good about noticing small details, which is why even as a kid he had retrieved all the valuable material from the cave on the first go-round. He backed away from the door, keeping his eyes locked on the front entrance. Once he reached his truck, he pulled a .38 Special from the glove compartment and checked the chamber. It was full and he eased off the safety.

With one hand tightly clutching the walnut grip, Brazden pushed open the door and stepped inside. A distant bathroom light filled the living room with a warm glow—a light he did not remember leaving on. He kept his right arm straight out in front of him, ready to fire.

At first glance, the place seemed untouched, but personal papers on the Mexican desk were out of place.

"Someone was in the house," he thought, terrified at the idea.

A very slow and complete search of the premises and grounds revealed nothing missing. He did discover a fresh set of tire tracks and one set of loafer-clad footprints. Although the trail went around the entire perimeter of the house, including the spring garden, nothing appeared to have been touched. The footprints were deep, so the person who made them had to either be heavy or carrying something that weighed a lot.

The intruder had most likely been in his house last night.

Convinced he was now alone, Brazden plopped down on the worn-out couch. His right arm began to shake and his breathing became labored. The gun that only moments before was an extension of his hand now felt like it was made of cast iron. He switched the safety back on and put the weapon down.

Brazden stared at the ground, trying to make sense of a break in which nothing was taken. Someone was looking for something. They didn't steal his precious pots; maybe they were wise to the skeleton?

"The Feds would have waited until I was home," he thought. "Could Felix have done this? Was he trying to avoid paying me?"

That seemed unlikely, and he shook off the idea. Tomorrow, when he met with the rich art dealer on Canyon Road, Brazden would watch his reaction when he told him about the break-in. For now, the looter was spent. A large slug of a decent malt liquor—the last in his arsenal of anesthetics—did the trick and the pothunter fell asleep on the paisley couch, the gun not far from his reach.

CHAPTER 26

UPDATE

Jonathan Wolf's $1,000 appraisal of the artifacts Bloom and the Sandovals found would have been a good ballpark figure if the pre-Columbian head were an ordinary piece—but it was an outstanding three-thousand-year-old example of Olmec culture and the archaeologist/historian knew it.

There was a possibility the body of the figurine was buried not far from where Bloom had excavated the trunk; no one had ever looked further. If the remaining piece could be recovered—with Wolf confirming its excavation from an early New Mexico house site—the sculpture could be worth $50,000—more if it were indeed an early Spanish trade piece. There would be no problem with any trade laws in this case as the piece would have come into the United States long before New Mexico even belonged to Mexico—a bullet-proof provenance.

The question for Jonathan was how much of what he was learning he should divulge to Felix. After all, he decided, he was on retainer to the man, so he set up a meeting with the art dealer to discuss his findings with regards to the Bloom project.

Jonathan wanted in on any deal related to the buried treasure. He had leverage, he believed, because he would be providing the provenance on the Olmec head and any other artifacts found on Bloom's property. That, plus the important deed history, would allow Jonathan to negotiate the best deal possible for himself. Or so he thought.

❋ ❋ ❋ ❋

At the meeting, as Jonathan laid out the evidence he had been gathering for potentially high-stakes loot and an important historic property, Felix became even more fixated on buying Bloom's buildings.

"We must make Bloom willing to sell by whatever means necessary," Felix said to his de facto partner.

The dealer devised a rough plan to find the weak spot that could force Bloom to sell the property. Felix was a master of shady deals—one of the best in the business—and Jonathan never let laws or morality pollute a deal that was in his favor.

Felix made money not only from selling art but also by badmouthing his competitors' inventory, thus making his own pieces seem more important in his clients' eyes.

He did this very subtly, under the guise of protecting the client's welfare. Anytime he became aware that a client was considering a piece from another dealer, Felix would undertake supposedly exhaustive research—at no charge, of course—on his client's behalf.

In truth, Felix would contact the other dealer and either cut himself into the sale or, if his competitor wouldn't play ball, destroy the deal.

His "free and unbiased opinion" included determining an object's age, condition and other factors the client might not be aware of—all of which would come back unfavorably unless the other dealer was willing to give Felix a piece of the action. His most successful strategy was to say the piece wasn't quite as old as had been represented. It wasn't the dealer's fault—poor fellow, he's just not as knowledgeable as me—but the piece is not worth the money he's asking.

Five years difference in the age of an object could kill a sale, so it was easy to take the high ground—and Felix loved the power that came with being all-knowing.

Clients were impressed that Felix was making sure they were not being taken advantage of; he was, after all, a leader in his field.

The truth was that Zachow would quash all deals that didn't involve him. He knew that if clients spent money with the competition, they would have less for him in the future—unless, of course, he could get in on the deal from the get-go.

If the art he downgraded were particularly compelling, he would come in after the client had passed and try to scoop it up for himself for less money, then sell it quietly to one of his big clients. Having three galleries in different cities allowed him to move material from one location to another, with no one the wiser.

Occasionally he got caught in his lies. But, because he was such a powerful presence in the field, most of the other dealers and even some clients would continue to work with him; they never wanted to chance losing a deal or access to the next great piece.

Bloom was no different from these other marks, Felix thought. The weakling dealer would bow to him voluntarily or he would break the man and just take the property. The skill set for either outcome was the same; only the bait would be different.

Spanish silver coins and pre-Columbian figurines brought to what was now New Mexico by early colonists were buried under Bloom's property—bounty that, in Zachow's eyes, was rightfully his.

❈ ❈ ❈ ❈

A fine layer of dust lined the tops of the files that filled the New Mexico State Records Center and Archives on Camino Carlos Rey. The drafty building filled with history was Jonathan's favorite place in the city. He was the master of this domain. And he loved the smell of moldy old paper, an odor that meant money for those who knew how to profit from it.

The archives staff recognized Jonathan on sight and respected him. He had once worked at the Smithsonian Institution—impressive credentials to any small town researcher. What the librarians didn't know was that Wolf had been terminated when research documents went missing under his watch. No charges had been filed, as the evidence was circumstantial.

Jonathan had taken the documents all right, but he hadn't been caught in the act. He reasoned that he deserved the items he had removed from the institution as they related directly to his studies—and he alone was qualified to comprehend their meaning and divulge their secrets to the world at large.

He had originally planned to return all the stolen papers once he was close to publishing, but, since he had been terminated, he sold them off through a broker when his research ground to a halt.

Once Wolf was no longer a publish-or-perish academic, the documents were more important for their monetary value than their content. His profits from selling off early American ephemera were substantial, which helped him set up shop in Santa Fe—a city off the beaten track that just happened to be rich in old documents just ripe for the stealing. Jonathan's favorite clients were the extremely wealthy—people who would buy documents from him, then tuck them away where they would never be seen again.

Jonathan had done well enough that he only occasionally appropriated a library document when he needed a little something extra. As a general rule, he led a quiet life in Santa Fe, nestled in his books and papers, doing historical reviews and the occasional archaeological examination required for many New Mexico building sites.

He had done an exhaustive search of the A to Z buildings' histories and produced deeds that allowed Felix to undertake his current renovations. Now his first order of business was to review those papers once more, focusing in on the structure that shared a wall with Bloom's casita.

Maybe there were some clues he had missed that would explain the silver coins and pre-Columbian head. Maybe he had mistaken the age of the buildings, and maybe the shared wall gave Felix some legal position for part ownership of Bloom's property. In Jonathan's mind, everything was open for discussion and interpretation.

The lines of A to Z's property ownership seemed straightforward. The Martinez family constructed two adobe compounds in the mid- to late-seventeen-hundreds, early by Canyon Road's timeline.

Jonathan decided to follow Juan Ignacio Martinez's genealogy to see if there were more to the story, Martinez apparently being the owner of that piece of land. After two days of running into dead ends, the answer revealed itself: Martinez was related by marriage to the Peralta family—the same Pedro de Peralta for whom Santa Fe had named a main thoroughfare that just happened to connect to Canyon Road.

Peralta's history, in turn, led back to Don Diego de Vargas—who, if Jonathan were reading the material correctly, may have had a direct connection to the first governor-general of Santa Fe, Don Juan de Oñate. It might be a revisionist history flying in the face of commonly accepted timelines, but Wolf was thrilled with the possibilities of his discovery. Dating the building that much earlier gave him a thread that led to Oñate, which in turn gave credence to the theory that the coins that dated from the fifteen-hundreds could have been deposited on the property by Oñate, de Vargas or Peralta.

Madeline Sandoval's bloodline was not just parallel to that of the inhabitants of Jamestown, it was older. She could trace relatives back to de Vargas, so it wasn't much of a leap to assume that Martinez and Sandoval were also related—most likely cousins.

Jonathan could find no significant scholarly references with regards to the Martinez home or suggestions linking it to de Vargas or Oñate in any published periodicals. The oldest house listed on CanyonRoadArts.com only dated to the seventeen-fifties.

The largest section of Bloom's building was constructed in the nineteen-forties and had little to no historic significance. The enlargement of the small casita on the edge of a large apple orchard had been a gift to Madeline Sandoval's father

Bloom's casita had the same Martinez family history as Felix's place, but with a small twist: one line of text dating from the mid-seventeen-hundreds referred to a pre-existing structure on that land: *"the ancient casa of the great one that was reinforced and added to..."*

"Who was 'the great one,'" Jonathan wondered. "Could the pre-existing structure be Bloom's casita?"

"The great one" was not a familiar reference from early Spanish documents. The diary he was reading was written sometime in the seventeen-fifties in Old World Spanish, and clearly noted the home in question as being of ancient origin.

"Could 'the great one' be Oñate?" he wondered feverishly. "Is it possible he had a home in Santa Fe by the end of the sixteenth century?" That would explain the silver and even the decorative pre-Columbian ceramic head from Mexico.

Jonathan's mind was leaping to a groundbreaking conclusion: "Oñate's wife was the great-granddaughter of the Aztec Emperor Moctezuma Xocoyotzin. Maybe the Olmec piece was an heirloom from his wife's lineage—not a simple decoration but a piece of patrimony."

The thought that the casita could have been Oñate's home or even that it had a possible connection to him—and that the uncovered objects could have been "the great one's" personal holdings—was exhilarating. It would signify a previously unknown and important historical discovery.

There were minimal written documents attributed to Oñate. The coins could be dated prior to the sixteen-hundreds. Oñate came to New Mexico in fifteen hundred-ninety-eight, and Santa Fe was officially founded sometime between sixteen hundred-seven and sixteen hundred-ten, but there was so little paperwork on the conquistador that maybe those dates were incorrect. It's possible the accepted timeframes were misinterpretations, or that Oñate had a home away from the more commonly recognized encampment, not far from where the Acequia Madre had been constructed next to what is now Canyon Road.

Various schools and community buildings are named after Oñate, a hero to many in the American Southwest. With a $2 million, 34-foot-tall monument funded partially by the city and partially by private donors in two thousand-seven, the conquistador literally stands larger than life in El Paso, Texas.

Charged with cruelty to natives and colonists, Oñate was first recalled by the king of Spain in sixteen hundred-six; he didn't get the message and was again recalled and finally banished from New Mexico in sixteen hundred-thirteen.

"Could he have left some treasures behind for what he thought would be his eventual return to the capital city?" Wolf wondered.

When Jonathan closed the diary, his hands were trembling. He took photos of the text with his smartphone, and hurried home to look again at the artifacts Bloom had given him. Maybe there was a clue there that he had missed.

CHAPTER 27

IT'S HIM!

In Bloom's cache there were four ingot silver coins dating from the late fifteen hundreds, an early brass bell and crucifix, a couple of what appeared to be ceramic beads, and a metal, wood and leather box that had housed two of the coins and the ceramic head.

The container was 14-inches long, 8-inches wide, and 10-inches tall. Much of the leather had disintegrated. The wood, though in poor shape, was intact. The planks appeared to be of sabino wood, indicating Mexico as its place of origin. The interior of the trunk, lined with a grayish fabric, was in relatively good shape.

Holding a pair of forceps in his right hand and a microscopic light in the other, Jonathan lifted up the ancient cloth, peering under it with the light—and there it was: "Property of Juan de Oñate," the signature of the first governor of Spanish colonial New Mexico, in what Wolf recognized as the conquistador's handwriting.

It was impossible—yet there it was, revealed for the first time in over four hundred years! The signature alone was worth a small fortune.

Jonathan couldn't stop shaking as he gently set the box down. The small trunk was Oñate's personal cash box and had been buried in Santa Fe earlier than any scholar had ever documented. His discovery totally upended the conventional wisdom.

But what should he do with this information? Jonathan's mind was racing.

He couldn't let Bloom or any of the city or state historical committees know about his find. If local historians and officials found out about it, the whole world would soon know, and Wolf would be unable to claim rights to what he had discovered. It wasn't enough for him to be the genesis of this new knowledge; he literally wanted to possess it.

It was quite possible the rest of the Olmec figure was somewhere in the vicinity, yet to be unearthed—and who knew what other treasures might be buried nearby. Perhaps there were more artifacts that could be attributed to Oñate, even relics of his raids on Acoma Pueblo. If Oñate collected pre-Columbian artifacts, he could have collected objects from the pueblos as well—and they would be worth a fortune. Maybe there were even some additional documents tucked into some nook or cranny of the casita.

The fact that the existing artifacts had been found buried under the portal made perfect sense. It was definitely the place to begin digging for more treasure. But if Bloom got his certificate to start construction, something might get uncovered in the process and then it would belong to Bloom.

Jonathan and Felix devised a plan: Keep Bloom's construction permit dangling for as long as possible while they found a way to wrangle away the rights to the buried treasure.

Jonathan would become an international star for his important New Mexico history discoveries, and Felix, ever lusting after things that escaped his grasp, would turn the compound into his own private museum.

Felix considered tunneling under the shared wall, fracking his neighbor's treasures as it were, if Bloom wouldn't sell. There were other incentives that could be applied as well. If business was poor or—god forbid—if something bad were to happen to Bloom's family, then the money he offered would be gratefully accepted.

✳ ✳ ✳ ✳

Jonathan laid out the casita's history, including the possible provenance of Bloom's artifacts, to Felix. There was no way to hide the truth; the historian needed the art dealer's power and money to coerce Bloom to sell.

Felix wasn't interested in laying claim to the historical discoveries; he would gladly turn over any paper or other records found to Jonathan, along with the accolades that came with them. Jonathan would get one-third of the current retail value of any artifacts, silver or gold discovered as a finder's fee. Any treasure discovered along with the Olmec figurine and trunk would become the property of Felix, who would make his offer for the compound contingent on Bloom including all archaeologically significant material discovered there in the final contract.

The easiest path to success was always the one of least resistance: Be a good neighbor and buy the buildings straight up for a significant profit to Bloom.

County records revealed the purchase price of the property, which had been seriously undervalued in Felix's opinion. He would be a good neighbor, then, and offer Bloom considerably more than he paid—a deal the second-rate art dealer would have to consider seriously. To sweeten the pot, Felix would let Bloom lease his Canyon Road annex rent-free for up to two years while Felix took over the casita and began major renovations.

In reality, Felix would go treasure hunting and plow up the casita's grounds. If, in two years, nothing more was unearthed, he would have Jonathan break the shocking news of the Oñate discovery in Bloom's wooden trunk. A major paper on the casita and its history would be published. The property would then be turned into an Oñate museum, charging visitors to view the artifacts while selling art from an adjacent gift shop.

Felix could staff the museum with docents, locally recruited free labor, under the premise of promoting a new Santa Fe institution. The museum would be incorporated as a nonprofit, with Felix

Zachow as the sole beneficiary and Jonathan Wolf the museum's curator. This would allow for monies to be skimmed and a yearly loss reported. Donations of art would be accepted and immediately sold to cover operating expenses, including Felix's ever-growing salary.

The plan was a good one, and Felix couldn't lose as long as the property's current owner cooperated. Felix knew what would do the trick—and Bloom would never see it coming.

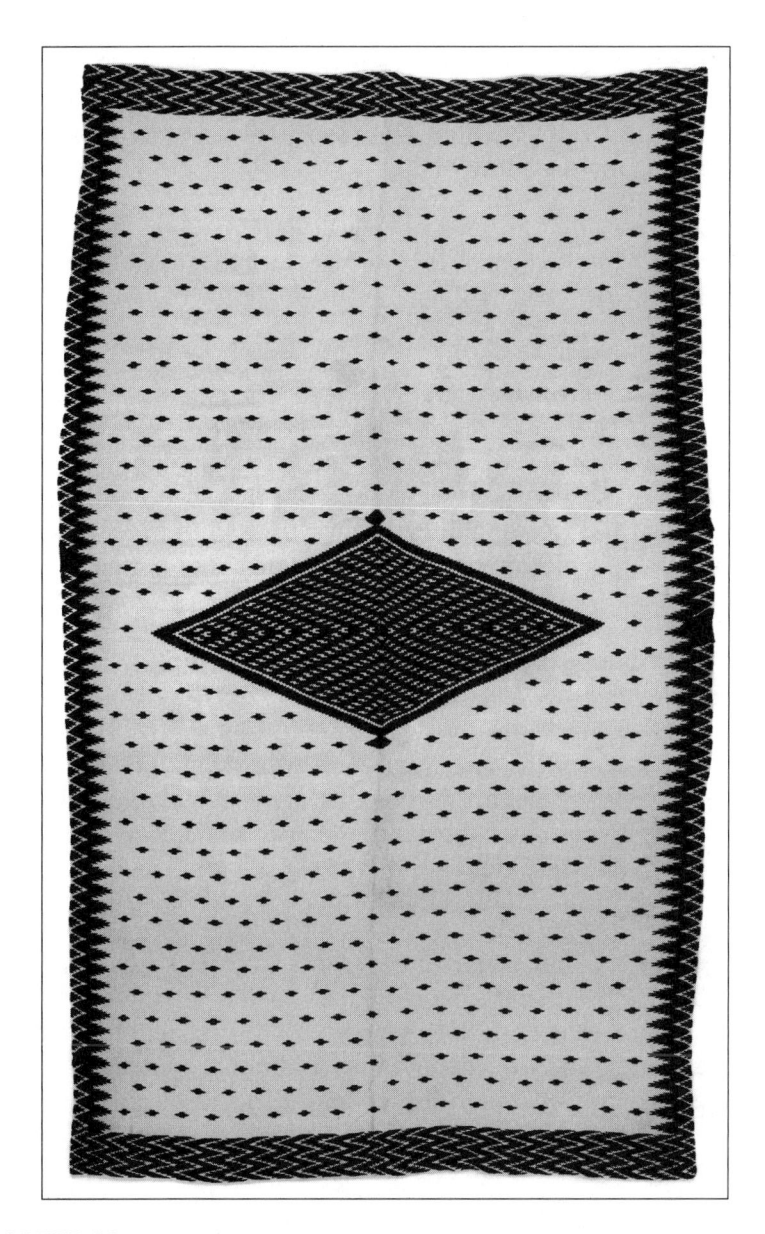

CHAPTER 28

MASTERPIECE TEXTILES OF THE SOUTHWEST

During Indian Market week, A to Z gallery had scheduled a show featuring the finest textiles by indigenous artists of Southwest America, Mexico, Central and South America. The centerpiece was the Butterfly Twins' manta, even though viewing the ancient weaving would be limited to those who could pay for it. The only way the general public would ever see it was in the catalog that would accompany the show.

Most quality art galleries have a plush side room whose sole purpose is to close art sales—a room that emphasizes comfort, with a single well-lit easel or wall to perfectly present the piece under consideration.

Felix had designed the ultimate in closing rooms, a work of art unto itself. No doors to the room were visible from the outside. You would have to know exactly where to push against a flat wall to gain entrance—a wow factor that would both facilitate the close and keep prying eyes at bay. Accessible only through Felix's office, the inner sanctum was a major part of the building's current construction project.

The twins provided the ideal exhibit for the closing room's début. Their fragile body would be suspended from fine stainless-steel wires as if floating from the heavens, the manta draped over the skeleton as it hung in life. The heads were positioned at severe angles to accentuate the fact that these were two individuals living in a single body. Ultraviolet lights were the primary illumination for the display, with two additional pinpoint LED lights focused on the manta.

Inside the room, a dozen white orchids graced each corner, the flowers glowing under the black lights. To top off the spectacle, a small trap door that opened when the room was entered released two dozen monarch butterflies to flutter about the enclosure. Music filled the background. Near the ceiling, a one-foot stone-inspired ledge with a large, buff-colored Hohokam olla tilted at a 45-degree angle helped create the ambiance of an ancient world.

The butterfly manta carried a $2,000,000 price tag.

Felix made it clear that he was selling the manta only; the skeleton was included in the deal for free. That way, no laws would be broken and he would not be trafficking in human remains because the bones themselves had no value—at least on paper.

Laws, Felix believed, were for people of lesser means. His prize piece would most likely end up in a billionaire's man cave and never be seen again.

Once the manta was sold the rest of the show was gravy. Felix figured he could sell the weaving simply by sending images of the piece to select buyers via email—but that was no fun at all; a major piece deserved better treatment. The theatrical flare of the closing room made the event memorable not only for him but also kept his fans wanting more. The price was not important; this was Art Theater.

The Indian Market textile show as a whole was an impressive display of monetary prowess, with a Navajo First Phase Chief's Wearing Blanket and a serape priced at $1 million each; a classic Saltillo blanket valued at $100,000; a Bolivian poncho tagged at $75,000; a nineteenth century Acoma Pueblo embroidered manta for $500,000; and a large variety of secondary pieces.

Bloom would fit into the fill portion of the program. Felix was aware of Rachael Yellowhorse's skill as a weaver. Though contemporary textiles were not normally what he bought or sold, he decided to visit Bloom's to see if he could purchase her next weaving—and put Charles and Rachael in his debt.

❉ ❉ ❉ ❉

Two weeks had passed since Charles and Rachael purchased the buildings. Rachael had wasted no time getting her loom set up in the casita and hanging some Two Grey Hills rugs that were on consignment from the Toadlena Trading Post for the summer.

Having her loomed rug in the gallery gave Rachael hope that she would be able to turn daily weaving into a full-time activity. She had been afraid to let Charles count on her large rug being finished for Indian Market. She had not started the rug until late February; it was now late May and the piece was coming along faster than she anticipated. If she could work on the rug continuously and not have to do too much babysitting, there was a chance it would be completed by August 1st. Rachael was pushing herself hard, putting in eight-hour days, and the progress was impressive.

Felix's unannounced visit to the casita with a gift for his new neighbors was a surprise to Rachael, who was hard at work at her loom. She recognized him from magazine spreads showing the well-dressed art dealer relaxing in elegant gallery settings.

In person, though, he seemed to lack something. He smiled, yet not. Then Rachael realized why his presentation was so odd: Botox treatments. Felix's eyebrows didn't move when the rest of his face did. She couldn't help but smile, happy her husband would never be so vain.

Strong features and a razor-sharp nose complemented Felix's Sleeping Beauty turquoise-colored eyes. The dealer was pushing fifty-five, yet had the face of a forty-year-old.

"Hello there, you must be Rachael Yellowhorse. I'm a big fan of your work—it's so wonderful to finally meet you. I brought you a little housewarming gift."

Felix handed Rachael one of the wreaths of Indian corn that Brazden had given him.

Rachael blushed. "Thank you. It's a lovely gift. I'll hang it in the kitchen."

"I'm surprised that I actually have a fan—it's not like I've produced enough rugs to develop a following—but I will say I do give each and every piece my best effort."

Rachael looked proudly at her latest masterpiece, sitting in front of her on the floor. She started to get up.

"Please stay seated," Felix cajoled. "You look so perfect next to that magnificent weaving. Would you mind if I took a photo?"

Rachael felt like she was ten years old again, sitting at the side of her grandmother Ethel Sherman, charging the tourists a dollar per photo.

"It will cost you a dollar," She giggled. Felix pulled out a small, professional-quality German camera and started shooting.

"How about instead of paying you a dollar, I buy the rug. Then could I get the photos for free?"

"Of course, you can use all those images at no charge," Rachael laughed, thinking the art dealer was joking.

"I am not kidding," Felix said, his vocal inflection reinforcing the seriousness of his intent. "Do you have a price on your rug yet?"

Felix looked intently into Rachael's chocolate-colored irises. She broke eye contact in surprise, turning her attention back to her rug.

"No, I haven't priced it yet. It's not finished and I try not to even think about price until I'm done. Lots can happen before the last weft is in place."

Rachael had learned this lesson all too well, having lost a rug to a maniacal killer once before.

"You'll have to ask my husband, Bloom, that question. He's also my agent and chief bottle washer."

Rachael cupped her hands and called loudly for Bloom. He came trotting across the open courtyard breathing hard and covered in sweat. He had been trimming trees and wondered what might be wrong.

"What's up?" He wiped the sweat from his brow with a dirt-stained sleeve.

"What do we have pricewise on my latest masterpiece?" Rachael asked, looking at Bloom. Her gaze told him they had a live one.

Bloom, the consummate salesman, reacted to Rachael's cue without missing a beat.

"Hi, Felix. Last year we sold Rachael's big rug for $15,000. This one has a finer weave and more complex design, so I'm afraid we would need to get $25,000 for it. It's the first piece Rachael has made for sale in nearly a year."

Bloom locked eyes with Felix. Rachael was in shock at the high price Bloom placed on the textile.

Felix had rehearsed his approach before he ever walked through Bloom's door. The plan was simple: gain trust. Timing was of the essence. He would buy the Yellowhorse rug without hesitation regardless of the price Bloom put on it. There would be no negotiation.

Under normal circumstances Felix would eviscerate any adversary when he knew he had the upper hand. But in this case, what he coveted was not the rug but Bloom's buildings. Felix thought that if he gained the dealer's trust by paying fairly, or even above retail, he would then have a good chance of buying the galleries.

"Done," Felix said without flinching.

Rachael and Bloom couldn't hide their surprise. They weren't expecting a $25,000 sale on a cool May morning.

The shock caused Bloom to blurt out, "Really?" like an amateur art dealer. Then, recovering, "Of course, that's a great buy, a true work of art."

Felix, recognizing the standard dealer moves, smiled—even though the grin did not reach his forehead.

"Yes, I love your wife's work, Mr. Bloom, and this piece will fit nicely with my holdings for this year's Indian Market show: Masterpiece Weavings of the Southwest. I'm going to put a hefty price tag on this rug. I hope that won't be a problem for you."

"Not at all. A high price will justify Rachael's current price structure. When is your show?"

"The exhibit opens August 14th, a week before Indian Market. The weaving will be finished by then, right? It looks nearly done to me now."

Bloom blurted out "No problem," without consulting his wife.

Rachael's facial muscles worked just fine, and she arranged them into a slight frown, which Bloom noticed.

"Of course, it might take right up to show time to complete it. Will that work for you?" He wanted to give Rachael a couple of weeks' leeway.

"That's splendid," Felix replied. "If you don't mind, I will use the photo of Rachael sitting in front of her masterpiece for the illustration since the rug isn't done. I need to get going on my catalog, and my understanding is there will be no photo charge."

Felix winked at Rachael.

"A catalog? That's so cool," Rachael chimed in enthusiastically.

"Yes, I will have approximately twenty weavings in the catalog, with curator's text and a full-page illustration of each textile. Your work will be in good company, Rachael. I have a Navajo First Phase blanket and a serape included in the show. In fact, yours will be the only textile from a living artist in the exhibit. The pieces date from twelve hundred C.E. to the present—you."

Rachael beamed. The rug would be finished by opening night, most likely with time to spare. Suddenly she realized today's wardrobe was weak at best. Old ripped jeans, a faded plaid shirt and hair that hadn't been washed in a day—that was the image people would see of Rachael Yellowhorse.

Her look of concern returned, then vanished just as quickly as a smile crept over her face. It was the rug that was important, not her wardrobe. Grandmother Sherman had reprimanded her once before when the teenaged Rachael had the same issues standing in front of one of the matriarch's masterpieces.

"The weaving is the star, my granddaughter. You are only a speck of dust floating in the air. Soon gone and forgotten is the speck, but the rug will live for generations."

Rachael had not forgotten her grandmother's words.

"Great. I can't wait to see my rug in the catalog."

Bloom wrote up the sale and Felix paid in full, three months in advance. It was looking like the kids' college fund would not have to be tapped for the renovations after all.

❄ ❄ ❄ ❄

Bloom and Rachael couldn't believe their good fortune in buying the property for nothing down and then receiving a full retail advance on her latest rug.

They spent the rest of the day chattering with each other about her weaving, the upcoming show, and how lucky they were to have Felix as their neighbor. The dealer next door had a less then stellar reputation on the street, but from all Bloom could see he had been straightforward about what he wanted. Felix paid Bloom's price up front and in full, something even Charles' retail clients sometimes had a problem doing.

The extra money would provide a nice cushion for any expenses that came up with regards to architectural drawings, fees, and building-out the back room. For the first time in many years, Bloom felt like his life was solidly back on track. A good summer would mean security for his family, and they were off to a great start.

Rachael hung the wreath on the kitchen wall, noting how it truly did look like Indian corn of the ancient variety. Herding sheep as a kid, she had run across Anasazi ruins that still contained remnants very similar in size to these. This wreath, though, also had intact kernels.

It was a perfect gift as far as Rachael was concerned. Bloom agreed. Felix was a godsend.

CHAPTER 29

ONE FOR THE ROAD

Brazden arranged a meeting with Felix to hand off the Butterfly Twin's remains. Felix didn't want anyone to see him receiving a human skeleton, so he reluctantly arranged the rendezvous at his Las Campanas home. With no close neighbors in the exclusive community just north of Santa Fe, the art dealer felt the transfer would be safe, though he didn't like the idea of Brazden seeing how and where he lived.

The break-in at his home weighed heavily on the pothunter's mind. He wasn't sure Felix hadn't done the deed himself, maybe looking for the skeleton so he wouldn't have to pay in full. The idea of meeting at Felix's home was disconcerting. Could it be a set-up? There was only one way to find out.

Zachow's Las Campanas compound included a palatial adobe in a forest of a hundred transplanted aspen. The rambling golf course twisted around the home, although the grounds were out of reach of eyes, voices, and errant golf balls.

Felix liked his country-club lifestyle, with sales to members easily making up for any dues he paid. He only lived in Santa Fe May through August, as did many of the other residents, but that didn't dissuade him from building a seven-thousand-foot home at the end of a cul-de-sac. To assure his privacy, he had purchased all the surrounding lots. Endless views of the Jemez Mountains to the west and the Sangre de Cristos to the east greeted him daily.

To gain entrance to the gated community, Brazden scrolled through a litany of Anglo-Saxon names before reaching the "Zs". It occurred to him later that if he had gone in the other direction with the up key, Zachow would have been the first name on the list.

Brazden punched in the code and waited. No one answered, but the gate opened with an annoying buzz and the pothunter drove through the first of two security gates. He missed a few turns before finding the correct cul-de-sac off Santo Domingo Circle. The front of the home had a giant abstract sculpture that Brazden vaguely recognized. Similar to the one at the museum in Fort Worth, the large bronze by Henry Moore had been a gift from his late father when Felix turned thirty. It was one of the rare objects in the dealer's life that was not for sale.

Felix was outside swinging a golf club, something Brazden couldn't relate to unless there were a rattlesnake at the other end.

"Hello, Mr. Shackelford. Nice you could visit. Did we bring me a treat?" Felix made a full swing with his nine iron.

"Yep, got her here. Where you want me to unload?"

"Let's go inside where it's more private. You have her in a bag, I assume?"

"Sure do, no prying eyes. I didn't want to chance getting pulled over. It would be hard to explain a skeleton." Brazden smiled at the thought.

"Can I offer you a cocktail?" Felix asked. Brazden never declined free alcohol, especially when quality booze was part of the action.

"Sure. Whatever you're drinking is fine."

The two entered a giant foyer plastered in a glossy, eggshell-white Italian finish. The house was impressive even by Santa Fe standards. Large Roman and Greek sculptures were interspersed with abstract expressionist paintings. The butterfly manta was draped on a mannequin in the living room, the twins' heads propped up on a nearby Adrian Pearsall coffee table. The incongruity of the skulls set against a classic piece of mid-century modernist furniture was surreal even for a looter.

"Many years since I've seen you," Brazden thought to himself when he saw the white manta.

Waves of déjà vu washed over him, and he plopped down in another uncomfortable Milo Baughman chair, his head spinning. Brazden was out of his element and regretted agreeing to meet here. Though it seemed safe enough, renegotiating his original deal in Felix's home territory might be tricky.

Felix brought back two vodka martinis with olives on a Paul Revere colonial silver platter.

"Hope you like them dry. You said you'd have what I was drinking."

Brazden smiled and took a long drag of the cocktail, looking for courage.

"Let's see the little girls' body. Whaddaya say?" Felix gave Brazden an evil wink.

The looter opened the large duffel bag and gingerly brought out the arms, then the torso, laying them on the table next to the twins' heads.

Felix's bleached teeth flashed as he swished the toothpick holding the olive side to side in his mouth, like a snake smelling for its prey.

Brazden placed the skulls on top of the skeleton and arranged the body as he had found it in the pot.

"The twins looked pretty much like this, knees bent in a fetal position, their arms folded over their chest, heads at different angles, one facing forward, the other the reverse."

"Why are the arms so white, with so very little flesh?"

Brazden explained how he had tossed them to the ground as a kid and how the resulting half-century of degradation had taken its toll.

"Pity they don't quite match up, but I'm sure my restorer can help with that. Can you believe I have someone who works on material like this? I've handled a couple of significant wooly mammoth skeletons—there's surprisingly big money to be had in bones."

Brazden shook his head. There must be big money in everything but dug pots, he thought, as he looked around at his surroundings.

The pothunter took another big swig of courage.

"So, Felix, can we discuss our arrangement? I've been thinking I'm kind of getting the short end of the stick on this one. You're going to make a fortune and I'm struggling. Do you think you could maybe throw me a bone?"

Felix didn't see the humor in the request.

"Well, that's interesting. You seemed quite happy the last time we talked—you even brought me a little wreath as a gift. What's happened in between now and then?"

Felix was no longer smiling. He stroked the heads of the twins while looking intently at his guest.

"Nothing. Just had time to think. We made a quick deal and I thought it would be fairer if I got a percentage of the sale. It doesn't have to be much—say 5 percent.

"Five percent, huh? You know the bones are of no value to you as is, only to me, and the pots—well, we both know they are going to be difficult to retrieve.

"Do you have any images of them by the way?"

Brazden pulled out his camera and scrolled through the photos, showing Felix the pots' impressive size and condition.

"They're nice, I agree. I'll tell you what. I will give you an additional $10,000 if you get the pots. Is there anything else you have to offer up or are we done with negotiating—for good?"

Brazden considered the question. The pots were going to be difficult and dangerous to go after, at least on his own. He had two other pieces of bait to trade—the amulet and the dead butterfly in his Skoal can—but he hated to sell the amulet and the butterfly carcass seemed worthless.

"Yes, I do, in fact, have a special object I've had since I was a kid. I hate to give it up, but I will sell it to you if you go the additional $10,000 plus $5,000 now for what I'm about to show you."

Felix was intrigued even if his paralyzed forehead muscles didn't show it.

"By all means, let's play show-and-tell, one of my favorite pastimes..."

Brazden pulled a turquoise amulet in the form of a butterfly mounted with a gold clasp from beneath his worn shirt. He retold the story of the jar and how the fetish came into his possession. Felix was clearly interested.

"That is indeed special. And it should remain with the twins. I agree to give you the additional $10,000 up front and the $5,000 kicker—but you still have to retrieve the pots. Getting them down with drones doesn't seem like a possibility. You may need to break them in large pieces to get them off the cliff without being seen.

"OK, then we have a final deal," Felix said, and stuck out his hand to solidify the agreement.

Brazden removed the necklace he had worn for most of his life and its new owner placed the fetish around his own neck, stroking the turquoise as if to summon up a genie.

"One more thing, Brazden. If you screw me over on this deal, there will be consequences. You realize this, don't you? I'm not the kind of man who doesn't get what's owed him, even something this small."

As Felix's eyes locked with those the pothunter, their color turned from blue to gray and a cold chill went up Brazden's spine. At that moment, he decided not to bring up the home invasion. Even if Felix were behind it, this was not a man to mess with.

"I hear you loud and clear, Felix. You'll get your pots as sure as I'm giving you my cherished fetish."

Felix's mood switched back to happy and he was once again his cheerful self.

"One more drink for the road, my good man?"

Brazden gulped. "Sure, why not."

CHAPTER 30

WEDDING BELLS

An intimate gathering of close friends and a who's-who of Santa Fe gathered for the Shriver-Sandoval wedding, which was being held on the large outdoor courtyard of Madeline's home.

The long swimming pool was filled with deep, saucer-shaped pots holding purple hyacinths. Gas heaters were stationed in pivotal positions in case the evening turned cool, which often happens in May. A whole lamb from Tierra Amarilla was roasting over an open pit, to be served with a wide variety of vegetable sushi for the local vegans.

Bloom and Rachael arrived early to offer help and encouragement to the long-time bachelor.

Bloom, who had only recently tied the knot himself, thought he knew the pep talk that might be needed. Surprisingly, though, Shriver was not worrying about making a mistake. He had had his fair share of crazy Santa Fe women and was looking forward to spending his life with someone stable.

His former life as a gallerist was also a fading memory; Shriver would now enjoy collecting art for fun. He had moved in with Madeline the second week of their relationship, and was developing a penchant for the early Taos Founders' art as a consequence. He would consider spending any extra money he had on these artists.

Bloom and Shriver sat on a nineteen-twenties William Penhall Henderson couch and sipped a fine brandy from Madeline's stash. The painting by Sheldon Parsons, TREASURES OF CANYON ROAD, had been moved over the fireplace—a place of honor for its part in bringing the couple together.

"Shriver, what do you think the deal is with that painting?" Bloom asked. "Is it possible there is any treasure on Canyon Road?"

Bloom and Shriver had long ago stopped using each other's first names.

"You mean like, literally, treasure?"

"Yes, you know what I turned up under the casita's portal. I've given the artifacts to Jonathan Wolf, an archaeologist/historian in town. He's evaluating them for historic significance."

"It's possible, and part of me hopes it's true. Another part says why the hell did I sell so cheap if it turns out to be on your property."

Shriver laughed at the thought of treasure being found under his old gallery right after he had sold out to Bloom.

"Sheldon Parsons lived for years on the upper part of Canyon Road, and my understanding is that he was quite the historian. Did you know that, Bloom?"

"I think I knew the Canyon Road part, but he's not an artist I follow."

Shriver's professorial edge popped out and he saw his opportunity to educate Bloom, who specialized in Native artists.

"He trained at the National Academy of Design under Willam Merritt Chase and built a successful career in New York as a portrait and landscape painter whose subjects included President William McKinley. He was an interesting guy."

"Wasn't he involved in the whole preservation thing with Santa Fe's architecture?" Bloom queried.

"Yes, he was a big proponent of preserving Santa Fe's adobe architecture and buildings in the Spanish-Pueblo Revival style. That's one of the reasons you see so many adobe homes in Parsons' paintings. He loved early New Mexico history and was the first director of the Museum of Fine Arts in 1918.

"So maybe, Mr. Bloom, this last painting of his is a cryptic road map to treasure buried on Canyon Road. All you have to do is start digging."

Both laughed at the thought of Bloom doing manual labor, and polished off the first of what would become many brandies.

The music started and the time was at hand to face the reality of a lifelong commitment—something that has no maps to steer by.

✽ ✽ ✽ ✽

The service went without a hitch. Bloom smiled the entire time and felt a true happiness that his friend had found someone to cherish as much as he cherished Rachael. He understood how rare it was to find that special person who could overlook your faults and laugh at your bad jokes.

Shriver glowed during the wedding dinner. Bloom sat next to his best friend at the head table; Rachael was next to Madeline. The talk was of the future and traveling.

Shriver, half-lit, said in a goofy, semi-loud voice, "Remember, if you sell that place we have to split the profits."

Bloom was also feeling no pain and the remark jogged his memory. "You know, my new neighbor, Felix Zachow, has made overtures about wanting the place."

"Well, he has the money to buy the place, so I understand. The rumor is that the family money came from illegally acquired Jewish paintings sold after the war. A guy named Bloom should be careful of a guy named Zachow."

"You ever have any dealings with the man?" Bloom asked.

"Nope, he's even out of my league for the most part. But if I did, I would make damned sure to be cautious. From what I hear about his reputation from my New York cohorts, he will screw you if he can—though that's par for the course back East."

"Thanks for the heads up," Bloom replied. "I'll be careful if we tango. Guess I'll have to hold onto the place until I find a more suitable buyer—or discover that treasure and retire like you."

Both men laughed, each enjoying the moment.

CHAPTER 31

DETECTIVE WORK

Billy Poh's calendar of pueblo events and responsibilities was looming large. The Feast Day for St. Anthony—the twelfth century patron saint of lost articles and travelers—was in less than two weeks. As a member of the tribal council at San Ildefonso, he was expected to devote a significant amount of time cooking for the masses of visitors who invariably arrived with empty stomachs.

A fifteen-year veteran of the Santa Fe Police Department, Poh had recently been promoted to detective specializing in homicide investigations. The force would respect his pueblo duties as long as they didn't interfere with his real job. Being Native was challenging in a non-Indian world, even in Santa Fe. Poh had considered being a tribal cop. That would make the feast day and dance schedules an easier part of his routine, but he wanted more.

"Detective" was a position he had sought for years, and with the job came added responsibilities. Now, on top of a demanding work schedule, he was going to have his first two-person jewelry show at Bloom's Traditional. Poh was a third-generation silversmith and, while police work came first, jewelry wasn't far behind on the importance scale.

A fourth of the jewelry he had promised Bloom for the show was completed; the remainder was due August 1st. Poh was dropping bracelets by Bloom's today so the gallery could start marketing them early and get some money coming in to cover the cost of the silver and gold. Public school was out for summer break, so it wouldn't be long before the tourist season would be upon them. Poh hoped Bloom would be able to presell part of the show.

※ ※ ※ ※

A month had passed since Rachael had moved into the casita and set up shop. She had purchased a dozen doggie gates—not something she had needed on the rez, but perfect for the in-town gallery. She lined the gates around the casita's portal like dominos to keep the kids herded in. What worked for sheep would work for kids, she reasoned. And to be sure all remained under control, she set up her loom within grabbing distance.

For the most part, the kids had adapted well to their new environment. Simon, the local gallery cat who answered to no master, had taken up residence at Bloom's and was encouraged to stay around for his amazing mouse-catching capabilities. The kids loved him.

Santa Fe averages 12 inches of rain a year, and the best way to hold the moisture is to liberally mulch the flowerbeds each spring. For the last two years, Bloom had made the mistake of using a pecan-shell mixture, which, unfortunately, proved to be a mouse magnet. The insides of the shells made wonderful breeding material and provided food for all sorts of rodents. Simon showed up last year to help out, and Bloom supplemented the cat's diet to encourage him to stay around. Willy, Bloom's two-year-old son, enjoyed chasing Simon around—and the black cat also enjoyed the game.

Bloom had hoped to start construction on the casita build-out by now, but the wheels of historians apparently turned slowly. At this point in the selling season, he would have to plan to begin work in earnest after Indian Market, the third week in August, so as not to interfere with the busiest retail time of the year.

Bloom gave Rachael the go-ahead to arrange the casita into her own gallery, Bloom's Traditional. The transformation was remarkable. The building took on a nineteenth-century trading post feel, the exact opposite of its next-door neighbor, Bloom's, with its modern aesthetic and sparse furnishings.

Rachael's domain was dominated by a 10-foot-long oak case salvaged from the old Nambé grocery store. The centerpiece of the room, the case was filled with small Navajo weavings on consignment from Toadlena.

The rugs were small enough to grow legs and walk away on their own if one wasn't careful. Santa Fe has a group of professional thieves that drop by from time to time searching for unlocked valuables. Small Navajo weavings were ideal targets, but they would not be going anywhere on Rachael's watch.

The adobe walls were pinned with a crazy quilt of brown, gray, black and white colors—the larger Toadlena/Two Grey Hills weavings for sale.

Rachael's own significant weaving sat in front of the kids' chamber. On the floor next to her weaving mat was a tip can with a paper sign —"If you like what you see, feel free to contribute"—written in red crayon.

Bloom was appalled when he first saw the Arbuckle's coffee can and the plea for money, but Rachael reasoned that if you wanted an old trading post feel, tip cans would help make it authentic. Besides, she confessed, "I can use the money to buy baby clothes and the tourists eat it up: A real live Indian weaving a rug."

She laughed at the thought, knowing her education was probably better than that of most of the people who entered the gallery.

Bloom relented, as he often did where Rachael was concerned. He was surprised by how many dollars they collected each week, though Rachael reminded him these were her tips.

"If you want extra cash, set up your own tip jar," she suggested, then added, "A modern chrome cash box might not interfere with your minimalistic aesthetics as much as an old coffee can filled with dollars."

Making money on her terms felt right, as did kidding her purist husband.

❋ ❋ ❋ ❋

Bloom was excited to see what Poh had produced for the upcoming August show. He had first met the jeweler in February at his San Ildefonso home when he was looking for advice about the fake Indian jewelry that was contaminating the Santa Fe art market. The two developed an immediate rapport, and now Bloom's Traditional was representing Poh's silverwork, which was exceptional.

Poh's style was Native in its roots, but also had an elegance to it. Bloom was still educating himself on the subtler points of Native jewelry, but from what he could tell the great Navajo silversmith Kenneth Begay had influenced Poh and the detective confirmed as much—which encouraged Bloom, who was still learning the field.

The tall, lanky Poh ducked under the low Spanish colonial door jam of Bloom's Traditional, dressed in what appeared to be an uncomfortable suit. Bloom was waiting for him.

"Hello there, Mr. Bloom. I like what you've done with the place. Nice touch with the tip can. It reminds me of my grandmother's home. She used to sell black-on-black pottery, and I swear that tip can helped pay for college."

Rachael, who was within hearing range, peeked out from behind her loom and stuck her tongue out at Bloom—then went back to her work, laughing.

"If that's you hiding back there, Rachael, hi."

"Hi, Billy. Sorry I can't get up. I just got my babies to sleep and Bloom has me on a strict work schedule. I've got to get this rug finished by August 1st—sound familiar?"

Poh started to laugh, a hardy deep chuckle. Bloom blushed, knowing what Rachael said was true.

"So, Mister Taskmaster, I've got your first load of jewelry. You know we Indians have the bad reputation of waiting to the last minute to bring you our work, but I'm here to tell you that won't happen with me."

Bloom smiled, his face still flushed. He knew tardiness crossed all racial borders and was part of being an artist; creative people often lose their bearings when it comes to time management.

"Great, Mr. Poh, you'll be the first. Makes me wonder if you are an artist after all—you may be more of a detective if you keep showing up on time with your work."

Bloom was getting in his own jab in response to Poh's "taskmaster" dis.

The two men spread the goodies out on the scratched glass top of a small jewelry case and reviewed the work. Poh described the stones and materials used in each piece, and, in a couple of cases, elaborated on what he was trying to represent. Bloom took notes.

They both helped set prices and completed a consignment contract for the jewelry. Poh reviewed the terms carefully; he was not one to sign his name to any legal document without reading it first. The artist would receive 60 percent of the proceeds. Any discounting and advertising expenses would come off Bloom's end of the sale.

"What if there is a break-in and all my jewelry is stolen," Poh asked. "Is my stuff covered?"

Bloom had never been asked this question, but he also had never had a cop as one of his artists or dealt in jewelry, which people like to steal.

"Well, we keep everything locked up so that shouldn't be a problem unless we get a smash-and-run. Have you seen anything like that on Canyon Road?"

"No, can't say we have…"

"I'll ask my insurance agent what needs to be done to cover it, but for now let's assume your work is not insured."

"Sounds reasonable. Maybe I'll send a patrol car past the gallery a couple of times a night until you get me an answer." Poh winked at Bloom.

After the gallery business was complete, Bloom decided to take advantage of his silversmith's other line of work.

"Billy, I was wondering—and if I'm out of line you can say so—but I was hoping you could look at a picture and let me know if you recognize the fellow."

"Sure. What's the deal? Do you think he's stealing from you? We don't want any jewelry thieves around here…" Poh continued ribbing Bloom about his lack of insurance, but this time there was a hint of concern in the detective's voice.

"No, nothing like that. He was hanging out in the parking lot the other day and met with my neighbor Felix Zachow, who owns the gallery right next to mine. The guy seemed a bit odd and I just wanted to be sure he wasn't a problem. My wife works here now, and she's often alone in the casita with the kids."

This was only partially true. Bloom wasn't that worried about the man, but wouldn't mind knowing more about whom Felix was buying from. His art dealer neighbor seemed perturbed when he realized Bloom had seen them together, and he wanted to know why.

He opened his laptop and brought up the photos he had taken.

"Pretty good surveillance there, Detective Bloom. These were taken over the coyote fence, I assume?" Poh pointed at the top of the fence on one of the images.

Bloom's face got red for a second time. "Thanks. That was the best I could do with my iPhone. I'm not a professional Peeping Tom like some we know."

"Touché."

Poh took a few more minutes to look at the images, zooming in and moving the cursor from the man's face to the Indian corn hanging from the pickup's rearview mirror.

"I do know this guy. I gave him a warning a couple of weeks ago at the farmers market for having an out-of-date business license.

"It was a slow day so I went looking for the fake Indian art that occasionally gets sold at the nearby artists' market. We wanted to crack down on vendors and get the word out that we take that kind of stuff seriously before the tourist season kicks off.

"I remember this guy because of that corn. It's some kind of Indian corn, but none I've seen before—and I should know, having just paid my $25 plowing permit at San Ildefonso to plant my summer garden.

"Anyway, I have this guy's info back at the station. I'll do a search and let you know if there's anything to worry about."

"Thanks, that would be great. I owe you one."

"I'll remember that, Mr. Detective."

Poh smiled again and Bloom wondered if he was now going to be working for the Santa Fe Police Department. He hoped Poh was only joking.

※ ※ ※ ※

The next day Poh found the information on Bloom's perp. He did have a file on Brazden Shackelford, but nothing of substance. He had been swept up in a pot-digging case five years ago and accused of digging prehistoric pottery on Indian lands, but the evidence was improperly collected and he had gotten off on a technicality. No charges were ever refiled.

Poh made a call to the tribal officer in charge, who remembered the case. It was clear to that officer that Brazden was guilty even if he had gotten off scot-free. No other citations had been noted. The pothunter's last known address was near Galisteo.

Poh wrote the information down and called Bloom. The detective explained what he found and told Charles that if he had trouble with Shackelford, he would be happy to send somebody to the man's house to put the fear of god into him. Bloom thanked him and assured him that shouldn't be necessary.

"A pothunter who sells at the farmers market," Bloom said to himself. It seemed odd. He wrote the name down: Brazden Shackelford.

Felix had probably bought something questionable from the man, which would explain the dealer's peeved look when he had been caught in the act. This was the same man who now owned Rachael's big rug and was going to promote her work.

It might not hurt to drop by the market for some fresh vegetables; you never know what might turnip.

CHAPTER 32

THE BIG SALE

Money had been flowing out of A to Z's coffers since January. New York and Switzerland were both doing well enough, but the Santa Fe gallery was a different story. Construction had destroyed any hope of making serious walk-in sales. Felix's annex was closed for now, and the activity had shifted from renovation to demolition.

The revelation of an Oñate connection and possible treasure next door to the annex property had totally captivated Felix. He had the gallery's newly installed floor removed and cut a gaping hole in the concrete.

Jonathan Wolf was acting archaeologist on the property. Phosphorus (P) samples had been taken and analyzed, and they were promising. The building had the markers for being built on an ancient trash midden. The P levels were high, indicating the presence of organic material. Ground-penetrating radar marked a probable cache, and today was the day the men hoped to uncover what the radar had promised was there. Unfortunately, the process required destruction of the annex's beautiful blonde fir floor.

Concurrent to the search for treasure in the annex, Felix had just completed the work on A to Z's closing room. Conservation on the Butterfly Twin's skeleton was complete, and the remains and manta were now suspended from a massive, centrally located metal beam in his special room.

The first order of two dozen live monarch butterflies had arrived via FedEx, and they set the tone for the room. Felix was surprised at how easily insect delivery could be obtained, but pretty bugs apparently were the new must-have for Millennial weddings. He ordered delivery of twenty-four butterflies per week; there was no sense in being cheap with the ambiance.

The annex floor was stacked with large piles of debris. Digging had been going on for four hours when an object was unearthed and Felix was summoned.

"PAY DIRT," read the text on Felix's phone.

"What did you find, Jon?" (Jonathan hated being called by this diminutive, but put up with it from Felix.)

"Anything worth me destroying my beautiful gallery?" Felix asked sarcastically, knowing it would cost him dearly to replace the annex's floors.

"I'm just digging it out," Jonathan replied. "Looks like it is an early cache all right—this is good news. Means a greater likelihood there is something else here or nearby."

Felix started to pace; he loved new art finds—especially if they came from his own property.

Five tense minutes later the object was dislodged from its underground chamber.

"Not what I hoped for, BUT it is Spanish colonial," Jonathan announced.

"What is it?" Felix frowned.

Jonathan pulled up a pile of broken dishes.

"Oh, it's better than I thought, much better," the archaeologist announced. "This is a Spanish colonial midden cache as we hoped. Look at this…" Jonathan pointed to a viceroy's insignia.

"This is early material, in the Oñate timeframe I would postulate—one of the earliest findings of its kind. Ceramics is not my field, but a New World find from this period, even in this condition, has to have substantial value."

"That's great! Put it back where you found it, Jon, and document where it was discovered. Make sure there is no doubt it's from my property."

Jonathan started taking photos with his Nikon DSC3200, knowing Felix had a larger plan in mind.

"Keep up the good work and see if you can't find some real treasure. If broken dishes are valuable, imagine what a gold idol could be worth."

Felix was convinced the mother lode was near. He would make an offer on Bloom's property tomorrow, or at least feel him out. A month had passed since he consummated the deal for the Yellowhorse textile. Checking on the progress of his investment would be his excuse for dropping by Bloom's gallery.

✳ ✳ ✳ ✳

Felix's buyer arrived an hour late, not unusual for the super rich. The client, who Felix felt was his best shot for buying the manta for big money, was the head honcho of AgraCon and a serious collector of rare and unusual tribal objects.

The CEO had spent his life traveling the world for his work, and that had given him a taste for aboriginal arts. He owned the largest private collection of authentic shrunken human heads from New Guinea and the Shuar people of the Ecuadorian Amazon.

Buying a summer home in Santa Fe two years ago had turned the collector toward Southwest art. Felix already had sold him many important pieces in Santa Fe and New York. The dealer planned to price the manta at an inflated $2 million, but when it comes to art who's to say what's a piece's true value. The manta was a one of a kind and the skeleton reinforced its rarity. Felix knew the combination would hit home with this mark.

The scent of expensive musk cologne filtering through the gallery alerted Felix to his guest's arrival and he released light bulb-warmed butterflies into the twins' room in preparation for the meeting.

Felix left his office to greet his client. "David, so nice to see you. It's been a while."

"Yes, it has, and I remember the last time we got together it cost me $500,000. But don't get me wrong—I'm very happy with the piece, such a classic example. So what's all this about?"

David Rolland was not one to waste time, even when he was on vacation.

"Follow me and I will change your perception of Indian art forever."

Felix explained as he walked back to his closing room that what he was about to show Rolland was the star textile for his upcoming show. The exhibit would open in just over a month and David was the first person to see the weaving.

Felix told the buyer the manta's history, how the weaving had been his father's and had been discovered in an ancient cliff dwelling. Felix saved the tastiest detail for last; the skeleton would tell the rest of the story.

The men entered the dark room and paused as their eyes adjusted to the low light. The butterflies had warmed up nicely and were flying about, iridescent slow-mo missiles under the black lights.

"David, let me introduce you to the Butterfly Twins."

Rolland was clearly impressed. A wide grin filled his tanned face as he watched a butterfly land nearby.

"My god. They were conjoined twins, prehistoric, correct? What's the timeframe, Anasazi?"

"Yes, carbon dating puts the skeleton at the last part of the thirteenth century, a date supported by the exquisite complexity of weaving."

"I must say that is remarkable, Felix. Your build-up didn't disappoint."

"Notice the red ocher butterflies lining the dress. Look closely and you'll see they're conjoined too!"

"I'll be damned. You're right, they are," David agreed.

"It's also very rare to find a mummified Anasazi skeleton in such remarkably good condition, with hair and skin almost intact. To my knowledge, Siamese twins have never been documented in prehistoric people. Seems to me this dress and skeleton would be a natural addition to your trophy room.

"I would surmise that Oxford's Pitt Rivers Museum would love to have a specimen like this."

Felix knew this last observation would help close Rolland. The museum had a great shrunken head collection that he knew the CEO admired.

"Is it legal—the dress, skeleton, heads, papers and all?"

"I have papers for the manta. It came with my dad's estate. He bought it decades ago, and it's well documented. I wouldn't want to flaunt the skeleton, if you know what I mean. I'm selling the manta and *giving* you the skeleton—but they all come together as a single package."

"Sure, I understand. That's culturally sensitive, smart."

"Correct, quite sensitive to some," Felix let out a breath.

"The manta is the valuable artifact, and I can honestly say that no one else will have something as rare. Once this private show comes down, I have a custom-made humidity-controlled box to store and preserve the skeletal remains. It even has a special two-head foam liner."

"What's the ticket?"

Felix had been going to ask $2,000,000 but his patsy seemed excited, so he spontaneously jacked up the price. He could always come down. If he needed to, he could throw in the butterfly amulet that rested beneath his shirt, though he had grown to appreciate its power.

"Two and a half million is not inexpensive," the dealer continued, "but it's a fair price for something this rare. It's truly one of a kind. I'm also including a custom-designed bust for the manta so the blanket can be shown as sculpture if you prefer. I don't think you would want the dress to be displayed on the skeleton in your home. But, if you do, I'm happy to throw in the pulley device and wires as well."

"I'll probably just show the manta on the mannequin and put the heads in my shrunken-head case. The bones would be great for Halloween hanging from the rafters." David laughed at the perverse thought.

"OK, consider it sold, Felix. Send an empty box to my Connecticut address; you know the drill. I don't pay tax—ever.

"I'll pick the girls up after the show. You are going to exhibit the skeleton and manta with the other weavings, correct? I'd like to send a couple of friends by to see my new trophy."

Felix agreed to Rolland's terms. Even though sales made in New Mexico were taxable, Felix made his own rules and would ship an empty box. Every sale he made was to an out-of-state buyer as far as he was concerned. He was not worried he would be the next Dennis Kozlowski, the ex-CEO of Tyco International who did six years in jail.

That happened in New York. How smart could the authorities in New Mexico be? "It's barely part of the United States," he sneered. Then he turned his attention back to his buyer.

"Of course, David. I'll keep the Butterfly Twins hanging through August in case you want to drop in with your wife or special friends. Just let my staff know when you're coming. I'm the only person with access to the back room and we want the viewing to be perfect, butterflies and all."

"The wife won't like this one, but a couple of my Chile fishing buddies that like my shrunken head collection would love to see the Siamese twins—though I doubt they will understand the manta. I'll let you know when we'll come by. Keep a bottle of your best wine chilled. Love the butterflies by the way, nice touch."

Felix, the consummate salesman, gave his catlike grin and said, "Thanks. I had good inspiration."

CHAPTER 33

BATHROOM ART

The two went back to Felix's office and worked out the details of the sale. When the business was complete, Felix popped open a bottle of Vina Almaviva and the men engaged in a lively discussion of art, money, and the twins.

Two glasses later, David excused himself to the restroom and Felix, feeling a nice buzz, leaned back in his nineteen-fifties Adrian Pearsall chair to soak in the moment.

Tomorrow he would have the funds wired into his account—a cool $2.5 million, mostly profit. He would owe a hefty tax bill, but even accounting for the taxes he couldn't skirt, there would be more than enough money to acquire Bloom's buildings without spending much out of pocket.

Felix was convinced there was treasure on Bloom's property—and that it would be the next big score for the man who liked to win.

David returned from the bathroom and tossed a wreath of Indian corn on Felix's desk. As he skipped the trinket across the expensive surface, the CEO's smile vanished. Felix had not witnessed this side of the man before.

"What's the story on this?"

Felix was perceptive. It was clear to him that Rolland already knew the answer to the question.

"I got the wreath from a local man. He calls it Indian corn and I thought it gave the bathroom a nice Southwestern look. Do you agree?"

"What's the guy's name, Felix?"

It was another test. Felix had $2.5 million in his grasp and wasn't about to blow it over some damned Indian corn wreath. His mind was spinning.

"Brazden—is that his name?" David blurted out, not waiting for Felix's answer. He knew the name because an AgraCon thug had already searched Brazden's house for clues to the origins of the wreaths.

"Yes, his name is Brazden, Brazden Shackelford I believe. Why the interest, David?"

"I met Mr. Shackelford at the farmers market a few weeks back," Rolland replied. "Let's just say I'm interested in his farming practices, which is why I wanted to know how you ended up with this wreath."

Felix felt a twinge of panic. If David was investigating Brazden and a connection between the twins and the pothunter was discovered, there could be trouble in paradise. Rich CEOs didn't like getting gouged on prices.

"And the corn is important somehow? By the way, you're welcome to have the wreath if you like."

"Thanks, Felix. I will take you up on that. As I'm sure you know, I'm CEO of one of the largest agra companies in the world. What you may not know is that we specialize in seeds.

"This bozo Brazden has a corn variety we have never seen before—and we have seen them all, including one that was reputedly descended from prehistoric corn. I bought the same wreaths as are in your bathroom from him and had the seeds tested at one of the top labs. Genetic analysis shows that the corn has only the slightest contamination from local varieties and the lowest glycemic index ever recorded—not to mention that it tastes great.

"In laymen's terms, it's a new variety, one that could be ideal for diabetics and quite honestly could be worth millions—and you have the seeds hanging on your damned bathroom door.

"Pretty funny, huh. I spend $2.5 million on a manta and you give me a million-dollar wreath. Of course, it's only worth that in the right hands, like AgraCon."

"So how can I help, David?"

"I've got to shut this loose screw down. I can't have him selling these damned things to Joe Public at a damned farmers market. If growers get hold of this, they won't need my very expensive seeds, and we don't want that. I need information."

Felix's mind was moving at warp speed. All he could think was "worth millions" and I gave two of them away, and told Brazden he could give the corn to the birds—and it turns out to be a variety that has sat untouched for a thousand years.

Coming back to present reality, he said, "I'll call around and see what we can find out about Mr. Shackelford and where he does business. If possible, I'll also find out who knows about the corn and where it comes from."

"Good, that's what I need—inside leverage."

"Once you get this information, David, what will you do?"

"If we can get a patent and the corn turns out to be drought resistant, as this Brazden fellow claims, AgraCon will make a bundle. We will genetically engineer a portion of the seeds with other varieties to bring out the best in the corn's biologic code and provide us with yet another patent.

"Do you have any idea how many corn chips Doritos sells in a year?"

"Not a clue."

"At least $1.5 billion worth. Hell, PepsiCo, which owns Frito-Lay, and the Doritos brand will sell a million pounds of the stuff over the July Fourth weekend. Do you see the possibilities?"

"I do indeed. I'll see what I can do for you, David. I'm sure I can track him down. He sells pots on the side so I'll make an offer on his collection and see if I can't loosen his lips a bit."

"Once we get this guy's source for seeds, assuming it's not him, and we put him out of business, I will make sure I buy a lot more art, expensive art. Brazden needs to go away…"

Felix wasn't sure what Rolland meant by "go away," but the man's tone was very serious.

David took the wreath, put it around his wrist and walked out of the room. Looking back, he smiled and said: "Thanks for the wine. I'll let you know when my buddies and I will drop by.

"Felix, you're a good businessman, as am I, so don't disappoint me on the Brazden issue. That's where the real money is."

The tables had been turned and Felix was now the one being pressured. Some loose ends needed to be tied up fast and his first order of business was to find out what happened to that pot full of prehistoric corn kernels. If he could get his hands on the cache, maybe he could go in as a partner with Rolland.

In the face of big bucks from AgraCon, Bloom's buried treasure was looking more like icing on the cake.

CHAPTER 34

FRESH VEGETABLES

The larger number of vendors at the farmers market said the summer season had arrived. It was June, hot, with few clouds and humidity hovering around 12 percent. Bloom rode his bicycle over to the downtown Rail Runner Express station from Canyon Road, assuming it would take as long to secure a parking place for his truck as it would to get a little cardiovascular exercise and avoid the stress of garage traffic.

Balloon artists, kid musicians and the usual assortment of Santa Fe characters wove through the long line of vendors. Bloom was on a mission to find Brazden, but couldn't help but shop for dinner while he was at it. Lettuce, peas, beans, and radishes seemed to be the fare of the day.

Bloom picked his way through the crowd, and by the time he made his way to the tail end of the booths, his Trader Joe's bags were bulging. Across from the main vendors was a rag-tag line of what Bloom could only think of as the leftovers—and the man he had come to find was lounging there among the misfits, looking bored.

His first thought was that Brazden seemed less well than when he had last seen him sitting in his beat-up truck. A long, greasy, gray ponytail and unkempt beard surrounded thin lips from which an unfiltered hand-rolled cigarette lazily dangled. His market offerings were lying on a knockoff Navajo blanket, surrounded by a few chipped Indian pots. The sparse vegetables on display were wilting in the hot summer sun, as was the man selling them.

"How goes it?"

Brazden looked up, squinting in the sun's harsh rays.

"Fair to middling." The man popped to life. "Can I help you? Need something for dinner?"

Bloom figured he would buy some lettuce and see what developed.

"Sure, a bag of lettuce. You grow this yourself?"

"Yep, I have a nice little garden. In a couple of weeks, I might have some tomatoes."

"When do you expect the corn to be ready? The Fourth of July?" Bloom was probing.

"Corn's at least a month away. Depends on when the monsoons come and how much rain we get. I raise Indian corn that only needs dryland farming, so late July maybe."

Bloom saw his opening.

"I own Bloom's on Canyon Road. I'm married to a Navajo, Rachael Yellowhorse. She's a weaver, and she would love to get some Indian corn."

Bloom watched for his reaction.

"Hell, yes, I know the gallery and your wife's work. She's a great weaver. I knew her grandmother Ethel too—she was one fine human being. I'm a picker by trade, used to hit all the trading posts on my route. Toadlena was a favorite. You know if old Sal is still around?"

"Yes, he's there but starting to slow down. Now he only works twelve hours a day."

"That's funny. You deal in new stuff, right? Contemporary Indian art?"

"Yes, that's correct, though we just opened Bloom's Traditional. I'm going to handle rugs and jewelry, see how it fares. I might add additional art, pots, etc., later."

"Pots, huh? How about prehistoric ones? I occasionally get them, high quality, the real McCoy, all guaranteed to be legitimately old, lots better than these old junkers I brought today."

Brazden was hoping Bloom was a novice who was not aware of the strict laws dealing with prehistoric pieces.

"I hadn't thought about that, but I do love Native American history, especially petroglyphs. Do you sell to any other dealers on the road?"

Bloom was fishing to find out what kind of deal Brazden and Felix had done.

"Your next-door neighbor buys from me occasionally, so you know I must sell the good stuff. Felix Zachow. He's big time."

"Yes, he's one of the movers and shakers," Bloom agreed. "Has he purchased anything lately that I could go see to get an idea of the quality and price?"

Brazden paused, then answered: "No, nothing recently. But I've got some Polaroids of good pieces I keep at my house. The photos are in my truck if you want to see them."

Bloom had the answer he was looking for. Whatever Felix had bought from Brazden must have been illegal, or the pothunter would not have lied about it.

"I don't have time today, I'm afraid." Bloom held up his bag of vegetables. "I need to get back to the gallery. Maybe another time. I'm still trying to figure out what the traditional place's mix of inventory is going to be. Once you get that Indian corn in, please let me know."

Bloom gave Brazden his business card, then rode off on his bicycle loaded down with groceries and a much better understanding of who his neighbor was. He would be careful in his dealings with Felix—it was obvious he played loose with the law and that wasn't the way Bloom did business.

His first impression of Brazden was that he was an OK guy who was down on his luck.

The pothunter took Bloom's "maybe later" as an invitation to make an unannounced visit with his portfolio of photos to see if he couldn't make a sale. Brazden could use some new customers.

CHAPTER 35

JUST A FEW MEASUREMENTS

Brazden's financial difficulties made Bloom reflect on the business of art. A couple of deals go south and wham! You're selling wilted lettuce at the Santa Fe Railyard to survive.

Convinced that Felix's art dealings were sometimes questionable, Bloom would now be more cautious about selling his property to the high-end gallerist.

"Did Felix own any illegal prehistoric pottery?" Bloom wondered. "Would he admit to doing business with Brazden Shackelford? Maybe it was not Felix but the pothunter who was playing coy…"

These questions were important to Bloom. Felix now owned his wife's rug and, to some extent, Zachow's dealings could affect her reputation.

From Bloom's perspective, Brazden didn't appear to be a dangerous person. The old guy just seemed down on his luck—although offering to sell prehistoric pots to a stranger did seem risky, especially since Brazden had been busted once before for the same offense.

The casita's improvement hearing was scheduled within the next ten days — and Bloom wanted to make sure they were on schedule—so he arranged to meet Jonathan Wolf at the gallery to discuss what to expect.

The historian's answers were not what Bloom was hoping to hear.

"Mr. Bloom, I'm afraid I've had a difficult time uncovering any new information about your property. I brought back your artifacts—they are interesting, but nothing out of the ordinary. Unfortunately, I can't tie them into anything exciting."

Jonathan scooted a large plastic tub in Bloom's direction, avoiding eye contact with him.

"I feel it's important to gather measurements and document the property's landscape and interior structure," Wolf said. "Doing this will help protect your interests in case the review board wants to discuss the architectural details in more depth."

"OK. What do you need from me?" Bloom asked.

"You're closed Sundays, correct?"

"Yes, for now. In two weeks, Rachael will start opening Bloom's Traditional on Sundays at 11 a.m. and I'll get the kids to myself. Do you want to take your measurements this Sunday?"

"Yes, if you don't mind. I'll need to borrow that key again. Is it still under the flowerpot, with same code—1610? I promise not to touch any art."

Jonathan gave Bloom his most ingratiating, "Trust me, I'm a nice guy," grin.

That Jonathan remembered the casita security code and the key's hiding place so easily made Bloom realize he should change codes and key locations more often. Letting it be without making regular changes was pretty poor security on his part.

"Will it be just you?"

"I'll have an assistant, but only I will go inside the gallery portion of the building."

Jonathan felt Bloom's hesitation and added, "It's important to do this now so we'll be sure to be ready for the scheduled meeting with the board."

Bloom flinched, then acquiesced. "OK. The key is in the same place and you can use that 1610 code—that's my special guest code."

Bloom was lying, as 1610 was his password for all non-employee visitors, but he wanted Jonathan to understand that he could track all the comings and goings in the building.

"If you have any problems, Jonathan, or find anything of interest, please don't hesitate to call me. You won't be doing any digging, will you? I have a drip system in place."

"No, I don't even own a shovel anymore."

It was true that Wolf wouldn't disturb the topsoil though he would bring in the latest laser technology to see if he could locate the hidden treasure. Any information he gained would help his boss decide how aggressive he would need to be when he offered to purchase Bloom's property.

❋ ❋ ❋ ❋

Sunday was a blustery day, with large cumulonimbus clouds boiling over the Sangre de Cristo Mountains, the first serious sign of the arrival of the summer rains.

Jonathan arrived at the casita at 7 a.m. with his special projects assistant. Though deaf, the man was an accomplished lip reader and not much of a talker—Jonathan's favorite kind of human.

Operating the handheld laser, an amazing tool that set a new standard for archaeological research, was a one-person job. Contours under the ground appeared in different colors and registries, mapping out high-resolution images up to fifteen feet below the surface. The density of objects could be calculated and, in some cases, tentative identification of found objects could be made.

Jonathan designed a grid pattern that would allow his man to map the entire portal and grounds, starting where the other artifacts had been found. Amazingly, after only twenty minutes they got a serious hit: A large object one meter below the surface appeared to be a chest—a treasure chest!

Jonathan surveyed the area twice to make sure he was not indulging in wishful thinking, but there was no doubt: there was a dense object in the shape of a chest, its size and other details consistent with early Mexican design, under the ground. Even better, it was one-and-a-half meters off the edge of the existing portal and easily accessible.

The radar was also pinging on smaller items, in much the way boat radar could key in on fish suspended in the water. These items could be silver coins, or broken bits of the Olmec statue's torso, or even more ceramic artifacts like those Jonathan had uncovered earlier. These smaller objects were located in a two-meter radius from the trunk.

Jonathan left his assistant to complete mapping the remainder of the property while he went inside the casita to snoop around for architectural clues. He wondered if Bloom had any cameras monitoring the gallery but saw none.

The quaint adobe building was just one thousand-square-feet, so it was understandable why the gallerist needed to create more space. Jonathan was sure Bloom would be granted the construction permit he sought. If the treasure chest proved to be Oñate's, though, the Historic Districts Review Board might rule differently.

Although its basic bones were intact, the building had clearly been modified many times over the years. The door jams were five-feet, eight-inches tall with two-and-a-half-foot thick walls and what looked like the original latias on the ceiling. Using a small corkscrew-like tool, Jonathan took a core sample from one of the beams in an area where the hole would be hard to notice. He filled the tiny depression with a pinch of dark caulk.

There was a small kitchen in the building with a gas stove, refrigerator, and microwave. An air vent over the stove that led to the roof appeared functional. There was also a single toilet and sink in the small bathroom. Jonathan took photos and noted outlets, switches, gas hoses and anything else that might come in handy in the future.

He had already had a copy of the door key made. The antiquated alarm system would not be a problem. It was still hooked up to a hard, rather than wireless, line.

The casita's small windows, which were barely large enough for a medium-sized man to squeeze through, were locked and protected by decorative security bars.

"If someone were to be trapped in the building and there was a fire," Jonathan thought, writing his observation in his notebook, "it could be hard to get out."

Large, widely spaced raindrops started falling at 11 a.m. The timing was perfect as the two had completed the geographic map and Jonathan had seen and noted everything he needed to inside the casita.

Jonathan had no doubt he had located a treasure chest; there would be no turning back until it was unearthed.

He hoped Bloom would sell his buildings and walk away a wealthy and healthy man. If he refused to sell, Plan B would go into effect—and that would make for a much messier and less pleasant scenario.

CHAPTER 36

CORN FOR THE LADY

It was now July and the tourist season promised to be a good one.

Bloom was pleased with the money the galleries had brought in to date. Rachael turned out to be as great a salesperson as he had expected, and working with Dr. J at Bloom's Traditional gave her the time she needed to finish Felix's rug. With only two inches to complete, there was no doubt she would make the August deadline. Then she could concentrate more fully on sales when she was not babysitting.

The kids turned out to be a good draw. With people lingering longer to watch Rachael weave, the children play, and Dr. J sell, Rachael's tip jar was overflowing.

She began to wonder if they even needed to enclose the portal: the doggie gates were working perfectly well and were easy to clean when dirty. Rachael was lobbying hard to save the construction money, but Bloom would have none of it. He had done well this year and paying for the build-out with savings and summer sales was doable.

Bloom had wisely reinvested some of the profits into a couple of works he had originally sold twenty years ago, and an old client had consigned a nice pencil drawing by Rachael's late brother Willard Yellowhorse. Bloom would clear $20,000 once the small piece sold—and he knew it wouldn't take long. He thought about showing the drawing to Felix, but didn't want the other dealer to get into the Willard Yellowhorse resale business—something that was still an important income stream for Bloom.

He was having a very good day when Brazden strolled in with a large duffel bag and smiled at Bloom.

"How's it going, Mr. Bloom? You look busy. I've been sitting on the porch for nearly an hour waiting for the customers to clear out. If you've got a minute, I can show you a few things."

Bloom knew he wasn't going to be buying any prehistoric pots. He had looked up the laws and knew that if you sold these items you had better have great paperwork to back up their provenance. He doubted Brazden had the paperwork, so the risk of selling his looted pots would outweigh the profit.

"I have a little time, but I'm not sure I'm going down the pot route right now. Just so you know..."

"Not a problem," Brazden sighed, "but if you don't mind, I'd like to meet your wife before we get down to it. I have a little present I think she might like. As I told you when we met at the farmers market, I used to watch her grandmother when Ethel had a loom set up at Toadlena."

"Did you buy contemporary rugs from Ethel?" Bloom asked, hoping he might have one for sale.

"Nah. I couldn't afford her weavings even back in the day, but I would occasionally sell a nice rug to old Sal. He treated me good. Some dealers ain't so nice. They make you wait or have you come through the back door like you're a dirty dog, if you know what I mean. Sal never did that. He was always a gentleman."

Bloom understood Brazden all too well. He had seen pickers treated like subhumans, not good enough to use the toilet. He tried never to behave that way, even on a busy July day.

"Let's go see Rachael while no one's here. I'm sure she would love hearing a story about her grandmother."

Brazden opened his bag and pulled out a large freezer bag. "My gift."

"Great, you can leave your duffel bag here. I'll lock up so it will be safe."

Bloom put his "Gone for 15 Minutes" sign in the window and walked Brazden over to Bloom's Traditional. There were three women draped in oversized squash blossom necklaces talking to Dr. J, who nodded in Bloom's direction while he kept the conversation going.

"He must be close to a sale," Bloom thought.

Both kids were asleep in the doggie chamber and Rachael's weaving comb was moving in harmony with the rug. She was nearing the end of the work and her concentration was intense. Bloom hated to interrupt, knowing her rhythm would be broken.

"Hi, Rachael." No response. She was lost in the wool.

"Oh, Rachael. It's your husband Charles Bloom, the great art dealer."

Bloom's humor broke the spell and Rachael looked up and smiled.

"Sorry. You know how I am when I'm working. It's a good day and I'm pushing to finish the rug this weekend."

"Rachael, this man is a fan of yours and knew your grandmother Ethel. He used to visit her in Toadlena, and he's brought you a story or two and a gift."

"A gift—that's sweet."

Brazden blushed and pushed his scraggly gray hair back like a young boy in love.

"Yes, ma'am. I did meet your grandma a couple of times, once when you were there. I remember how pretty you looked then, and I believe you've gotten even better looking. Bloom's a lucky man."

It was Rachael's turn to blush.

"I brought something I thought you might could use. When I first met your husband, he said you liked to garden and while it's probably way too late for this year's crop, I can assure you these Indian corn seeds will be just as good next year."

Brazden smiled at his inside joke. "This is the real deal."

The looter handed over the freezer bag full of Anasazi corn dusted with ancient pollen. Rachael looked over the small, multicolored kernels and smiled widely.

"This is just like the corn on the wreath that Felix gave us, Bloom. What a wonderful gift. Thank you so much, Brazden. I can't wait to plant it. I'll put some in the ground tomorrow. Who knows? We might be able to get a few stalks to maturity if we have great monsoons this year."

Shackelford was a little hurt to learn Felix had given his corn wreath away—but he guessed that was to be expected. The wealthy dealer couldn't give a shit about the corn kernels in the prehistoric pot.

Brazden was happy the wreath ended up with Rachael Yellowhorse. She was Indian and her having the seeds was a good thing—even if her people feared the Anasazi spirits who had grown them. He wouldn't mention that part of the corn's story to Rachael.

"If I get any seeds to produce this year," she said, "I'll make you a batch of my posole with Santa Fe green chile. With this Indian corn, I can't go wrong."

Brazden's face lit up. It had been a long time since anyone had offered him a home-cooked meal, much less a woman as good-looking as Rachael Yellowhorse.

"I can't wait. Don't overwater the seeds or plants. They require less water than you might imagine and will do just fine on the monsoon rains. The bugs seem to leave them alone too."

Brazden asked Rachael if he could take a picture with her. "I have one of your grandmother in my scrapbook and it would nice to have another photo with you all grown up."

"Sure, I'm happy to do that."

Standing next to the young woman, Brazden was beaming like a sixteen-year-old at the prom. Bloom took a couple of shots of the pair with his iPhone. One image showed the entire loom; the second was a close-up of the two from the waist up. He emailed the files to the gallery computer so he could print off a copy for Brazden before he left.

Bloom and Shackelford said their goodbyes to Rachael and walked back to the main gallery as Dr. J finally closed the sale to one of the silver-and-turquoise bedecked women. It was indeed a good day.

No one was waiting to see Bloom, so he decided to leave the "Gone for 15 Minutes" sign up a little longer and give Brazden time to pitch his pottery collection. He had brought nice examples of a Mimbres, Tularosa Black on White, Gila River and even a Chaco pot, but it was clear to Bloom after a brief discussion that the pothunter's paperwork was scant at best. Brazden proudly showed him certificates of authenticity and provenance, but the collection's geography was vague and possibly contrived.

Bloom smiled, acted interested and let the man down gently by explaining that prehistoric pottery wasn't his field. He added that he was starting to buy old Navajo rugs and blankets now that he had a little extra money, so if Brazden turned anything up, he could bring it over. He didn't need an appointment; he could just come on in through the front door.

Brazden was also having a good day. For once he felt special, not like he was standing on the bottom rung of the art world ladder. And when Bloom gave Brazden the photos of him and Rachael, it cemented these positive feelings.

CHAPTER 37

THE PLAY

Felix was reviewing Jonathan's detailed report as the two men sat in the dealer's office.

"You see that?" the historian asked, waving a thin finger at an enlarged blip. "There are empty spaces between that structure and the outside—in other words, there are layers of content in that chest, which, by the way, is the correct size for something created in the conquistador period."

"Can we tell what's inside—metal, paper, wood?" Felix asked.

"We can tell the density. The nature of the material itself is more of a supposition on my part, but there are clearly different kinds of objects in the container, which is a good sign."

"And you think it's a meter down?"

"Yes. And those small pings also relate to a mass—coins would be my guess, but one would need to sift the dirt methodically to find out.

"There are two distinct areas to explore, one under the portal close to where the box is located and another a half-meter west. If Bloom proceeds with the construction on the portal, that brick foundation will come out and there is a better than not chance they will turn up some artifacts.

"You need to own the building and let me bring in archaeological professionals to excavate the property properly and document everything for your Oñate museum and my scientific paper."

"Is there anything else to report?" Felix asked as if he expected more.

"I did a thorough inspection of the inside of Bloom's casita. The beam's core carbon dates to a fifteen-hundred timeframe, give or take seventy-five years. It's the real thing. This is the oldest house in Santa Fe, and the case can be made that this structure is the most historically pertinent building in the whole state, if not the entire country. Can you believe Oñate's home appears to be intact?"

Felix smiled. He could see the possibilities and only two people understood the significance.

"Jonathan, did you appropriate the smoking-gun historical document related to the ancient homesite?"

"Yes, it's secure."

Felix's tone turned serious. "What about Plan B? Did you get the information you needed in case we have to go to Plan C?"

"Yes, it's easily doable. The wife and kids spend the day at the casita and Bloom is in the other gallery. In August Rachael will come in on Sundays without the children in tow—so that would be the least busy day, and the earlier in the month, the better."

"Ok, I'll make my offer to Bloom soon and see if I can't do this the civilized way. We have to have the building to get the value out of the chest—correct?"

Felix wanted to be sure he knew the score.

"Yes, it's definitely best to own the casita and Bloom's other gallery as a buffer, both to maximize your profits and for me to get the recognition I so justly deserve."

Felix grinned. He could care less about the building's historical significance or any academic accolades for Jonathan. Money was his mantra. This deal was within reach and nothing was going to stop him from closing it.

CHAPTER 38

DONE

Luck was on Felix's side; he would not have to make an unannounced visit to Bloom's. Being able to minimize his perceived interest in the property would strengthen his ability to negotiate.

Rachael had finished her weaving two weeks early, giving A to Z more time to place her rug. Unbeknownst to Rachael, though, Felix wasn't at all concerned with selling the piece. Her rug was the least valuable textile in the show, and he had no doubt he would easily find a buyer.

Felix decided to sound out Rachael first, to see how she might feel about selling the property before he hit Bloom with an offer.

Rachael's weaving had been hung on the wall of Bloom's Traditional with small carpet tacks—not the best for the textile, but not a problem in the short term. When Felix strolled in, Rachael was sitting on the side of a desk rocking her one-year-old, Samantha. It was naptime. Willy was quietly building a castle out of multicolored blocks.

"Very nice weaving, Rachael. You deserve to revel in your accomplishment."

Rachael turned around, blushing.

"Felix, the amount of time that goes into one of these rugs is shocking. The reality is that I might only be able to produce thirty of these in my entire career, so I try to soak in the moment of completion for all of them."

Felix nodded his head as if understanding the effort involved and responded affirmatively: "You're right. Life is precious and so often it's not in our control."

Felix sat down next to Rachael as they discussed the rug and what he should know about the meaning of the pattern and the time involved. He acted interested even though he knew that no hype would be necessary: the fine textile would sell itself.

"I was wondering, Rachael, if you would ever consider letting me purchase your gallery buildings. You know you could make a tidy profit, enough to pay the bills for many years and take the pressure off so you'd have time to have another child."

Felix was a good salesman; he understood the right buttons to push.

"Anything is possible, I guess. You'll have to talk to Bloom about that. This gallery is his baby; I'm just here for the ride. If he wants to sell the buildings, I'm good with his decision. He's in charge."

Felix smiled. He knew that Rachael controlled the family's decisions and, as much as she said it was Bloom's choice, it was clear to him that it was not.

"Is your husband around?"

"Yes, he's working at Bloom's. Go over there and tell him I said he should discuss the property with you."

"Thanks, I'll do that. Could I bother you for a bottle of water on my way out? It's a hot afternoon..."

"Sure, there's some in the kitchen fridge. Help yourself. I would get you a drink but I've gotten Samantha down and I don't want to move right now—unless you'd like to hear a high-pitched scream."

"No problem. I can handle this."

Felix pushed open the brown curtain and slipped into the small kitchen. An avocado green nineteen-seventies refrigerator hummed in the corner next to a small New Mexican WPA hutch. Perched on the tabletop was a large freezer bag full of Native corn kernels. A yellow Post-it Note stuck on the bag read, "Owe Brazden a meal soon," with a happy face next to the word "meal."

Felix froze. Brazden had brought a bag of what appeared to be the very Indian corn that David was trying to obtain. He considered pocketing the package then and there, but that would be risky. More worrisome was the fact that the idiot was giving the valuable corn away—Felix's corn—and that Rachael apparently was on friendly terms with Brazden.

What else did she know?

Felix had a bigger and more serious problem than he had anticipated. His fingers stroked the turquoise butterfly fetish as he searched for an answer to his dilemma. He smiled as he decided what he had to do: "Brazden has to go."

"Did you find the water?" Rachael asked, wondering what was keeping Felix in the kitchen for so long.

"Oh, yes. I certainly did…"

❋ ❋ ❋ ❋

Bloom was in the process of hanging a large painting, something that's difficult for one person to manage. No one warns you about how physically demanding the art business can be. The daily routine is not all wine and cheese openings.

"Here, let me give you a hand." Felix grabbed one of the corners of the three- by seven-foot painting.

"Thanks. It's not all that heavy but it's more cumbersome than I thought."

"You should have your man do this for you."

Bloom smiled at Felix's suggestion. His was not one of those Santa Fe galleries that had a designated person to hang artwork.

When the piece was hung, Bloom stood back to gauge the spacing. It was perfect. His eye never lied.

"Thanks again, Felix. Is that Rachael's rug under your arm?"

Bloom pointed to the large black garbage bag in which Rachael had placed her masterpiece before giving it to Felix.

"Did she have you sign a receipt for the weaving?" Bloom tried to ask diplomatically.

"I wondered about that—your wife is a very trusting woman. No, she did not."

"Rachael is new to this business and still believes no one would ever take advantage of her when it comes to purchasing a Navajo rug. I know you understand. If you don't mind, I'll have you sign for the piece."

"No problem. I'm thrilled with what I purchased."

Bloom handed a dated, handwritten bill of sale to Felix and had him sign off.

"Mind if I take one more look at my wife's work since I may never see it again?"

Bloom loved his wife's rugs and hated to see them go, even for big money—but that was the retail business.

"Sure, have at it old man."

Bloom pulled out the rug and caressed the wool like it was a woman's cheek. Sighing, he carefully folded it, replaced it in its ugly trash bag and handed it back—creating the perfect opening for Felix's gambit to buy Bloom's.

"You know, Charles, if you sold me your buildings you could keep Rachael's masterpiece for your children and not ever have to sell another one.

"I'm very interested in the property, and I happen to be able to write a big check right now. It would be an all cash deal, and you could walk away from all this responsibility. I'm even willing to give you my annex rent-free for a year, or until you get a new place."

Bloom was interested, but his radar was up. He knew Felix was a very rich man who could make his life miserable if he so chose.

"What would you want to pay for the place, hypothetically speaking?"

Felix felt the traction and didn't want to screw around with low-ball offers. It was now or never.

"Two million cash. You could pay off your mortgage and walk a way a rich man, with clear sailing for the near future. What do you say?"

Bloom was stunned. He had paid $1.4 million less than three months ago, with nothing down. He did the math in his head. Even splitting the profit with Shriver, he would walk away with $300,000 profit. Free rent for a year would save him another $60,000.

"That's generous," he responded, watching for Felix's reaction. "You must really like this part of Canyon Road."

Felix revealed nothing.

"Yes, that's why I'm here. I like my spaces and yours would add to mine in the long haul. Buyers like me will not knock on your door very often—and with no Realtor fees. We both know that $2 million is overpaying, but I'm willing to do that because I can."

"Let me think about it and talk to Rachael. It's her place too."

"Of course. I'll give you a week to make a decision. I can use the money for other projects, so I want to know one way or another. I'm sure you can understand."

"That's more than fair. I have been here for over twenty years, so that's an important part of the equation too. It's not all about money I guess, or I would already have said yes."

The two men shook hands and Felix walked out of the gallery with a piece of Rachael's lifework under his arm.

Tough decisions would have to be made—but first Bloom wanted to do some investigating of his own.

The possibility of treasure on the property still haunted him. Could this be part of Felix's reason for wanting to buy the property? It seemed farfetched, but it was definitely possible. Standing there, watching Felix walk away, he couldn't help but see Sheldon Parsons' painting in his mind: TREASURES OF CANYON ROAD.

CHAPTER 39

NEED A SECOND OPINION

Bloom called Wendy Whippelton before Felix cleared the grounds. He had given her the artifacts right after Jonathan brought them back and she had promised to investigate his property a little further. In the art world, you rarely solicit and accept only one opinion. In Bloom's mind, the artifacts warranted a second look.

"Wendy here," a perky young voice answered the phone.

"Hi, Wendy. Charles Bloom. Sorry to bother you. I know it hasn't been that long since we talked, but I was hoping you might have found some information on the casita or the artifacts I gave you."

"Well, it's interesting that you ask. I have learned a few things. The coins are Spanish but of New World mint, which points to a possible early building site. The head is even more interesting. It's a very rare Olmec piece and quite valuable. If you have the rest of the body, I'm told it could easily be worth $30,000 or more. The head alone might be $3,000 to $5,000."

Jonathan had played down the value of the head, saying it was insignificant.

"You're sure about these estimates?"

"Yes, I checked with three separate dealers specializing in pre-Columbian work. They all had similar estimates, and they were all puzzled by the fact that it had been buried in New Mexico. They said to let them know if you found the other part of the body. My guess is they were hedging—the piece may be worth even more with the right provenance."

"And the history of the casita—anything there? Jonathan Wolf doesn't seem to think there are any compelling findings so far."

"I would have to agree with him up to a point. There is one document that I can't locate. The librarian is looking for it now. Hopefully, it's just been misplaced."

"Is it important?"

"Hard to say, but it's clearly a piece of the puzzle. Here's the part you might find interesting, although not in a good way. The last person to check out that file was Jonathan Wolf."

"Uh-oh," Bloom said out loud. "Do you think he stole it?"

"I would never accuse someone of something as serious as stealing historical documents—especially a man like Wolf, who has had a long and distinguished career. All I can say at this point is that it's missing and his signature was the last one in the file."

Bloom wondered what the missing file might contain.

"Wendy, are we on schedule for the permit hearing?"

"Yes, that's all good, but we need to get the property report from Wolf before we can proceed. How is he coming?"

"It's still in process, I'm afraid. I'll try to move him along a little faster."

Bloom paused then asked: "Do you know which historian was hired for the A to Z gallery board meeting?

"Jonathan Wolf."

"Interesting. I'll get back to you about his report. And thanks again for the information regarding the artifacts. Please let me know right away if the librarian finds that missing document."

"Sure thing. And for what it's worth, Bloom, my gut feeling is that your little casita is a lot older than we might believe. But even if it is older, it shouldn't keep you from doing your project."

"Thanks, we'll talk soon."

Bloom's inner voice was telling him something wasn't right. Felix had made too good an offer on his place.

"What am I missing?" he wondered. "Could it be the treasure? Is it possible?"

CHAPTER 40

TIME FOR A VISIT

Breathing was becoming more difficult for Brazden. He knew this was a bad sign, but was afraid to get medical help. Doctors were not his friends. They never listened and gave him prescriptions for pills he couldn't afford.

His father had died of a heart attack at fifty-six, and he was older than that now. Brazden had never respected his body. It was probably too late to start now, he thought, as he let out a stream of blue smoke. The drag on the cigarette felt good, invigorating.

Brazden hoped that if he did have some horrible medical condition he wouldn't linger long. For the time being, he would keep his physical activity to a minimum, tend the garden in the morning and rest in the afternoon.

His condition made it clear he would never again be able to climb the cliff wall. His time as a pothunter had passed and he was now the mirror image of his grandfather Sidney, but without a grandchild to help him find and retrieve artifacts.

"Not in the cards," he thought to himself, "no kids, no wife, one of many missed opportunities."

His mind dwelled on the butterfly amulet. Brazden felt lost without the fetish and its power. He was sure its loss was contributing to his failing health. The twins were gone too. All his treasures were now in the hands of the greedy art dealer, Felix Zachow.

Brazden was angry with Felix for screwing him out of such great objects for so little money.

"He'll get rich off my finds," he groused. "I took all the risks and he took none." He said it out loud, as if there were someone nearby to hear him.

Looking around, he wondered what would become of his pots and precious seeds. The authorities would most likely confiscate the pottery, and it would collect dust forever in some government basement.

But Brazden had begun to think of his seeds as his children and felt he had a responsibility to at least pass them on to someone who would care about them. Rachael Yellowhorse treated him as kindly as her grandmother had. If he were on his way out, it was Rachael who would care for the seeds.

If he had the energy, he would drive out to Bloom's tomorrow and drop off all the remaining seeds with an explanation of why he was giving them to Rachael.

He slept well that night, for the first time in a long time.

✽ ✽ ✽ ✽

Images of seeds encased in dollar signs danced in Felix's dreams after seeing Rachael's bag of Indian corn.

He had called the AgraCon CEO and explained he might be able to run down the mother lode, viable Anasazi seeds untouched for a thousand years. He had found the source of Brazden's stash.

David was excited and promised him a 1-percent royalty on all gross sales if he could obtain an exclusive on the seeds—and if they were as viable as promised.

Felix kept replaying Rolland's words in his head:

"One percent doesn't sound like much, but think of it in terms of $100 million per year, that's a million dollar payday every twelve months, and all the transactions take place via our Irish corporation, which has low tax rates. Dryland farming is still huge in much of the world.

"This deal could make your manta sale look insignificant over time—and the payout from the seeds is in perpetuity."

Felix knew the easiest pickings would be Brazden's seed stash. The pot he had found them in was huge, so he must have more. If he couldn't get his hands on Brazden's seeds, he would somehow get Rachael's—maybe even have Bloom throw them in on the building deal, which he was sure his neighbor was going to accept. It was too much money for a man like Bloom to turn down. He would take the easy money.

Felix was more excited about the corn seed deal than the property sale now. Rolland's 1-percent offer could make the treasure and historic building a small payout compared to what he could make dealing in prehistoric seeds.

The time had come, he thought grimly. Brazden's pothunting days would soon be over.

CHAPTER 41

GIFT FROM THE BUTTERFLY TWINS

The phone call from Felix surprised Brazden. The high-ticket art dealer said he wanted to purchase a few prehistoric pots as decoration for the Butterfly Twins exhibit. For the first time, the pothunter heard a friendly timbre in Felix's voice—not his usual rush to be done with the conversation and the picker.

Brazden was feeling better today, or so he tried to tell himself, and the unexpected additional income boosted his spirits. Maybe he would see a doctor after all. Maybe it wasn't too late.

Felix wanted to meet that night at Brazden's modest home south of town, a structure about the size of Felix's guest casita.

Brazden was ashamed of how he lived and worried about what Zachow would think. He knew he shouldn't care, but he did. He hadn't had guests in the house in years, and his place was dirty even by a bachelor's standards. It was useless to clean, easier to just push things in piles and cover them with the quilts his mother had left him.

Working as hard as his lungs would permit, Brazden arranged the most expensive pots on a mesquite coffee table and put his lesser pots away. He wanted Felix to focus only on the best objects. With Felix, provenance wouldn't be a problem; he could fabricate what he needed if he ever sold the pots. In Felix's world, everything was legal.

Brazden decided to try to trade Felix out of the amulet, maybe exchange a couple of great pots for his old necklace. He knew his time was short and he wanted the charm to be on his neck the day he died—which could be soon if his lungs didn't improve.

But before he checked out of this world, Brazden had to take care of his precious corn kernels. He knew Felix would just give them away, like he gave his wreath to Rachael or, worse yet, feed them to the Canyon Road ravens. If Felix were going to dispose of them anyway, Brazden would make sure the hand-off was done responsibly. A trip to Bloom's was in order.

He packed up all of the corn, including the two remaining wreaths, and put the loot in an old Tide detergent box. He wrote a small explanation about how he was dying and he hoped Rachael would take on the responsibility of the ancient seeds. He stuffed a couple of old socks into the top the box and sealed it, then remembered he had one other message. He reopened the box and put in the Skoal can that contained the butterfly carcass and added a sticky note: "P.S. Here's a gift from the Butterfly Twins."

Responsibly disposing of the sacred butterfly remains eased his mind and he felt at peace, like he finally was square with the twins.

Brazden drove to Bloom's and delivered the package.

"Hi, Bloom. I'm sorry to bother you. Have you got a minute?" the old pothunter asked, his breathing labored.

"Sure. Do you have a rug to show me?" Bloom looked quizzically at Brazden, who was obviously physically taxed.

"Are you OK? It looks like you're out of breath. Why don't you sit down and I'll get you some water."

"Oh, I'm fine, some days are harder than others. It's this damned humidity and too many smokes." Brazden smiled and put the box on Bloom's desk.

"I have another gift for your wife. I thought I could drop it off and you could give it to her later. I don't want to bother her."

"I'm not sure my wife will like a box of Tide, but I know I sure do. We can work on her laundry skills together," Bloom kidded Brazden.

"Sorry about the box," Brazden tried to smile as he pursed his lips to keep some oxygen flowing to his brain. "It's what's inside that counts."

"We can walk over and give it her now. She's not going to start weaving again for at least two weeks. She's enjoying her time with the kids and making the occasional sale."

"I wish I could do that, but I'm pretty tired. Maybe you could just give her the box for me and tell her to keep true to Spider Woman's gift." Brazden gave Bloom a weak smile and walked out the door without looking back.

Bloom was concerned. The man did not look good; his color was ashen and his breathing was not normal. He was clearly ill, but what could Bloom do? He walked the box over to Rachael and revisited the drop-off and his conversation with Brazden.

"Great, I get to sell *and* do your laundry?" Rachael laughed, knowing full well that Bloom washed most of the clothes.

"I wish," he parried. "This is a gift from Brazden. He wanted you to have it and he didn't look so good."

"Really? Is he sick?"

"I'm not a doctor, but if I had to guess, I would say he's very ill."

Rachael opened the box and read the notes, then looked at her husband.

"What's this all about? Ancient seeds? Gift of the twins? I don't understand—and what's with the dead butterfly?"

Bloom couldn't make sense of it either.

"I guess he's dying, and maybe he wanted to give these seeds to someone who would appreciate them. For whatever reason, that's you. It looks like we will have a good garden next year," Bloom said, trying to make light of the situation. It wasn't working.

"I'm worried about him," Rachael mused. "You should ask Billy Poh if he can check on him." Bloom assured her he would do that.

Rachael reread the letter and decided that if the seeds were that special to Brazden she would treat them as though they were sacred. She put the box in a small ground safe Bloom had installed for her precious wool.

Rachael had good instincts and her inner voice told her this box meant trouble—though what kind of trouble she couldn't say.

CHAPTER 42

WHERE IS IT?

The Mercedes-Benz slid up the red dirt road. The howling wind and sheets of rain made it difficult to find Brazden's small, ramshackle home.

Felix finally spotted Brazden's beat-up Ford and turned in and parked. He was dressed in black, wearing gloves, and carrying a .38 pistol. He was there for only one reason: to get the exact location of the pots, collect his seeds and eliminate Brazden.

Felix had done a lot of nasty things in his life, but had never taken a human life—at least not yet. Surprisingly, though, the concept didn't seem to bother him as much as he had expected.

Brazden and his grandfather were longtime acquaintances. Felix even liked the man well enough, but he was in a no-win situation. If David discovered the link between the looter and himself, a lot could go wrong. The manta deal could be at jeopardy and he would be cut out of the seed royalty for sure. The easiest way to protect his interests was to kill Brazden, make it look like a pot deal gone bad, and move on—with the seeds, of course. No one would ever suspect him of the crime.

Trying to stay dry, Felix ran for the entrance. He gave a muffled knock on the door with his gloved fist, pistol behind his back. There was no answer. He waited a few minutes, took off a glove and knocked harder. The rain on the tin roof made it impossible to hear if anyone was moving around inside.

Felix turned the doorknob. It opened and he peered in. There was music playing in the background, the kitchen lights were on, and a half-dozen prehistoric pots were arranged in a neat row on a worn coffee table in the living room. There was no sign of Brazden.

Elton John's voice filled the small space: "Someone saved my life tonight." The song resonated even in the poorly insulated room. The lyrics took root in Felix's mind: "You're a butterfly and free to fly... bye bye."

Something was wrong. Felix holstered his weapon and went to the back of the house. Brazden was sprawled on the top of his bed surrounded by a mosaic of different colored beer cans. He was smiling, but his breathing was shallow and his color ashen. He appeared to be dying.

Felix walked over and sat next to him.

"Hey, Brazden—You don't look so good."

"I've been betterrr," Brazden said, slurring his words. It looks like I could check out tonight, so I'm afraid I can't do no deals. If you want any of the pots, just take them. I won't need them where I'm headed —unless maybe we could trade for my turquoise butterfly. I'd love to die with it on."

The music was playing in a loop, the words of the song mirroring the action in the house: "coming in the morning with a truck to take me home."

"Brazden, where is the big pot, the one with the corn?"

The pothunter pointed to the coffee table in the front room and said, "Take the camera. I took photos. The pots are at Wupatki National Monument, over by Flagstaff. You can follow the butterfly rock marker grandpa Sidney made."

Brazden's shallow breathing, oxygen deprivation, and beer consumption made talking difficult.

"The corn, is it still in the pot?"

Brazden smiled. "No, and I didn't give it to the birds neither."

Felix leaned in, and for the first time Brazden saw him clearly—the black clothes, the gloves, the holstered gun. It all sunk in.

"What do you really want, Felix?" Brazden's eyes locked on the dealer's and his voice turned serious.

"Where's the damned corn, Brazden?"

"First you didn't give a shit, now you'd kill for it?" Brazden was struggling to speak.

Felix tried a gentler approach: "It's valuable, my old friend, very. And you know how I like precious things. It won't do you any good now, so tell me where it is."

"You shouldn't have given my wreath away..." A big grin contorted Brazden's blue lips as he gasped for air.

Brazden's dying defiance tripped Felix's angry switch.

"Where is the corn? You're not dead yet, you know, and I could make your last few hours very unpleasant."

Felix reached into his pocket and a pulled out a switchblade. Putting the knife into Brazden's right nostril, he flicked the blade, sending a splash of blood over Brazden's face.

The dying man let out a weak yell and then started coughing and gasping for air, finally regaining his voice one last time: "Is that all you have—some CHINATOWN rip off? I'd have given you the damned corn if you'd asked. You don't give a shit about the corn or the twins—they're all just a product to you.

"I may just be a lowly pothunter, but I loved what I did and I have no regrets. Goodbye. I won't see you again. I'll be in heaven and you're going to hell."

Then Brazden took his fate in his own hands and held his breath. His face started to turn blue. Felix was furious. The pothunter couldn't die without telling him where the corn kernels were. He punched Brazden hard in the solar plexus with the butt end of the gun to force him to breathe. He gasped in pain then held his breath again. This time his heart gave out from a massive myocardial infarction.

Grabbing Brazden's limp body, Felix shook the old man and slapped his face with his gloved hand. Nothing. The pothunter was dead.

Felix was overcome with rage. He started to pace around the small house, then grabbed the closest pot and flung it against the fireplace, sending sherds in all directions.

"What a fool," he thought. "He died alone, with no money and in a shithole."

Felix searched Brazden's house until he found something he could use. It wasn't the seeds, but it was nearly as good. There were two photos in a keepsake album showing Brazden standing next to Rachael Yellowhorse—recent images by the appearance of her loomed rug. Rachael's left hand held a Ziploc bag full of Indian corn kernels. The remainder of the corn must be at his neighbor's gallery. Felix took the photos, which he would destroy later. He would leave no loose ends.

Felix waited for the rain to slow, then took three of the best prehistoric pots Brazden had so kindly given him, placed them on passenger side floorboard of his Mercedes, and wrapped them with cheap pink bathroom towels.

"Decorations for my office," he growled as he pulled away. "The spoils of war."

A half a mile down the muddy road he passed a Santa Fe police cruiser heading toward Brazden's house. Felix felt a moment of fear. He had not killed Brazden, but he might have left incriminating evidence that could make it look as if he had.

A broken pot, tossed house, cut nose, bruised abdomen? He hoped the cop had not noticed the make of his car and gunned the engine, sending mud flying. He took only secondary roads back to his Las Campanas home.

Thinking about the tracks he had left in the wet soil surrounding Brazden's casita, he decided to park the Mercedes in his four-car garage and drive the Jag this month.

Felix would not dwell on the "ifs," or other possible consequences of his actions. After all, he reasoned to himself, this was Santa Fe and the cops weren't all that bright.

Tomorrow he would see if Bloom had reached a decision. He now knew for sure that Rachael had the seeds, and he would get them from her one way or another. Felix did not play to lose.

Adjusting the satellite radio station to his new favorite, the Elton John channel, he stroked the butterfly fetish and smiled. "No trade, Brazden. The amulet is mine, and soon the seeds will be too."

The car fishtailed as Felix hit blacktop. He would be home in five minutes and tomorrow would be a game changer.

❋ ❋ ❋ ❋

Billy Poh pulled up to Brazden's house three minutes after Felix left. Bloom had called Poh, asking him to check on Brazden. Normally, Poh would have sent a patrolman to do the job as he had just gotten off duty and was heading home in the other direction—but Bloom sounded concerned and he was his art dealer, so he figured a little TLC on his end couldn't hurt.

The front door was ajar and Poh noticed fresh footprints in the mud. The detective drew his weapon and slowly entered the house. Music was playing and the remains of a broken pot were scattered across the living room—the scene of a possible struggle?

Entering the bedroom he found Brazden, who was blue, still warm, and not breathing. Poh put his ear to the pothunter's chest but heard no heartbeat. He called for an ambulance and started CPR. After five minutes, he checked for a pulse and stopped compressions. The man was definitely dead.

It looked like Brazden could have been the victim of a homicide. There were broken blood vessels on his face and his right nostril had been cut with a sharp object. There was an expansive bruise in his mid-abdominal region. The detective's guess was that the pothunter had been smothered, but it would be up to the coroner to determine the cause of death.

Poh would call Bloom later to thank him for alerting him to a possible homicide, but first he had to secure the crime scene. He could hear the sirens in the distance. It was going to be a long night.

CHAPTER 43

HOMICIDE?

Informing loved ones of an unexpected death—especially late at night—was not Billy Poh's favorite part of the job. At least, he thought, Bloom wasn't a relative. He could just give the art dealer a heads-up that he'd need to interview him in the morning since he was the one who had sent him to Brazden's house.

Bloom answered on the second ring. He sounded like he was still asleep.

"Hello??" Bloom blinked his eyes, trying to focus.

Rachael sat up immediately. She was wide awake.

"What's wrong, Bloom?" Rachael asked, as her husband tried to make sense of who was on the other end of the phone.

"Hi, Charles. It's Billy Poh. Sorry to wake you."

"No problem. What's wrong?"

"I've got bad news. Mr. Shackelford is dead."

"I was afraid of that. He didn't look good today. Was he alive when you got to his house? Did he make it to the hospital?"

"No, he was already dead—and it looks like it might be a homicide."

Bloom was now fully awake.

"Homicide? Are you sure??"

Rachael was listening intently, her husband's body language telling her something was very wrong.

"Yes, in my opinion it was most likely a homicide. There were physical signs on the body and the house had been disturbed. I'll need to come by the gallery tomorrow to take a statement from you. You may have been the last one to see him alive. How about 9 a.m., before your gallery opens?"

"Yes, that will work. It's hard to believe Brazden was the victim of a homicide. He gave Rachael a gift yesterday."

Bloom explained the contents of the Tide box and told Poh about the other pack of seeds Rachael had received from Shackelford the week before.

"Don't touch anything," Poh warned. "The box and packet could be evidence. I'll take a look tomorrow morning."

Bloom hung up and explained what Poh had told him. Rachael started to cry. He wasn't sure why, but Bloom teared up too. Maybe it was just that someone needed to grieve for the lonely pothunter—and he believed that no man should die at the hand of another.

Both Bloom and Rachael were waiting at the gallery when Poh arrived promptly at 9 a.m., dressed in his business attire. Bloom was thankful for the unmarked vehicle, as a police car parked in front of the gallery would be bad for business. People gossiped in Santa Fe—especially competitors.

Poh was all business, a side of him Bloom had never seen before. His respect for Poh was growing, and he was happy the detective was on his side.

"If I could, Charles and Rachael, I'll take some notes. I'll also need to look at the packages Mr. Shackelford gave you. At this point we're treating his death as a possible homicide, although all I can officially say at this point is that it's very suspicious, to say the least."

Poh reviewed yesterday's events to be sure he had the chronology right, then asked Bloom once again why he had decided Shackelford's health was failing. He asked if Charles knew if Brazden had any enemies or others who might have had recent dealings with the pothunter.

Bloom, who had only recently met Brazden, knew nothing about possible enemies. He told Poh about Felix's meeting with Brazden again, and explained why he had taken the surveillance photos from his back yard.

Poh asked Bloom to email him the images so he could add them to the file and look at them again.

"Charles, what do you think was in the grocery bag Brazden brought to Zachow's place?"

"I would assume it was a prehistoric pot," Bloom replied. "The reason I initially asked you to look up Brazden's file was the look on Felix's face when he realized I had seen him with Brazden. It could all be perfectly innocent, but my gut is telling me he wouldn't have acted that way if there weren't something questionable going on. But that's purely supposition on my part. After twenty years in this business, you become jaded."

"Anything else you can say about Mr. Zachow that could help me understand how he might fit into all this?"

"Well, yesterday morning Felix came over and, well… he made an offer to buy my place, quite a lucrative one I might add."

Rachael turned to Bloom with a look that was a cross between peeved and stunned.

Bloom had not told Rachael about the offer because he was still trying to figure out how he felt about selling the gallery. It was a big decision and he wanted to be clear about what he thought would be best for his family and his business in the long term, before discussing it with his wife.

"How much, Bloom?" Rachael asked.

"Two million dollars."

Rachael's mouth fell open. "WOW. That's a lot of money. When were you planning to tell me about it?"

The look she gave Charles no longer signaled mixed emotions. She was not happy.

"Honey, I'm sorry. Honestly, I was trying to understand all the ramifications and was going to discuss the offer with you last night but we both passed out. Then Brazden's death took precedence in my mind."

Rachael's hard look softened.

"OK. Sorry about the family drama, Billy," Rachael apologized.

"No need. I'm used to a lot worse. I'm no expert on Canyon Road prices, but that seems like a strong offer in today's economy."

"Yes, it's above market by about $500,000—but Felix knows I don't want to sell and he really wants the property, so I guess it's not too crazy for a rich guy like him. I deal with a lot of these people. They want what they want when they want it and they don't take kindly to getting shut out."

Poh smiled and added, "I hope these guys like Indian jewelry too."

His wry humor made them all laugh and eased the tension that had been building up in the room.

The detective then examined the Tide box and looked in each sock to make sure it was simply packing material. He sketched an image of the butterfly carcass and took photos of everything. He opened each individual bag of corn and smelled it before resealing the Ziploc bags.

Rachael told Poh about her earlier meeting with Brazden and his gift to her, showing him the bag with her Post-it Note promising the pothunter dinner. Trying to hold her emotions in check, she focused her attention on Poh.

"Do you think these are ancient corn kernels, like the letter said?" Poh asked Rachael.

"I haven't a clue. I've raised Indian corn but have never seen any seeds this small or in these colors. And they smell nuttier than what I think of with Indian corn.

"What do you think, Billy?"

"I'm with you," Poh replied. "I've grown corn for years, including a lot of traditional stock, and this is different. I guess anything is possible. Brazden was a pothunter, after all, and we know the prehistoric Indians used to leave caches of seeds for lean times. Even my folks did that when I was a kid."

"I would like to take a few kernels and the butterfly carcass in its little can and see if I can learn anything about them. I have an entomologist friend who consults with the department, and his wife is a botanist. I don't see any reason to impound these packages as evidence yet. It's clear he gave you this gift well before he died. The photos are all we need for now.

"But don't go making any stew with these kernels, Rachael." Poh grinned, showing all his white teeth.

"I'll try not to do that," Rachael teased back. She liked Poh more and more, and hoped he and Bloom would become good friends.

CHAPTER 44

WHAT NOW?

A silence fell over Bloom's after Poh left. The gallery would open in less than five minutes and Rachael needed to retrieve the kids from a neighbor's house. The elephant in the room was the $2,000,000 offer that Bloom "forgot" to mention. This was the first time he had not shared an important decision with her, and this was a monumental one for their family. Rachael was hurt to hear about the offer in front of Poh, and not in her own home.

"I know you're mad at me, Rachael, and you have every right to be, but I just needed to work it out in my own mind before I talked with you about it," Bloom said. "If I sell the gallery and move away, a part of me will be lost forever. But it might not be fair to our family if I don't sell. Plus, I have Shriver to consider. Three hundred thousand dollars of that sale would belong to him, and I don't know if I should discuss it with him or not."

He couldn't read Rachael's face.

"Bloom, you know I would stand behind any decision you make, no matter what. I love you. And I want you to be happy and successful because that is what will keep our family strong.

"So what do you think?"

"My practical side says we could make a lot of money for not too much work, and we still would have a Canyon Road address with frontage access for a year. My heart says no—I love this gallery and have a dedicated following, not to mention seven parking spots." Bloom tried to inject a little humor to lighten the conversation.

"There's also this whole treasure scenario, which is such a long shot it's laughable. But Felix is a shrewd businessman and I have to ask why he is willing to overpay for the property.

"Ultimately, I feel it has to be a gut decision—and my gut is telling me it's no sale. We should stay on the path that we know works for us. We can always sell sometime in the future. And, after five years, I don't have to split any profits with Shriver, so even if we just got our money back, we would be OK.

"It's a risk to turn Felix down, but life is risky too. That's my take."

Rachael looked into his eyes, put her arms around her husband and gave him a big bear hug.

"I love you, Charlie Bloom, so tell Felix thanks but no thanks. He's already got our rug; that's enough from the Bloom-Yellowhorse family for one year."

Bloom gave Rachael a passionate hug. He was a lucky man and Rachael knew it.

Bloom would let Felix know his decision shortly. He hoped they could still be good neighbors.

❊ ❊ ❊ ❊

An unexpected call from Wendy Whippelton later that afternoon brought good news. She had tracked down Jonathan Wolf and explained that if he couldn't give her a written review of the property, she had done enough research herself to help the committee render a decision on the casita's building permit. The meeting was tonight and if he wanted to have any input he had to turn in his report now.

She also told him a specific document was missing from the state archives and that his signature was the last recorded. Did he know where the file might be?

Jonathan deflected the question, saying he would need to review his records. The original plan was to smuggle the document back into the archives folder once the Bloom building was in Felix's hands. He would need to do this sooner than they had planned or risk being exposed for the thief he was.

He told Wendy he would drop a preliminary report by her office. He wanted it noted in the official record that he had a few more documents to research and that she would have to take responsibility if something significant turned up at a later date, which she agreed to do so.

Bloom was granted the permit he sought that night. He now had up to three years to start construction without having to go back to the committee.

Felix Zachow was aware of the meeting and had considered showing up to protest to keep Bloom from starting any construction. He knew the treasure chest was there for the taking. But he also knew the property could soon be his, and the construction permit would transfer to him along with the property. If things didn't go his way, he could always activate Plan B. His best strategy for now, he decided, was to wait for Bloom's answer.

Jonathan and Bloom sat next to each other waiting for his case to be called. The hearing was short and sweet: permit granted, no surprises.

As they were leaving, Jonathan asked Bloom when he would start construction. "Right away," Bloom replied. He'd start by laying footers and moving some of the fruit trees. The more disruptive part of the construction would have to wait until after Indian Market.

Jonathan's first call after leaving the building was to Felix. He was nervous.

"Did Bloom say anything about selling?" Felix asked, then answered his own question. "If he's talking about construction, that's not a good sign, is it?

"So, Jonathan old boy, we'll put Plan B into effect immediately if Bloom turns me down. I'll meet with him tomorrow to ask how his permit process is coming along and feel him out. Then, if I can't get him to commit to selling…

"Don't go anywhere in the next few days."

Felix hung up. Bloom was about to find out what the cutthroat dealer was capable of when he didn't get his way.

CHAPTER 45

PLAN B

Today Bloom would give Felix his answer. He was expecting the man to be disappointed, but Zachow was an art professional and Bloom was sure he had lost out on deals before—probably bigger ones then this.

Bloom's mind was made up: There would be no sale. He would focus on Indian Market and proceed with the build-out of the casita as planned.

Two landscape firms were scheduled to give him estimates next week for moving a row of pear trees away from the portal so the overhang could be extended. He would also ask the workers to explore the old raccoon hole carefully, just in case the Olmec body or some other treasure turned up.

He wasn't sure how to explain the kind of excavation he wanted them to do; he didn't want them to think he was crazy. Buried treasure was a ridiculous idea, he thought, but on the off chance it was real, he didn't want anything destroyed because he had been careless.

Zachow's receptionist Tiffany greeted Bloom as he entered A to Z. Her height and weight were those of a runway model, something that may have been a prerequisite for working for Felix. Her perfect features and tightly fitting dress left little to the imagination.

She buzzed Felix and escorted Bloom to his office—a large, elegantly designed inner sanctum straight out of a MAD MEN episode. Bloom noticed two inviting lemon-yellow Papa Bear chairs, something he had only seen on 1stdibs.com, the online marketplace for rare midcentury-modern goods. Felix offered him a seat.

"Nice and comfortable," Bloom sighed. "Are these original Hans J. Wegner chairs?"

"Would I have anything else?" Felix teased. "I'm impressed that a man who sells Indian art recognizes a Danish masterpiece. What other surprises do you have for me—a building sale maybe?"

Felix fixed his eyes on Bloom's face, reflexively stroking the turquoise amulet around his neck for luck. The answer was not what he had hoped, and the twisting of the butterfly fetish stopped immediately after Bloom responded to the question.

"Sorry, I can't sell her yet. I know your offer is more than fair, way more. But I have an emotional connection to the buildings and the gallery and I'm just not ready to let it all go. It's not a money decision; it's one of the heart."

Bloom gave Felix his most empathetic look. He had been on the other end of art deals that didn't go the way he wanted.

"Clearly not from the head," Felix retorted sarcastically. Then, with a change of tone: "OK, I understand, Charles. Our timing is off. I will still be interested if you have a change of heart. Life is funny. One minute you think you know exactly where you're headed, then boom! Something happens and your perspective changes."

Felix slapped his hand down hard, rocking the spindly legs of his George Nakashima desk. Bloom flinched.

"Sorry. I didn't mean to startle you. I'm a passionate man, tightly strung."

Felix changed the subject. "So when can I expect to hear the sounds of your construction starting up?" He was fishing for information.

"Maybe a week or a little longer. I'll start working on the grounds first. I won't get to the noisy stuff till after Indian Market.

"When is your new show opening?"

"I'm hanging it tonight. If your wife is coming in tomorrow morning, she might want to come over for a look-see."

"It's her day to work, but she'll be alone, so I doubt Rachael will want to break away. Maybe she could come by on Monday when I'm in. I get to play father on Sundays—it's my one day to pitch in and spend time with my kids."

"Rachael's a good woman. It sounds like she's your rock."

"That she is. I'd be lost without her," Bloom said, reflecting on his wonderful life.

Felix smiled, thinking to himself, "Yes, you would be lost. With two kids and a mortgage payment, a man might change his mind about selling property that's eating up precious capital if he were all alone."

Felix brought his mind back to the present.

"OK, then, thanks for the quick response and good luck with your construction."

Bloom left, surprised at how civil Felix had been. Maybe he was all wrong about the man.

❋ ❋ ❋ ❋

As soon as Bloom left, an angry Felix Zachow called Jonathan Wolf. It was time activate Plan B.

"Well, if you can believe it, the jerk passed up $2,000,000. You ever watch SHARK TANK, Jonathan?"

Jonathan didn't own a TV; he thought they were for idiots.

"No, I can't say I have. It's a television show, I assume?"

"Yes, a hit show. There's this guy on it called Mr. Wonderful. He's a charming man, straight up about the fact that money rules his life. When contestants don't take his money and it's obvious they should have, he always says, 'You're dead to me now.'

"Well, Jonathan, Bloom is dead to me now. Or should I say his lovely wife is. I'm going to raise the price of that great weaving of hers because it's the last rug she will ever make."

Felix laughed into the receiver and Jonathan chuckled along with him, hoping he would never get on the man's bad side.

"You know what to do, Jonathan. Wait in my closing room until everything is set. When the little red light above the door comes on, that's your cue that the coast is clear. *Verstehen Sie mich?*"

"Yes, I understand," Jonathan said, noting that Felix's German accent was excellent.

"Tonight requires precision," the dealer continued. "There's no room for screw-ups. If you get caught, you're on your own. I never heard of you.

"Time is of the essence, so don't mess around looking for insignificant coins. And the cleanup must be perfect. Once the package is ours, head directly through my back door. It will be unlocked and you know what to do. I will be out to dinner in a crowded restaurant. Check-in exactly one hour after you retrieve the chest."

"I'm ready to go, Felix. You can trust me. Remember, I was an archaeologist so I know what needs to be done. And it's not exactly my first time taking something that isn't technically mine, if you know what I mean."

Felix was well aware of Jonathan's sticky-fingered past.

"Tomorrow's a big day, Jonathan, a moment in time when we both we become rich men if you do your job right. Good luck."

"Thanks, Felix. You don't have to worry. Luck won't be any part of the equation."

CHAPTER 46

NIGHT OPS

Canyon Road at one in the morning was dead. The last of the stragglers had stumbled home from the bar at El Farol and only an occasional car meandered up the street. It was the perfect time for a night op.

The red light blinked "Go" and Jonathan and his mute friend slipped from Felix's back room. They peered down Canyon Road and looked both ways, even though that segment of the street was one way. Empty.

The two slipped into the back alley that A to Z shared with Bloom's casita and, using the copy Jonathan had made of the door key Bloom had so generously supplied, they entered the gallery grounds. They were prepared with a pick, shovel, night-vision glasses, and small miners' lamps.

They positioned the laser map directly over where they expected to find the chest. A heavy-duty black plastic sheet with wooden perimeter handles and a precut hole was laid on the ground where the digging would occur.

Jonathan took the first shift. He was out of shape but still knew his way around the back end of a shovel. The adrenaline rush added to his speed. He could be aggressive with the blade knowing they had two feet of soil to move before they'd hit pay dirt.

The monsoons were in full swing and the ground was pliable. Rolls of thunder and an occasional distant flash of lightning pierced the cool summer air. Thirty-five minutes passed and, as the dirt pile grew, Jonathan and his accomplice dug more cautiously. CLUNK. The pick hit something solid. THE TREASURE.

Normally neat to the point of neurosis, Jonathan scrambled into the hole, digging vigorously with his hands. Time was of the essence.

It took another thirty minutes to extricate the large iron trunk. The metal was badly corroded and the leather straps but a tattered memory. The chest was so heavy it took both men to lift it out of the ground.

Their first order of business was move the treasure chest closer to the gate and stash it behind a massive purple butterfly bush. They then emptied a bag of peat moss into the hole the trunk had once occupied.

The men strained as they lifted the wooden handles on the black plastic cloth, easing the dirt back into the hole. Once the ground was level, the plastic was rolled up, placed in the empty peat moss bag and shoved into a large backpack. A Ziploc bag of fine dirt, leaves and elm twigs that Jonathan had concocted earlier was sprinkled over the disturbed area. A small hand broom wiped out any remaining signs of disturbance.

A creaking noise stopped the men's work and they retreated to the butterfly bush. The gate was slightly ajar and Simon the gallery cat was rubbing against its rough edge, producing the sound that had disturbed them.

Jonathan shooed the cat away, then used his night-vision glasses to peer down the alley. All was clear. Each man grabbed one of the rusty handles on the trunk and headed for Felix's gallery. Once the loot was safely inside friendly territory, Jonathan went back to Bloom's courtyard and retrieved the pick, shovel, and backpack. He then secured the gate and wiped out his footprints.

Simon reappeared once the men left and made the freshly dug dirt his new litter box.

With the job complete, the thieves donned blue hospital booties and entered the back door of Felix's gallery. They hauled the trunk into the dealer's office and placed it inside a huge wooden crate made for shipping sculpture, reattaching the top with wood screws. A large red sticker that read FRAGILE DO NOT TOUCH was prominently displayed on the front of the crate. A postage label to Zurich was already in place should shipping the loot become necessary.

Not knowing what was in the trunk was killing Jonathan, but it was clear that opening the chest would take some doing, and Felix had a plan to unveil the contents that made sense and required leaving the chest untouched.

The pre-addressed label to Zurich disturbed Jonathan, but there was nothing he could do about it. If something went wrong, the crate would need to leave the country quickly.

The colonial era lock and hinges were heavily rusted. There was no way Jonathan could take a peek without destroying the precious lock.

He hoped that whatever was in the trunk was valuable enough to compensate for his illegal activities.

Jonathan had taken two photos of the trunk with his smartphone before he placed it in the large wooden sarcophagus. For the most part, he trusted Felix, but the man was a cutthroat art dealer. They would open the trunk together soon; there would be no skimming on this deal.

He hoped Felix would play it straight up. If he didn't, Jonathan would soon have the kind of leverage that frightens men enough to play by the rules—even if they are thieves.

CHAPTER 47

CHEERS

A light, intermittent rain was caressing the courtyard garden as Rachael turned off the casita gallery alarm and blocked the door with her foot, her hands full of wool she had brought from home. She had arrived early, hoping to get started on a small rug. Indian Market was still three weeks away, and she could probably get a good jump on the new work today. Rain kept most people away.

The day was cold for July 31st, but Bloom had once told her he had witnessed snow flurries on the Santa Fe Plaza on the Fourth of July.

"My first Santa Fe winter in a long time and it's going to be a cold one," Rachael thought to herself. Santa Fe residents start thinking of winter the first time the weather turns cold, even if it's in July.

Rachael jumped when a large hand touched her shoulder.

"Sorry about that, Rachael. I thought you heard me come in," Felix Zachow said in his most polished European accent.

"I'm usually pretty aware of my surroundings, but my mind was elsewhere today," Rachael gasped. She was not used to being caught off guard.

"Rachael, I was hoping you could come over to see your weaving before you opened for business. I've had it hung and it looks fantastic. You will be the first person to see my show, if you have the time. I'm only open on Sundays during the peak months myself. I'm not sure why I bothered today."

"Is Bloom with you? He's welcome to view the exhibit as well." Felix had to be sure Bloom had not unexpectedly come to work with Rachael if Plan B were to work.

"No, he's not here. Sundays are dad's day with the kids and yes, I would love to see my baby hung. I've been wondering when the show would go up."

Rachael put down her wool and set her lunch in the refrigerator. She locked the front door but did not bother to alarm the building.

The pair walked over to A to Z. Felix let Rachael lead so he could survey the parking lot and alley. No people.

"Perfect," he thought. "Everything's right on schedule."

Felix raised his right hand in a kind of German salute, the signal for Jonathan to search the casita.

The A to Z gallery lights were perfectly directed on each piece of art, the spacious gallery making the textiles pop off the wall. Rachael could see why Felix was so successful: the gallery was like a museum, with the illumination focusing your attention on the walls.

The open space was decorated with early midcentury modern furniture for lounging and chatting about the art: "A perfect balance of art and space," she thought to herself.

"Can I offer you some coffee? It's fresh cappuccino." Rachael preferred her cowboy coffee, but when in Rome...

"Sure, black."

"You have to try my vanilla mix, too. It's imported from Zurich."

Rachael liked her coffee black and strong, but this was Felix's show and she didn't want to insult her host.

"I'll give it a try."

Felix went to another room, leaving Rachael to explore the exhibit on her own. She was shocked when she found her rug. It was hanging on a slate colored wall between a First Phase Chief's Blanket and a classic Navajo poncho.

Rachael knew enough about antique textiles to understand that these two blankets were worth as much as both her buildings.

Her rug had never looked better. She loved Bloom, but his gallery couldn't compete with the kind of display put on by A to Z. Her rug tag read:

RACHAEL YELLOWHORSE, b. 1979

Handspun native wool

72" x 48"

16 warps, 80 wefts per inch

Five shades of natural brown

POR

The wall tag with her birthdate made her Rachael realize how few weavings she could complete in a lifetime. One day the tags on her work would include a date of death as well. It was a wake-up call: life is not a dress rehearsal.

Rachael tried to decipher "POR," then the acronym clicked: Price On Request.

"How much could Felix have on the piece," she wondered. He had paid $25,000, full retail in her mind. How much further could he push the price? The galley business seemed to make its own rules when it came to value. Buying art was not like buying sheep, where you could figure out what was fair to pay.

"Here you go, my dear. It's the perfect temperature. I would like to make a toast to you."

Rachael blushed. "If you say so."

"I insist. Rachael, you're a remarkable artist whose rugs can only increase in value from here on out. Cheers!"

The two clinked their expensive porcelain cups and enjoyed the moment.

"You're right, Felix. This has a unique taste, not like what I brew," Rachael said as she took another sip of the lukewarm coffee.

"Do you mind if I ask—and if you don't want to tell me, I totally understand—how much you are asking for my weaving?"

"Well, as I told Bloom, I think it's an important piece. You can see that from the way I juxtaposed it against those early Navajo masterpieces. I have $55,000 on the rug."

"WOW! Do let me know if you get your price. It would be a record for me."

"Oh, I can assure you that I will get it. I always get what I want."

CHAPTER 48

I TRY TO PLAY FAIR

Jonathan had a very small window to complete his operation successfully. A client could stroll down the casita's dirt road at any moment. If a visitor tried the door and found it locked during gallery hours—or worse, noticed Rachael's truck parked out front and decided to wait for her to open—the consequences could be disastrous.

Securing the gate after entering the courtyard, Jonathan looked around. Everything appeared to be in place.

He had come prepared with gloves and a large knapsack. Plan B was now in full play and there was no turning back. The historian filled the bag with Navajo rugs, knocked over Rachael's empty loom to make it look as if there had been a struggle, broke the jewelry case with a small rug wrapped around his gloved hand, and took all of Billy Poh's silverwork.

He did a complete search of the premises, but could not find the Ziploc bag of corn seeds Felix wanted. This would no doubt be a big disappointment to the dealer. He did spot the corn wreath, which he threw into the bag with the rugs and jewelry.

As Jonathan exited the gallery, Simon the gallery cat slipped in the door and ran into the kitchen. A black cat crossing his path would be a bad omen for a superstitious man, but Jonathan was not at all bothered by it. He figured the cat's presence was a random occurrence and shut the door, trapping the animal in the casita. Exiting the building, he left the front door and gate closed but unlocked, and wiped away his footprints.

Jonathan slipped into Felix's annex, changed clothes and stashed the loot in a predetermined spot in the building. His car was parked across the street on Camino Escondido, and he escaped without notice. Now it just was a matter of waiting for Plan B to play itself out.

Jonathan was not one to take chances. He booked a room in a cheap Albuquerque hotel—to do some research if any one were to ask. He'd monitor news reports to see how things were developing in Santa Fe. He was now out of harm's way—or so he hoped.

❋ ❋ ❋ ❋

Rachael's head was woozy. The last thing she remembered was hearing the porcelain coffee cup shatter on the scored concrete floor. Her right hip throbbed as she struggled to sit up and orient herself.

"Hellooo...?" a muffled gurgle was all that came out of her taped mouth. Her hands and legs were tied too.

Consciousness was returning slowly, and fear shot through her body like a bee sting. She didn't know if she was having a nightmare or a stroke. She remembered Felix's voice and seeing him smile just before the lights went out.

Rapidly blinking her dry eyes helped restore Rachael's vision. She was in a dark, strangely lit room. Tiny feet landed on the end of her nose and she struggled to move her head. The bug flew away and for a brief moment Rachael felt relief.

Music was playing in the chamber, Elton John's BUTTERFLIES ARE FREE. She was now totally terrified. She tried to focus on regaining her composure, but waves of nausea washed over her and broke her concentration. Trying to yell through the tape was useless and increased her urge to vomit.

The gravity of the situation was apparent. She was bound, gagged and drugged, but by whom? Had some lunatic come to rob Felix as they talked?

Samantha's, Willy's, and Bloom's faces flashed before her. "Thank god the kids are with Bloom," she thought. "He is going to be so sad if I die." Tears poured down her high cheekbones, bathing her irritated eyes.

She pulled herself together once more. She was determined to survive.

She was lying flat on a hard surface, her wrists and legs bound to cold metal slats. Her prison was on rollers and, as she rocked, the bed shifted with her momentum. Just as her fears started to subside, she was hit with another rush of adrenaline. She tried to yell, but to no avail.

Over her right shoulder, suspended by a fine metal chain, she spotted a human skeleton partially covered in dried flesh and draped in a white, pueblo-style manta. "A mummy," she thought, "like those of Peru." But this one was even more terrifying because two human skulls sat atop the neck. Rachael couldn't imagine what it all meant and turned away from the circus sideshow.

Another insect landed on her face. She shook her head for the second time but now recognized the form as the monarch butterfly flittered away. Like particles of dust in the raking light, dozens of butterflies floated through the room's interior, flying aimlessly around the illuminated space. Was this some hideous art project or—even worse—a recreation of a scene from THE SILENCE OF THE LAMBS where Rachael was the new lead character?

A door opened with a sucking sound, heavy and ominous.

"I see we are awake. Sorry about the hip, my dear. I tried to catch you, but when those ruffies kick in they can be quite powerful. I'm afraid you landed rather hard on the concrete floor. You're heavier than you look."

The voice belonged to Felix Zachow. He had drugged her with that lousy coffee!

"If you promise you won't scream, I'll take that annoying duct tape off your mouth so you can breathe more easily. The room is soundproof, so yelling won't make any difference, but I have sensitive ears and loud, high-pitched sounds make my head hurt. Deal?"

Rachael nodded her head "Yes" and wondered how many women he had done this to.

"It hurts less with one pull." He grabbed a corner of the tape and ripped off her gag.

Rachael winced but didn't make a sound.

"Why are you doing this? I don't understand…" Rachael said, her mouth dry and voice rough.

"I know it's hard to imagine that the next door neighbor who spent $25,000 on your rug and is a big fan—which I truly am—could be so heartless. Believe me, I don't like going to Plan B either. I tried to play it straight, but you can blame Bloom for your predicament.

"My father, Wilhelm, taught me to play fair, but he also told me that if people don't want to listen, you should just chop off a hand and they will come to their senses. That's the golden rule that built our family business and the one I still follow.

"I offered your husband real money for your place, considerably above market, I might add, but he refused to sell. I was trying to be a nice guy, but he didn't want to be a team player, so I'm afraid you are the hand I must cut off."

"All this is about the building? My life for a building?" Rachael couldn't believe what she was hearing.

"No, not just the building. There is also the matter of Oñate's treasure, which actually does exist. The trunk was under your front porch. I know that because I just had the ancient artifact pulled from that very spot. And that's just for starters.

"You also have some corn seeds—not just any seeds, but a rare prehistoric variety that are quite valuable to my friends in the agricultural business. You may have heard of AgraCon? Believe it or not, those little, colored kernels are a multi-million dollar proposition. I saw that Ziploc bag of Indian corn in your kitchen the other day."

Rachael's mind was still fuzzy, but she did remember that Felix had taken a long time in her kitchen. Apparently, he had been snooping around in there.

"I don't understand," she said. "You gave me a wreath made from the same corn. If the kernels were so valuable, why would you do that?"

"A rare mistake on my part, I'm afraid. My friend and accomplice Mr. Jonathan Wolf visited your casita this morning but couldn't find the bag of seeds. Where are they my dear Rachael?" Felix purred.

"I'm not sure where I left them," Rachael replied. "I believe they are in the main gallery. They were just corn kernels to me. Why don't you let me go and we can look for them together," she pleaded. "I don't want them. They're Anasazi, and you know we Navajo try to avoid any contact with this kind of prehistoric material. It's bad juju for me, so they're all yours."

"Rachael, you're right about those seeds being bad luck. In fact, for you those seeds were terrible luck. Unfortunately, you've been unconscious for many hours, and the police are out looking for you as we speak. They're afraid you've been kidnapped or worse.

"So this is your home for now. Say 'Hi' to your roommates. The Butterfly Twins are a rare Anasazi cadaver, and they're what got you into this mess. Brazden and his grandfather found your flying roommates and their corn cache at Wupatki National Monument fifty years ago. It seems the corn was left for the twins to help them to pass to the next world.

"I, on the other hand, have already made $2.5 million off these lovely girls, so they're not bad luck for me. Once I round up the corn kernels, I will make even more money, lots more.

"I recommend you stay quiet. If you become a problem I will have to cut off your hand, so to speak—or maybe worse."

Felix chuckled to himself and walked out of the room, followed by the sucking noise.

Elton John's music continued to play in the background, and an occasional butterfly flew past Rachael's acute ears. She realized she was in serious trouble.

Bloom had to figure out where she was and mount a rescue. Her life was in danger and time was running out. The man in control of the operation was clearly a lunatic.

CHAPTER 49

NO SIGNS OF BLOOD

Bloom was enjoying fatherhood more than he could have imagined. Today's game was "I'm the cougar, and Willy's the sheep." Willy would run by Bloom, who would feign grabbing him and just miss. Willy screamed wildly with each pass, and Samantha couldn't stop giggling. The laughter was infectious, and all were rolling on the floor when the phone rang.

It was 11:55 a.m. "Probably Rachael needing some information to close a sale," Bloom thought hopefully.

"What's up?" Bloom expected to hear Rachael's sweet voice.

"Charles, it's Billy Poh..." Bloom had not heard this serious a tone in the detective's voice before. Something bad must have happened.

"What's going on, Billy? You sound official." Bloom prayed it was nothing.

"I'm afraid I am calling in an official capacity. You need to come down to the gallery. There's been a robbery."

Bloom panicked. "Robbery! Is Rachael OK?"

"Rachael is not on the property. We think she may have been abducted. The place is a mess, my jewelry is gone and some rugs seem to have been taken. There are no signs of Rachael even though her truck is parked out front. The good news is that there's no blood." Poh tried to lessen the blow to his friend and art dealer, knowing he would come unglued.

"OK. I need to get the kids to a neighbor and then I'll come right down. Do I need to bring anything? How can I help?"

"No, there's nothing you can do now. Just expect a long day. Let your friends know they may need to watch the kids overnight and bring a toothbrush and change of clothes. The next twenty-four hours are critical. I've posted an all-points bulletin, so now it's a waiting game. Hopefully, they will contact you soon if they're looking for ransom."

"And if they aren't?" Bloom asked, knowing the answer but not wanting to hear it.

"Let's not go down that road quite yet. Let's keep our hopes up and work the case.

"The gallery is all taped off. It's kind of a zoo out here even in the rain. The tourists all think it's a movie shoot for MANHATTAN. Give the officer in charge your name and come on through the barricade."

Bloom ran to get bottles and bags for himself and his children. His world had been turned upside down and he had a deep feeling of doom. A homicide detective was in charge of the case—not a good omen. His wife might already be dead.

❊ ❊ ❊ ❊

Bloom arrived at the gallery out of breath. He had made the drive in only 20 minutes, racing down side roads and nearly running a red light. Poh was in the casita double-checking his notes. So far they had no leads, so he just reviewed what they knew with Bloom.

The gardener, who had an 11:30 a.m. appointment with Rachael, realized something was wrong when he saw her truck and the casita gate was still locked. He jumped the fence and looked inside the building. When he saw the havoc, he called the police. The cops arrived within five minutes and broke the lock on the gate to gain entrance to the courtyard.

Poh asked Bloom to take a look around to see if anything other than his jewelry was missing, something the detective had already noted with disgust.

"Looks like six smaller Toadlena Two Grey Hills rugs are missing, and, of course, your jewelry. We don't keep money on hand. And the lunch I made Rachael is sitting in the refrigerator."

"Anything else missing?" Poh asked.

"Not that I can tell. We have a floor safe."

Bloom moved the smashed jewelry case, revealing the safe under a worn Persian rug and pulled the heavy door open.

"The seeds are still here." He pulled them out for Poh to see. "She usually keeps her yarn in here…" His voice trailed off as he noticed the wool Rachael was going to work with that day on the floor next to her overturned loom. Bloom took a moment to compose himself and looked at Poh intently.

"I'm sorry. It's just that this looks very bad. Is there anything I can do to help?"

"Charles, you can call around to all the galleries that someone might try to sell Indian material to. You could also email the Antique Tribal Art Dealers Association and ask them to put the stolen goods up on their website. Other than that, it's a waiting game."

Bloom then asked a question that got Poh thinking.

"Is there any possibility that whoever killed Brazden was involved in this? The seed gift was odd, and he gave them to us right before he died. It could have been a premonition of his own death, or maybe he knew someone was after him.

"Have you heard anything back from your botanist or entomologist contacts?"

"I'll call them now," Poh said, "and see if they can give me a preliminary report. It's not crazy, Charles. Sometimes these kinds of things can be related. It's possible both crimes share a common element—the key is figuring out which thread to follow. The clues are often right under our noses."

Poh's remark gave Bloom a purpose, something he could hang onto to stay strong. He had to rein in his emotions and try to save his wife.

"OK, Billy. I'll review everything I know about Brazden Shackelford. Let's get together again in an hour. Maybe one of us will have some answers by then."

"Do you own a black cat?" Poh tossed out casually.

"Well, there is a gallery cat named Simon. He doesn't live with us, but he comes by every morning for breakfast. Rachael always feeds him when she opens. Did you notice if there was an empty cat food can anywhere?"

"There's nothing in the kitchen garbage can, but when we got here, a black cat ran out of the gallery. What time does Rachael usually open?"

"She should have gotten here around 9:15 this morning, assuming she didn't stop anywhere. So the cat had to come in shortly after that—and she was interrupted before she could feed him."

"OK. This could be very helpful. It gives us a possible time for the abduction."

Bloom headed over to his gallery, feeling slightly better after making a contribution to the investigation. But he knew he would need to do much more if he hoped to find his wife alive.

He would review everything that had happened in the last few weeks. Maybe this wasn't some random burglary and kidnapping. Maybe the abduction was much more sinister.

CHAPTER 50

TIME FOR YOU TO FLY

Rachael Yellowhorse was securely locked away for now. The gallery would be closing in a few hours and Felix had a problem he needed to deal with.

Plan B had been flawlessly executed, but he hadn't thought past the abduction phase—a mistake on his part. Destroying Bloom's life was the focal point of the operation and Rachael's death was inevitable, but how and when would he kill her? A body is easy to hide and death ends any possibility of escape.

Felix had assumed that once Bloom was a widower burdened with two kids and the Canyon Road gallery overhead, he would find selling his buildings his best option. The corn seeds were in Bloom's possession and he was sure the grieving husband would not give them a second thought. Felix would get the seeds thrown in on the building deal. After all, Bloom wouldn't want the karma that had brought such bad luck to remain around his family.

Felix hoped that if the depressed Bloom struggled in August, the busiest art sales month, he could buy his place for a lower price. That Bloom wouldn't go ahead with the construction was a given; it was too risky to do on his own with two kids to look after. If Bloom still wouldn't sell, Felix would find the chest under the floorboards of his annex while doing renovations, turn the annex into the Oñate museum, and figure out a way to steal the seeds.

But for now Felix needed answers to two critical questions: Where was Rachael hiding the ancient corn? And how much did Bloom know about the treasure?

Killing Rachael would allow Felix to place a premium on the "last Rachael Yellowhorse weaving"—a sweet bonus of sorts. He might even make an additional $25,000 on the piece.

Rachael was tied down to the heavy couch and wasn't going anywhere.

His receptionist had come in at 11 a.m. and would leave shortly. The day was winding down and Tiffany was oblivious, as usual. The two gorillas from the Santa Fe Police Department had done a cursory interrogation and seemed satisfied with his answers.

"Such simpletons," he thought to himself as he reviewed the pathetic questions they had posed. "No officer, I'm afraid I didn't see anyone or hear anything today. I've been in my office the whole time working." A catlike smile crossed Felix's face; only a few precious feet away his captive was waiting for a much harsher interrogation and execution. His questions would literally be more pointed. His only real issue was when and how to dispose of the body.

The most reasonable way to eliminate Rachael was to smother and then dismember her in the gallery bathtub. The remains would fit nicely in the large lockable freezer he used to eradicate moth larvae. The protocol was to freeze all weavings before they went on the gallery wall—and he had the only key.

Felix would stuff the soon-to-be-frozen body parts in Ziploc bags wrapped in old kilims in case someone got nosy, then wait a month before burying them in a pre-dug grave. Rachael would never be heard from again. Jonathan's stolen loot would be added to the burial site as an interesting find for future archaeologists.

Felix thought this was a wonderful irony, given the Butterfly Twins' current proximity to Rachael. "Could the girls' lives have been as complex as Rachael's was about to become?" Felix chuckled at his own perversity.

First and foremost, before any bloodletting, he had to get the information he needed. His father had told him stories of the concentration camps and the atrocities he had witnessed. He still could remember Wilhelm's voice: "Fear can break a man even more than a hammer." It was a catchy phrase, one you could live by, and this was the approach Felix would take with dear Rachael.

It was time for her to fly.

A stainless steel chain was threaded through Rachael's bound arms and legs, then she was cut loose from the couch. Rachael watched in horror as Felix flipped the switch on an electric wench. A low, grinding hum mingled with Elton John's voice as she slowly began to rise.

"Rachael, do you wonder why I'm playing this song by Elton John?"

Rachael winced as the rope started to tighten around her wrists.

"Because you're a sick bastard," she said, anger overtaking her fear.

"Feisty. I like that. And yes that's partially true. I can be difficult at times. But the real answer is that this is the song Brazden was playing when I visited him a few nights ago. He's dead now. It's a pity; he was such a sweet man in his own weird way."

"I'm assuming you had something to do with his death," Rachael asked as the pitch of the hum shifted, the motor straining to lift her full body weight off the couch.

"Oh, yes, I certainly did. He didn't want to play so I made him pay. Remember my father's words?

"Where are the seeds my lovely Rachael?" Felix moved closer to the weaver's face, his blue eyes cutting into hers.

"I told you they're in the main gallery. Put me down and I'll draw you a map."

Her body was now suspended off the couch as she was pulled upwards, toward the Butterfly Twins. Rachael suddenly tipped forward and yelled in pain as the chain slipped, placing extra stress on her shoulder joints.

"I'm sure that hurt," Felix said sadistically. "It's hard to balance on the wires, I'm afraid, but it does looks like we've found the point of least resistance. Unfortunately, your own weight will destroy those magnificent shoulders.

"Time is your enemy, so you can start telling me the truth or we can play this game for a long time. Don't you ever want to be able to weave again?"

Felix asked questions about the treasure and what Bloom knew about it, which she answered to the best of her knowledge. Felix seemed satisfied but wanted more.

Rachael knew the location of the seeds, but that information was her only wild card. If she gave up the hidden floor safe, she had no doubt Felix would end her life. At least this way he would have to keep her alive for a while longer. Rachael hoped she could endure the pain and that her captor wouldn't try any more of his family's persuasion techniques on her.

Felix was correct: time was running out. Five feet off the ground, suspended by a metal chain, shoulders and wrists on fire, and two grotesque skulls with fixed smiles looming nearby, fear was scouring Rachael's soul—just as the mad dealer had hoped.

CHAPTER 51

WHERE DID YOU GET THE FETISH?

Bloom reviewed the last two months of his and Rachael's activities, along with the photos he had taken of Brazden on the day the pothunter met with Felix. This was the third time he had plowed through his notes. Something was gnawing at his subconscious. Could it be an as yet unidentified clue?

The cell phone's loud ring startled Bloom. The preliminary verbal report on the insect carcass and seeds was that they appeared related. Poh passed the information on to Bloom quickly, then hung up to get back to the investigation.

"Think, Bloom—it's there!" Fear was the common thread running through the Bloom family's minds at that moment.

The distant bells of the Cathedral Basilica of St. Francis of Assisi rang at 5 p.m. Canyon Road would be closing down, although the small crowd milling around the entrance to Bloom's had never totally left.

The gossip mill was in full swing. The crime scene was a robbery, not a movie shoot—something much more exciting. "Santa Fe has changed," the bystanders murmured. "Robberies and kidnappings on Canyon Road. Can you imagine?"

Bloom heard the voices as he wheeled the out-of-kilter trashcan down the gravel road for tomorrow's pick-up. He was surprised he even remembered this husbandly duty, but Rachael would have expected him to carry on. He was in shock at this point and running on autopilot.

Tears filled Bloom's eyes when a camera flashed unexpectedly, and a reporter started shooting video. Apparently he was the opener for tonight's local news.

"What do you know about what happened here? Was it your wife who was kidnapped? Why are you taking out the trash?"

Bloom could only shrug as if to say, "Sorry, I'm afraid I can't help."

He hurried back to the gallery, the noisy trashcan in tow, as he realized his refuse might be considered evidence. He worried that his abrupt turnabout with the can made him look guilty, like he was Nick in GONE GIRL and there was nothing he could do to stop the negative spin.

If only there were a magic pill to make the nightmare disappear. Bloom tried to focus. He knew his wife's safety was within his grasp; he could feel her presence.

Was she close by? And what was the information he couldn't quite grasp?

He had tried to clear his mind by taking out the trash, but it was a bonehead move. The reporters would be going through the bin when it was something the cops should do.

Bloom found Poh next door. The detective assured him he was doing fine and had his officers stretch yellow tape over the top of the trashcan. Bloom hoped no photos were being taken. A shot of him rolling the can to the curb juxtaposed against the police tape certainly would make for an eye-catching image on the front page of THE SANTA FE NEW MEXICAN.

Poh could see Bloom was falling apart, so he ushered him back to the gallery and took some time to review their progress. The two sat on the oak floor surrounded by Bloom's notes. The dealer had printed off large copies of the photos of Brazden and had a yellow notebook filled with questions.

Poh started the conversation: "The entomologist determined that the species of butterfly in the can was one that has been extinct for at least 800 years, the same for the corn. The kernels are ancient and of an undetermined type. Both experts felt the corn and butterfly originated in the Southwest, probably on the same site, as the same corn pollen was found on both specimens. They also surmised the artifacts came from a dry cave, which would help explain their pristine condition."

"Ancient artifacts? Was that the clue Brazden was trying to give us?" Bloom wondered aloud.

"OK, Charles. Let's talk this out. Brazden gave you the corn as a gift. It was obviously dear to him and he may have known he was going to die soon."

Bloom nodded his head affirmatively.

"He was a pothunter known to engage in illegal activity and he had met with your neighbor Felix Zachow on at least one occasion, which is when you shot this photo of Brazden smoking in his truck." Poh held up the photo.

"That's correct," Bloom answered.

Poh continued: "I remembered Brazden because he didn't have a valid permit to sell his corn at the farmers market, the same kind of corn that was hanging off his truck's mirror. Correct?"

"Yes, that's correct. You can see a similar wreath hanging from his truck's mirror in this photo."

Bloom pointed out the obvious in the enlarged image, then asked: "Did you check Brazden's truck last night? Was the wreath still there?"

Poh had not done that. Realizing that Bloom might be on to something, he called the impound yard and asked the officer in charge to take a look. Five minutes later he had his answer: the wreath was missing.

"Felix gave you one of these Indian corn wreaths as a gift, correct?"

"Yes, he did!"

Was this the clue Bloom was searching for?

Both men hurried over to the casita. The wreath was missing; a small gold hook sat empty on the wall.

The wreath had been taken in the robbery, but why? Stealing decorative bobbles made no sense unless the wreath had some intrinsic value they didn't know about, or the kidnapper was leaving a message.

The two were deep in thought when the moment was broken by a plaintive, "Meow, Meeeoww..."

Bloom looked down. Simon was rubbing his side against the dealer's pant leg. The cat rarely came around in the evening looking for food.

"Poh, do we know if anyone noted seeing this cat earlier?"

Poh rifled through his papers. "Yes, a cat of this description ran out of the casita as the officers entered the building. Apparently your buddy here scared the shit out of Martinez."

Poh smiled to himself at the thought of the big patrolman being frightened by a cat.

Bloom wondered if Simon had not been fed earlier in the day. Was this why he was coming around when he normally would be sleeping on a chair outside?

Bloom peered into the small cylinder that served as the kitchen's trash can. There was no food tin. Rachael apparently didn't have a chance to feed Simon.

"He's crying because he missed his breakfast," Bloom said. "Whoever kidnapped my wife did so just as she opened. Rachael is a creature of habit. The first thing she does when she comes in is open a tin of cat food."

"That's helpful information. It pinpoints the exact time of the abduction. It's more likely someone was staking her out when she opened up versus a random opportunity to rob the place. Do you have any other thoughts?"

"We're getting close…"

Bloom's heart was pounding when he suddenly saw what he had been trying to put together. He grabbed the photo he had taken of Brazden sitting in his truck. A shiver went up his spine.

"There's a fetish around Brazden's neck!"

"What does that mean?" Poh probed.

"The day I took these photos of Brazden from my back yard there was an amulet around his neck. You can see it right here." Bloom pointed out the obvious, his finger visibly shaking.

"What does this mean?" Poh repeated.

"This photo was taken right after Brazden left Felix's gallery without his grocery bag. The necklace was still around his neck, so it wasn't part of that deal. A month later, when I told Felix no deal on the building, he was playing with a turquoise fetish—I remember noticing the nervous tell. It was Brazden's fetish!" Bloom's voice trembled.

Bloom explained to Poh how he could see a deep anger in Felix's eyes before the other dealer was able to hide his rage.

"There is one other recent photo of Brazden when the smiling pothunter was standing next to Rachael and her loom."

Bloom pulled out his iPhone and enlarged the image of Brazden's neck. The distinctive two-headed butterfly fetish was there. Bloom was positive it was the same one Felix had around his neck just a day ago.

"Felix had to have acquired this necklace in the last few days. He may have been one of the last people to see Brazden alive. Do you think he could somehow be involved in Brazden's death?"

Poh switched gears. Felix was now a major blip on the detective's radar.

"Did Felix know about the supposed treasure at your place?"

"Felix may have found out something about it from Jonathan Wolf. We both used the historian's services to obtain building permits. Jonathan said the artifacts I showed him were not worth much, but according to Wendy Whippelton, who had them evaluated independently, they actually could have great value. She also told me in confidence that an important historical document was missing from the state archives, and that Wolf was the last known person to have accessed it.

"Poh, I've seen art dealers behave like this before, making low-ball offers to try to get an important piece on the cheap. Jonathan may have wanted my artifacts for himself. If he believed there were more buried on my property, he could easily have told Felix about it."

Poh grabbed a passing patrolman and ordered him to go to Jonathan's Wolf's house and hold him for questioning.

"Bloom, I think it's time you and I go next door to call on Mr. Felix Zachow before he leaves for the day. My officers talked with him earlier and saw nothing fishy. But I think another visit is in order. A few pointed questions need answers and, if he's guilty, your presence might make him nervous.

"Missing prehistoric corn, a murder victim's fetish around his neck, multimillion dollar offers, and hidden treasure should be enough to get a sympathetic art-loving judge to grant us a search warrant if we need one.

"Mr. Zachow's day is about to get a bit longer."

Bloom and Poh hurried over to A to Z. The door was bolted, but the lights were on. Poh rapped on the glass. The receptionist ignored him. He knocked louder, this time with the side of his metal badge.

Tiffany couldn't ignore him any longer. She reluctantly looked up, gave a weak smile, walked over and unlocked the door.

She opened it just enough to fit her perfectly coiffed head through the slot. "Sorry, gentleman. We're closed for the day. We'll be open again at ten tomorrow."

"There are few questions I need to ask your boss. Is he still around?" Poh ignored Tiffany and wedged his foot in the doorway. There would be no keeping him out.

"Mr. Zachow is finishing some paperwork, but he told me he doesn't wish to be disturbed. He's got a big day ahead. How about tomorrow? I'm happy to leave him a message." Tiffany gave an insincere grin.

"No, I'm afraid tomorrow won't do. I will see him now. Please show me the way to his office." Poh pushed his way in, Bloom following close behind.

"But we're closed and he's very busy. He asked me not to disturb him."

"Tiffany, I'm only going to explain this to you once. I'm not asking you. I'm telling you: I want to see your boss right now. Show me the way or I'll find it for myself and arrest you for interfering in a police investigation."

Poh's stern face told her he was not fooling around.

When Bloom saw Rachael's rug beautifully displayed on the wall, his throat tightened with emotion.

They marched on, Tiffany's pasted-on smile now replaced by a nervous grimace. Poh didn't give the receptionist a chance to knock on the office door. He pulled it open himself.

"I'm sorry, Mr. Zachow. I tried to explain that you were busy, but HE insisted." The receptionist pointed at Poh, who was in turn eyeing Felix.

"That's fine, Tiffany. You can clock out now. I'll lock up." She shut the door behind her, the sound of her clicking heals fading as she exited the building.

"So how can I help you, officer?"

"Detective Poh, homicide."

"Homicide? Do we have a murder? I thought it was a break-in. I'm sorry to hear about this, Bloom. It's a terrible thing, your wife missing and all. If there's anything I can do to help, please don't hesitate to ask."

Bloom said nothing. He was waiting for Poh to take the lead.

Poh peppered Felix with questions regarding the treasure, his relationship with Wolf and the corn wreath.

Felix stayed in his chair and answered Poh's queries succinctly. None of his responses seemed forced, but Poh continued to chip away on various timelines and the fetish hanging around the art dealer's neck. The detective was recording the conversation and watching Felix's reactions closely.

"Where and on what day did you get the fetish?"

"This little thing? I'm not sure—maybe two weeks ago? It was a gift from Brazden. He was an old family friend. It was terrible to hear about his passing. I was friendly with his grandfather…"

Both Bloom and Poh knew this was not true, as Bloom had photographed Brazden with the necklace only a couple of days ago.

Poh dug deeper. "Why do you think he gave you this gift?"

"Why does any man give anyone anything? I guess he liked me."

"Did he give you other gifts?"

"No, not that I can remember."

"What about the corn wreaths? Didn't the one you gave Bloom come from Brazden?"

"I don't remember, Mr. Poh…"

"Detective Poh, please." He wanted Felix to know exactly who he was and that he was the one in charge.

"Sorry DETECTIVE Poh. I'm a wealthy man as I'm sure Mr. Bloom can confirm. A small corn wreath is not something I'm going to remember. It's simply too trite to worry about."

"Yet good enough for a gift to me?" Bloom said sarcastically.

"I don't mean it that way. I'm just saying I don't know where I got it."

Poh kept hammering Felix with questions.

"What about the day Brazden visited you carrying a Whole Foods bag? Mr. Bloom says that when he came out of the gallery he didn't have the bag. What was in that paper sack?"

Felix was not prepared for this line of inquiry. He hadn't realized Bloom had been spying on him and, at that moment, wanted to kill the art dealer along with his pretty wife. Anger was showing on Felix's face when he remembered the pots he had taken from Brazden's home.

"I purchased these pots from Brazden as decoration for my office." Felix pointed at the three prehistoric pots on his bookshelf. Bloom stood up and went to look at the pots more closely.

Poh again took the lead.

"You got these pots that day, and they've been in your office ever since?"

"Correct. They're quite nice decorative pieces."

"Do you have a bill of sale for the pots?"

"I'm afraid not. Brazden was not the kind to provide receipts or take checks. I paid him in cash, and I can provide a record of the petty cash that I took out to purchase the pieces. Again, this was not a lot of money; I was just helping out an old friend."

"You know that dealing in looted prehistoric material is a federal offense?"

"Yes I do, detective. I'm not dealing in prehistoric pots. Brazden told me they were legal and I'm not planning to sell them. As I told you, they are purely for decoration, so no laws have been broken on my part." Felix gave Poh a grin that said, "Screw you, detective. I know the law and can play the game as well as you."

When Bloom spoke, he moved closer to Felix and his tone was accusatory, his voice loud.

"You're a liar. A god-damned liar. You're the kind of dealer who gives all of us a bad name. You skirt the edges of the law and when there's a problem, it's always someone else's fault."

Poh undid his holster and placed his right hand on the butt of his gun. He could sense Bloom knew something. The detective would continue to listen, but he wanted to be ready for action too.

"Brazden offered me two of the same pots sitting on your shelf three weeks AFTER you supposedly bought them AND they have never left this room? That's bullshit. I thought this Mimbres bowl, which he brought to my gallery last week, was beautiful—but I would never deal in a pot that has no legitimate history and was most likely looted. You got these pots much later than you're telling us."

Bloom took another step closer and bent over Felix, placing his hands on the desk. Felix, who had been smiling smugly, changed his facial expression as Bloom's six-foot, one-inch frame loomed over him.

"What was in the bag, Felix? Did you kill Brazden Shackelford? And where is my wife?"

Felix was looking to Poh for help when a monarch butterfly that had escaped from the hidden chamber fluttered past the two men's faces and landed at the edge of the hidden door.

Felix's eyes fixed on the insect, and his tanned face turned ashen. Poh and Bloom also tracked the butterfly's movements, realizing there was something behind the wall.

Poh stepped forward, his weapon now drawn.

"What's with the butterfly? And that looks like it might be a door. Is it?" Poh asked.

Felix fainted when he tried to stand, hitting his head on the Nakashima desk on the way down. Poh cuffed the unconscious man's hands, searched him and called for backup.

Bloom pushed at the hidden door until it opened with a sucking swish. Rachael was suspended by a metal chain in the middle of the room as if she were flying—and next to her was a human skeleton wearing a white manta. Dozens of live butterflies covered both her body and the skeleton next to her. Both were enveloped by the shadowy blue light.

Tears ran down Rachael's cheeks when she saw Bloom. He ran over and lifted her body onto his shoulders to lessen the pressure on his wife's shoulders and wrists.

Before he could speak, she cried, "I love you, Charles Bloom. You're my hero. I knew you would find me—you're so good with puzzles."

Bloom started to laugh between his tears as Poh came into the room and helped Rachael out of her bonds.

🦋 🦋 🦋 🦋

Felix was led out in handcuffs and an arrest warrant was issued for Jonathan Wolf for kidnapping, attempted murder, and burglary. The historian was not at his home and was assumed to be on the run.

Rachael's shoulders and wrists had been badly sprained, and Bloom insisted she go to the hospital for an evaluation. She finally agreed and, as they exited the A to Z gallery, Bloom went over to her weaving and pulled the textile off the wall.

A policeman tried to stop Bloom.

"You can't take that. What are you thinking?"

Poh interceded. "It's OK. That's his wife's rug. Please step aside officer."

Bloom went to Tiffany's desk, grabbed a Post-it Note and wrote in big letters: "NO SALE, SUE ME" and stuck it to the wall where the rug had been hanging.

Charles gently placed the rug over Rachael's shoulders as if to reassure her that everything would be OK. He kissed her on the cheek and said, "I love you. Now let's get you checked out. Indian Market is only a few weeks out and you still owe me a small weaving."

Rachael laughed as tears of joy streamed down her cheeks. Her stiff and swollen shoulders made it impossible to wipe them away, but Bloom was still the ultimate salesman—and she was never happier that she had married him.

CHAPTER 52

THE AFTERMATH

A month had passed since Rachael's ordeal. Indian Market had come and gone, and the neighboring A to Z gallery remained shuttered for now.

A monumental Two Grey Hills rug won best of show at market and was supposedly priced at $120,000. Though Bloom never left his gallery to verify the amount, he hoped the rumor was true and that the rug sold for that price. A sale of that magnitude would benefit all Navajo weavers.

His main concern was for Rachael, who was recovering from severe shoulder and wrist sprains. It was not clear when she would be able to weave again, but her doctors were hopeful she could be back at her loom full time within the next six months.

Felix Zachow was in the Santa Fe jail awaiting arraignment. Deemed a flight risk, he was denied bail by a judge who had once been screwed over by a shifty Santa Fe art dealer.

Bloom sent a certified letter to A to Z gallery with a $25,000 check the day after he rescued his wife, rescinding the sale of Rachael's rug. On the bottom of the check, he wrote, "NO SALE YOU PSYCHOPATH." The letter had been signed for, but the check had not been cashed, which was fine with Bloom; he could use the float money.

He promised Rachael there was no way in hell Felix would ever get her rug back, no matter what. Sal Lito had even offered to hide the weaving if it came to that, and Bloom's lawyer assured him he had nothing to worry about.

Jonathan Wolf was a fugitive and on the run for now. His house had been searched, and a large number of documents stolen from various institutions were discovered. Wendy Whippelton identified the specific record that had been removed regarding Bloom's property. In light of the new evidence, the Historic Districts Review Board rescinded Bloom's work permit until further investigation of the casita's historical significance could be completed.

Rachael talked with Poh about AgraCon World Enterprises, what Felix had revealed about David Rolland's plans to patent the corn seeds, and the millions the company would reap in profits. She believed the kernels belonged to all the Indian people that had descended from the Anasazi. Poh agreed and offered to quietly share the seed cache with the tribal councils of all the Southwest Indian pueblos.

"No corporation should ever have control over the gifts that were left to us by our ancestors," Poh said, and Rachael agreed.

David Rolland of AgraCon World Enterprises would be in danger of losing his cushy position if the full story surfaced. Prehistoric skeletons and homicidal art dealers make for poor press, and the board of directors wouldn't take the fall out lightly.

He had been questioned about his part in breaking the law by purchasing artifacts looted off of federal lands. That was a felony and he would be prosecuted to the full extent of the law if the accusations were found to be true.

David's team of lawyers were reviewing all the purchases he had ever made from A to Z gallery and were demanding a full refund of the $2,500,000 he had paid for the Butterfly Twins' manta.

Felix's lawyers had not yet responded to that demand; they had bigger problems to deal with at the moment.

After David's hours-long interrogation, Poh cornered the CEO in a side room for a little talk without the lawyers. Poh told Rolland he knew he was trying to steal ancient corn from Native people and let him know that a Starbucks coffee sleeve with his personal cell phone number written on it had been found in Brazden Shackelford's desk drawer—evidence potentially linking him to an active crime investigation. If Rolland didn't back off, Poh said, things could get very nasty. Certain Indian cops might not like that he had bought the remains of their ancestors and take matters into their own hands.

David saw Poh's reasoning. He put his Santa Fe house up for sale the next day and promised to never take the Indian seed to market.

The twins' remains, manta, and the fetish amulet were claimed for repatriation by the Acoma people. If no other tribes came forth, and the Wupatki National Monument didn't put up a roadblock, the relics would be turned over to the pueblo for burial as it saw fit.

No fight was expected. The twins would finally be back home and treated with the dignity they deserved. Like the kernels that would soon be dispersed throughout the Southwest, the genetic code of the Butterfly Twins and Caterpillar Boy was still running strong in their pueblo descendants.

The treasure chest hidden in Felix's office had finally been turned over to the Bloom-Yellowhorse family.

Felix initially claimed the chest was discovered on his property during construction on the annex, but once the hole was discovered at Bloom's casita and an independent researcher confirmed the dirt on the chest was from the same peat moss-filled spot, Felix dropped the lawsuit.

Bloom promised not to initiate a civil suit over the treasure chest, but left open the possibility of civil retribution on other pending charges. Bloom needed leverage if Felix Zachow ever tried to come after Rachael's rug.

A small group of invited friends and historians were on hand when the ancient trunk was opened, a process filmed by the state historian.

It took some doing to open the corroded locks, but the chest ultimately gave up its five-hundred-year-old secrets.

Inside was the intact body of a three-thousand-year-old Olmec statue that perfectly fit the head Bloom had uncovered several years earlier. There were ten round wooden altar figurines with mineral paints accenting the simple faces, and a bison leather bag filled with fine Cerrillos turquoise nuggets. Below these was a stack of official documents, in poor condition, from Oñate's governorship.

At the very bottom of the trunk, and taking up most of its interior space, was an exquisite and well-preserved weaving wrapped in a churro sheepskin.

The weaving was a historic manta in the Acoma style, made of fine, white handspun cotton. The blanket's center was decorated with an elaborately embroidered motif: a large two-headed butterfly, each head facing in a different direction. The butterfly's wings, accented in red ocher, were spread wide, as if flying, a rising sun beckoning it onward.

The End

Photography courtesy Mark Sublette, unless otherwise noted

Page 1:   New Mexican Conquistador Sword
Page 6:   *Sunset Crater, Arizona*
Page 13: Mimbres Bowl, c. 1200 B.C.E.
Page 17: *On the Road to Toadlena, Tsénaajin and Tsénaajin Yazhi*, New Mexico
Page 20: *Winter Afternoon*, 1943, Sheldon Parsons (1866-1943)
Page 28: *Sheep Grazing*, Toadlena, New Mexico
Page 32: *Cafe Pasqual's*, Santa Fe, New Mexico
Page 36: *Huevos Rancheros,* Santa Fe, New Mexico
Page 48: *Historic Review Sign, Santa Fe*, New Mexico
Page 53: *Wupatki National Monument*, Arizona
Page 58: Acoma Plate with Butterfly Design, c. 1960
Page 62: *Ancient Hideaway*, Northwestern New Mexico
Page 67: *Wupatki National Monument Window*, Arizona
Page 70: *Grandfather Juniper Tree*, Navajo Nation
Page 74: *Clouds over the Sangre de Cristo Mountains*, North of Santa Fe, New Mexico
Page 86: *Towering Pine*, 1920, E. Martin Hennings (1886-1956)
Page 92: *Coyote Fencing, Medicine Man Gallery at 602A Canyon Road*, Santa Fe, New Mexico
Page 96: New World Spanish Document, June 12, 1809
Page 102: *Ancient Footholds,* New Mexico
Page 119: *Adobe Among Cottonwoods, Arizona*, c. 1900, Maynard Dixon (1875-1946)
Page 122: *17th Century Spanish Cross Petroglyph*, Tumacácori, Arizona
Page 129: Mexican Colonial Leather Trunk, late 19th century
Page 133: Classic Mexican Saltillo Blanket, c. 1840
Page 141: *Las Campanas*, Santa Fe, New Mexico
Page 147: *Lamb on Open Pit Fire*
Page 149: Navajo Turquoise and Silver Bracelet, Kenneth Begay c. 1930-40
Page 151: *Santa Fe Police Department*, Santa Fe, New Mexico
Page 159: *Butterfly Bush, 602A Canyon Road*, Santa Fe, New Mexico
Page 170: *Farmers Market Balloon Man*, Railyard District, Santa Fe, New Mexico
Page 174: *Exploding Cloud, Santa Fe*, New Mexico
Page 179: *Early 19th Century Navajo Weaving Tools*

Page 186: Navajo Two Grey Hills Tapestry Weaving by Virginia Deal (1926-2015), 2005-6, 72 by 46 inches
Page 197: *White Necked Ravens*, Canyon Road, Santa Fe, New Mexico
Page 218: *El Farol Restaurant Sign*, Santa Fe, New Mexico
Page 221: *Navajo Wool and Tools*
Page 225: *Camino Escondido and Canyon Road Road Signs*, Santa Fe, New Mexico
Page 231: *Crime Scene Unit*, Santa Fe, New Mexico
Page 239: Cathedral Basilica of *St. Francis of Assisi Church,* Santa Fe, New Mexico
Page 251: *Best of Show, Lola Cody's Two Grey Hills Rug,* 2014